THE WHITE WEDDING MURDER

THE WHITE WEDDING MURDER

Elizabeth Silverman

DEDICATION:

For Wimsey without whom there would be no Rufus.

Chapter 1

Although technically I am a Sleuth Hound, never in my wildest squirrel-chasing dreams did I ever expect to be mixed up in an actual murder.

It happened like this:

One sunny October morning, I was peacefully minding my own business, ripping up some boxes in the kitchen, when I heard the front door buzzer of our brownstone.

"Yes?" inquired my human Cressida of the talky thing on the wall. It was a name that made her sound more like a salad garnish than a girl, but that's what happens when you had a father who had been a Professor of Literature at Yale before his untimely demise.

"By leave of their Graces, my Lord and Lady Kovac of Cincinnati, I hereby bring merry tidings for the fair Lady Cressida of Manhattan and Her Royal Hound Rufus the Red.

"WTF," muttered my generally lady-like human, except that she used the actual words.

She grabbed me and clipped a collar around my neck—the scary-looking kind with the prongs that was supposed to keep me from pulling but never did. The idea was that if our visitor turned out to be a nut—this was New York City after all—the collar plus the fact that I tipped the scales somewhere in the neighborhood of 125 would offer her some protection. Frankly, a chihuahua would be better suited to the task. Bloodhounds in general, and me in particular, have a strong sense of self-preservation, meaning that my idea of protection is to park myself firmly behind my human's legs and remain there.

The irony, of course, was that protection is the whole reason I ended up living on Manhattan's Upper West Side, where bloodhounds are as rare as reasonable rents.

It all began with my human's mother, who was firmly convinced that if her daughter was going to be living alone in New York City she should have an enormous dog to protect her. Like many an over-protective mother who was mortified at being thought so, she omitted the whole protection thing when she went to talk to an old friend who happened to be a bloodhound breeder. The result was that, instead of acquiring something purpose-built for the job like a Rottweiler, she acquired something purpose-built for making a mess of your house and dragging you all over Central Park. I did, however, come with an exquisitely refined pedigree—my father was Comedy of Errors Kennels *Ch. I Ate the Couch*, the number two bloodhound in the country, and my mother was that incredible bitch, *Ch. It's My Shoe Now* from Drop That Immediately Farms, who prior to a lengthy maternity leave pretending to look after her offspring, had taken the breed at Westminster. This was a vast improvement over all the other things she took, including time, money, and several Sunday roasts, but that's a story for another time.

My only real complaint is my name. My human is a writer and as a fan of mystery novels she had originally wanted to call me Wimsey, after the urbane sleuth Lord Peter Wimsey, but that name was already taken by a famous bloodhound. Her next idea was to honor her Shakespearean heritage and call me Horatio, until a friend pointed out that it had too many syllables and yelling the first one at me on the streets of New York might not be such a good idea. In the end, history triumphed over literature, and she decided to name me Rufus after William the Conqueror's favorite son and heir, Rufus the Red. Although most people think William's greatest accomplishment was to conquer England, it was really to introduce bloodhounds to the Saxons.

But I digress.

As soon as my human opened the door, a trumpet fanfare sounded from somewhere that was not a trumpet and a young man knelt in front of us with his head parallel to the ground as if he were examining some fascinating aspect of the concrete. He was dressed in a green velvet doublet, cream-colored hose, and had a tasty looking green plush cap on his head. In short, he looked more like he might be bringing Henry VIII urgent matrimonial news from France than delivering merry messages from Cincinnati.

I bayed in his face.

This being New York, I was probably the only one who thought that a 16th century page unrolling a large, ornate parchment scroll to the accompaniment of an invisible trumpet was anything to bay about.

"By Proclamation of their Graces, Lord and Lady Kovac of Cincinnati, the attendance of the fair Lady Cressida of the Isle of Manhattan is hereby entreated at the revelries consequent upon the nuptials of their daughter, the fair and virtuous Lady Brooke of the Upper East Side, the week of April 1 in the year next at Crackshaw Castle. Abide ye further instructions from mine Master of Revels." He rolled up the scroll, slipped a red silk ribbon around it, and presented it to my human, once again resuming his examination of the concrete.

As soon as she took it, he rose and unrolled a second scroll. The trumpet sounded again but this time my human put her hand proactively on my snout.

"By Proclamation of their Graces, Lord and Lady Kovac of Cincinnati, the attendance of the Most Magnificent and Esteem'd Royal Hound Rufus the Red is hereby most ardently begged and desired at the revelries consequent upon the nuptials, etc., etc., etc."

When our visitor had finished his spiel, he rolled up the scroll and tied a ribbon around it but this time he placed it in a thick cardboard tube. Then he kneeled, his head even lower if that were possible, and presented it not to my human, but to me. It was a tossup as to whether I would go for the scroll or the hat, but in the end the scroll won, since I probably had a better chance of keeping it.

As soon as I snatched it, the young man rose, executed a courtly bow, and capered down the brownstone stairs in search of his next wedding victim. As I watched him go, I idly wondered in which branch of the performing arts our time traveling friend hoped to make his home. As a writer, my human, too, has suffered the indignities of embarrassing side gigs, notwithstanding the small trust fund from her grandmother and the occasional help from her mother to make ends meet. Neither I, nor life in Manhattan, come cheap.

Once back inside—a one bedroom apartment of the kind realtors call "cozy" and the rest of us call small– my human removed the parchment and handed me the tube. Don't get me wrong, I'm not an ingrate, but ripping stuff up is always more enjoyable when it's ripping stuff up that you're not supposed to have. I would say you can't always get what you want, except that I usually do.

While I addressed myself to distributing bits of shredded cardboard all over the floor, my human picked up her phone.

"Hi Mother. Did you get..."

"Hello Cressida. Yes, I got my invitation about an hour

ago." I thumped my tail at the sound of this much-loved voice.

"What the – I mean what on earth is Brooke thinking. More to the point what is Percy thinking?" Percy, I should add, is Percival Dudley Alden Winthrop (call name "Percy"), my human's first cousin. Perhaps there are worse things than being called Rufus. Anyway, Percy is the groom in the affair, although I'm guessing he wasn't given the option of thinking anything since grooms at weddings are merely inconvenient accessories that like children, are expected to be seen and not heard.

"I wish I knew. Anne and I were discussing it earlier. According to Percy, Brooke got the idea from binge watching *The Tudors*. She and your Uncle Charles are very unhappy about it of course, but Brooke's going to be their daughter-in law so they're trying to make the best of it."

"And did you know that Rufus…"

"Yes. Anne told me. Apparently, Brooke thinks he adds tone."

"But does she have any idea what a dog like Rufus can do to a wedding dress with his slobber, let alone to the other guests?"

"Percy did bring it up, but Brooke insists it won't be a problem."

"I can't imagine how. I don't suppose there's any way to get out of it, is there? A day would have been bad enough but a week…"

"No, I'm afraid we have to go. The only one who has an excuse is Edmund." Edmund was my human's brother and a budding Egyptologist who was away digging something up. It's something we had in common.

"Let's just hope there's plenty of alcohol. And how on earth is anyone, let alone Rufus, supposed to get to Crackshaw

Castle. It's in the middle of nowhere. And why April? I would have thought June was more Brooke's style."

"As far as transport goes, you probably already have an email from someone called The Master of Revels. It has all the details. And April wasn't Brooke's choice. Anne told me that she and Percy had wanted to get married this past June, but this was the only date the wedding planner would let them have. Brooke absolutely insisted on using him and evidently, he's so famous that he tells brides when they can get married rather than the other way around. Promise me Cressida, if you and Ben ever get married..."

"Don't worry. If a Master of Revels is involved, you have my permission to drag me to City Hall."

At the sound of the name Ben, I thumped my tail again. Ben Prescott was my human's boyfriend and had also been Percy's best friend since their puppy days at prep school. It had been Percy who had introduced Ben to my human. It's all very incestuous, but kennels like Phillips Exeter and Princeton are like that. At least my human had the good sense to flee to Stanford.

They soon left wedding matters behind and moved on to how my human's novel was coming along and also to a lot of pathetic moaning on the part of my human about her latest freelance writing gig. It was ongoing feature for *Beautiful Beauty* called "1001 Ways to Look Younger", which had sounded like a catchy title when she pitched it until she realized that there weren't. But then again, asking a 26-year-old for tips on how to look younger is like asking me for tips on how to keep your house clean.

But this was still better than her most dreaded side hustle—working as an extra. She's been a reporter, a street drunk, a doctor, a lawyer, a nurse, a nanny, a teacher, a juror, a Nazi, a barfly, a banker, a factory worker, a global climate change delegate, a commuter, a sobbing funeral guest, a traveler, a prison visitor, and a train passenger, many times over, and in many different decades. She has attended any number of weddings, operas, sporting events, plays, parties, and galas, and has walked more streets in more ways and in more costumes than a working girl. Summer clothes in the winter, winter clothes in the summer, and soaked in rain in all seasons. Not to mention getting up at 3am and getting home at 3am. It's all part of the glamor of low budget life in New York City.

I think we both preferred having her chained to her laptop writing about wrinkles.

When the maternal moanfest was over, my human rang off and opened her laptop to read what The Master of Revels had to say. There were some unpleasant noises and a few bad words as she read through the email. A few clicks later, Ben appeared on the screen. He was a pleasant featured, if serious-looking young man as befits a junior member of a leading architectural firm. As soon as I met him, I knew my human had made a good choice. He never complained when I sat on him, drooled on him, or when he had more of my hair on his clothes than many men had on their heads.

I stuck my face in front of the camera. Joining video calls where one is not wanted is one of the great technological pleasures of modern canine life.

"I see you Rufus," Ben said. "You can get down now." Naturally I did not get down. I may have long ears, but they have nothing to do with hearing.

"I've just read the email from The Master of Revels," said my human, poking her head around mine. "He wants my dress size and all my measurements for 'bespoke nuptial attire.' Even when I go to a wedding, I'm an extra!" she groaned. "He also wants Rufus's measurements. And they're going to make him a hat."

"I don't see Rufus wearing a hat," said Ben.

"I'm sure Rufus doesn't see Rufus wearing a hat either." Actually, I am extraordinarily fond of hats, just not for their intended purpose. "In fact, most of the email seems to be about Rufus. They want to know his preferences in snacks, toys, and meals and they're sending a limo for him to take us to 'The Kingdom of Teterboro' so he can fly private. I'm sure if it were just me, I'd be on a bus. Are you on the same flight?"

"Unfortunately, no. The wedding party is going down earlier in the week to rehearse. I love Percy like a brother, but I just can't see the attraction of Brooke. None of us can. On the plus side, it's an excuse to visit Crackshaw Castle. There're supposed to be secret passages that I'm itching to hunt for."

"And should any of your firm's clients want a replica of Crackshaw Castle, you'll be their guy."

"Please God no. If we get one more request to design a Hamptons beach cottage but make it look like Versailles, I'm going to run away and join a hedge fund."

"Also, do you know what 'the keys to the kingdom are?' They said they'd send them when I RSVP."

"Yeah, they're personal QR codes to unlock the outer gate to the estate, which I understand is the size of a small country, and also the door to the castle. But I have a feeling most of us will want to break out and not in by the end of the week."

Ben disappeared from inside the screen and my human unearthed her measuring tape. By the time she caught me, her fitness tracker thought she'd run a 5K.

She replied to The Master of Revels with our measurements and her doubts as to the feasibility of me wearing millinery of any kind. She also added the helpful information that I am extremely large and consume a king's ransom in kibble, to which the addition of pieces of poached salmon and finely roasted meats would not go amiss. Also, that I require an elevated feeding station because bending is bad for my back and that it would be prudent to drape any and all furniture in my room with sheets. (Not that this is entirely effective either as I have been known to shed hair under sheets via a mechanism that remains a mystery). She added that the sheets have to be of a high thread count, as I am immensely fussy about the fabrics upon which I lie and ruck up and reject any I deem substandard.

I am not The Royal Hound Rufus the Red for nothing.

Chapter 2

April 1st was soon upon us. Although to be fair, the activity ratcheted up weeks before. There were endless consultations with girlfriends about what clothes to bring, what clothes to buy—shopping being to human females like chasing squirrels is to me, it's more about the chase than the capture—and many convivial evenings spent sipping adult beverages and speculating as to what exactly was going to go down at Crackshaw Castle. Now I like sticking my nose into adult beverages as much as the next hound especially while sitting on laps into which I manifestly do not fit, but the real highlight of my human's preparations was the purchase of a number of extremely large rawhide bones with which she hoped to keep me occupied and out of places I didn't belong. As if.

On the morning of our departure, my human and I were up as usual at the proverbial crack of dawn to conduct my morning perambulation around Central Park. It was a suspiciously long and vigorous one. This generally meant she was trying to get me tired, which was just about as effective as her trying to get me to do anything else, like behave in the bath the night before. Although I did eventually succumb, it ended as it usually did with the meat of a small turkey on the inside of me and a tub full of water on the outside of her. I have my pride after all.

I was just relaxing after a hearty breakfast of scrambled eggs and kibble when I was interrupted by the sound of the door buzzer. My human grabbed the shortest of my many leashes which was always a promising development since it meant she needed to control me; and if she needed to control me it meant that there was something to control me from.

Much to my human's relief, although not to mine since I was hoping to have another crack at that plush cap, it was not a ridiculous costumed character who awaited us, but a pudgy smiling man wearing an ordinary chauffeur's uniform. I was ecstatic and greeted the gentleman in my usual effusively hospitable way while my human labored to keep drool streaks off his pants with the large washcloth she kept about her person for just such occasions.

I hurtled down the front steps and after a quick leg lift on one of the tires of a large limo to let everyone know it was mine, we and our luggage were soon locked, loaded and on our way. The limo was a vast improvement over my usual means of transport since unlike New York City taxis, our driver did not appear to be auditioning for NASCAR. Also, I liked the leather seats that were covered in a soft protective fleece and the large bag of Kobe beef treats. For my human there was the usual assortment of nuts, nibbles, booze, and bottled water. The only downside was that the distance to the front seat precluded me from resting my chin on our chauffeur's shoulder and poking my cold nose in his ear. But nothing's perfect.

Road trips, however short—Teterboro is a disappointing thirty minutes from Manhattan—are a rare and invigorating treat since we New Yorkers generally use our feet rather than wheels to get around. But thirty minutes is better than no minutes and when we arrived, I attempted to separate my human's right arm from its socket as I charged into the low building. We burst through its door, one of us yelling and one of us baying. We were checked in rapidly.

It was a fine day and as I towed briskly across the tarmac, I pointed myself towards a strange looking contraption that had three wheels and a staircase. I gazed longingly at the wheels.

"Absolutely not, Rufus" said my killjoy human. I turned my attention to the triad of smiling humans standing by the staircase, all of whom were dressed in appealingly immaculate uniforms and wafting an admiring scent.

"We heard that we had a special guest flying with us today," said one of the male members of the group, (my human and I both knew he wasn't talking about her) "and we wanted to extend a personal welcome." It was nice to know that I was just as much of a celebrity on private jets as I was on the streets of Manhattan where I've been photographed so many times that my human should have carried a red carpet instead of a drool rag.

I wagged and snuffled. Six hands delved into my wrinkles. My human produced the washcloth.

I love being me.

My entourage escorted me up the stairs with the deference due a dog for whom limos are sent, and we entered what appeared to be a long, skinny room with a number of nice wide chairs and a long couch. The place reeked deliciously of previous passengers, rich leather, and food.

"It's just the two of you today," beamed the female member of my retinue as she placed a stuffed, squeaky, pink pig in my mouth. She ushered us over to the long leather couch. "I think you'll be more comfortable here. We have a special padded seat belt harness for Rufus, but he only needs to wear it during takeoff and landing since we're expecting a smooth flight. Our flight time should be about two hours."

My human secured a seat belt around her lap while our

hostess helped me into my safety apparatus, which I found was surprisingly comfortable. And although it didn't permit me to get all of me into my human's lap, I did manage to finagle my front end on top of her anyway.

"We have Evian water, poached salmon, cold chicken breast, and a sliced New York strip," said the flight attendant. "There is also a very good cheese plate. And for you Ms. Pennington, we have champagne, white and red wine, beer, mineral water, spirits, and a selection of sandwiches. Would you and Rufus like something now or would you like to wait until after takeoff?"

"I think we'll both wait. Rufus has never flown before, and I want to see how he reacts." I knew it took a lot of fortitude on my human's part to refuse a drink because I had the distinct impression that she felt she was going to need one.

The engines sprang to life, and we bounced along for bit like we did in a car; I tried to stick my head out the window but had to settle for leaving large nose prints on the thick glass. Suddenly we were accelerating like we had found an empty lane in the Lincoln Tunnel, and we rose into the sky.

Our gracious hostess reappeared to release me from my harness and to offer me some Evian from a large ceramic bowl.

"Have you and Rufus decided what you would like to eat?"

"Yes thanks. I'll have a Bloody Mary. A large one please. And some sandwiches. I think Rufus would like the sliced steak." I approved of her choice since the family exchequer seldom ran to New York strip.

It was as promised, a short trip. Between all the noshing and sloshing it went by rather quickly. We came to a smooth stop on a secluded airstrip and the crew gathered round the exit door to bid me a tactile farewell and take a few selfies.

They also clipped a pair of wings onto my collar.

I bounded down the stairs and inhaled deeply of the fresh forest air. Then I lifted a leg on a tire of the waiting limo.

"Welcome Rufus and Ms. Pennington," said our new chauffeur. "It's about an hour's drive to Crackshaw, so make yourselves comfortable. We have truffle treats, air-dried venison, and a small bar with both alcoholic and nonalcoholic beverages and some human snacks. Cell phone service will be spotty so if there is anything you'd like to download, I'll give you some time to do it while I deal with the luggage." He opened the door of the long black car with a flourish. I hopped in and my human pulled out a rawhide bone and placed it on the floor. I picked up the rawhide bone and placed it in her lap. While I settled in for a lengthy chew she read the Wikipedia entry about our destination:

Crackshaw Castle is one of the largest private homes ever built in the United States. It was constructed in 1885 in western Pennsylvania by Alaric Blicester Whitscomsbyworth, the disgraced 8th Earl Crackshaw, who, after being found in flagrante with the wife of a neighboring earl known for both his temper and his proficiency with firearms, fled to the U.S. with the family fortune. Using this fortune, Lord Crackshaw reinvented himself as Oily Earl, the oil rig robber baron. It has always been claimed that Crackshaw Castle, which has over 100 rooms, contains numerous secret passages necessitated by the Earl's frequent need to make hasty exits from ladies' bedrooms. Upon the death of the 8th earl, which doctors said was due to an absence of liver function, the impoverished English 9th earl sold the property to a railroad robber baron who was too lazy to build his own castle.

In the wake of the 1929 stock market crash, the Castle was sold to bootlegger "Ginger Gin" O'Malley who built a gin distillery in the basement and who is rumored to have added additional secret passages to the property. Following the repeal of Prohibition, Mr. O'Malley found the legitimate liquor business to be unsuited to one of his talents, so he expanded into more interesting business ventures such as gun running and extortion, which unfortunately resulted in his permanent incarceration. The Castle was then sold to Harry Shiseberg, the founder of Starlight Studios where it famously served as the setting for such popular hits as The King and the Showgirl,

The King and the Shopgirl, The King and the Stenographer, The King and the Seamstress, The King and the Servant, and The King and the Songstress. Following the demise of the Golden Age of King movies, Shiseberg became a wealthy recluse and spent his days obsessively trying to remember the name of a sled he had as a boy.

After the death of Shiseberg, the Castle was purchased by a local politician who bought it with "an inheritance." Following his indictment, the Castle passed to Abdul Zayt Habibi, a Saudi prince who added it to his collection of luxury homes he never lived in. When the prince moved on to collecting yachts he never sailed in, the Castle was sold to the Termite Hill Development Corp., who were going to convert it into luxury condominiums before extensive market research revealed that no one wanted to pay vast sums of money to live in the middle of nowhere unless there was a beach. The Castle was finally acquired by its current owners The Lemming Event Group who realized that people would pay vast sums of money to host events in the middle of nowhere if they thought it was a celebrity secret.

Having completed work on my rawhide, the drool from which gratifyingly made my human look like she had failed to make it to the toilet in time, I stretched out to take a restorative nap. As my deafening snores and gas from the New York strip filled the car our driver put up that plastic barrier thingy and opened the windows while my human resumed work on her novel, *The Thief of Time*, which I suspect is about a bloodhound. But then again, we bloodhounds are the thieves of everything else also.

It was just as I was in the midst of a wonderful dream in which I had actually captured a squirrel, that I was awakened by the slowing of the car. I stuck my head out the window and saw that we were winding back and forth up a seemingly endless drive with large trees packed densely on either side. The trees cleared and suddenly there stood the most monumental structure I had ever seen that was not vertical and made of glass and steel. It had wings. It had turrets. It had towers. And if Pennsylvania were ever to be attacked by Ohio, it looked ready to withstand the siege.

We had arrived.

Chapter 3

The car door flew open and I flew out. A tall, barrel-chested young man done up in full Renaissance regalia was waiting for us. From his velvet hat to his silk shoes, he looked the business.

"I bid thee welcome Royal Hound Rufus the Red and the fair maiden Lady Cressida," he boomed after he had gotten up from bended knee. I liked him immediately. He had the proper reverential spirit, although to be fair, referring to my human as a maiden was a bit of a stretch. I also liked the fact that his doublet had a large interlocking RR embroidered on it in gold as did the soft cloth that he used to delicately remove the drool from my flews when I shoved my nose along his tights. If you've ever been wanded by an overly enthusiastic TSA agent at an airport you know what it's like to meet a bloodhound.

The immense door to the castle opened and disgorged a bevy of individuals to deal with our luggage while My Attendant, who looked like he should be called Ambrose, escorted us through the door and into a large entrance hall that was all dark wood and heraldry. There were doors and corridors leading in every direction and we threaded our way through a labyrinth of them many of which featured (sadly empty) suits of armor and displays of sharp pointy things whose purposes appeared to be less than friendly. When we reached an imposing stone staircase, we ascended and continued down and along a number of richly decorated and tapestry-laden hallways with nary a lethal weapon in sight. A last, My Attendant stopped at a door, took a key from his leather pouch, opened it, and handed the key to my human.

"Prithee enter, Royal Hound Rufus the Red. And Lady Cressida. Me'thinks yon bedchamber will mayhaps prove pleasing to the Royal Hound Rufus the Red. And Lady Cressida."

My human dropped my leash, and I began the methodical process of acquainting my nose with every square inch of our temporary abode. It consisted of two rooms. The first was a large wood-paneled chamber featuring comfortable-looking furniture that included a bloodhound-sized couch and several cushioned chairs perfect for trying to wedge myself into. All of it was draped in soft fabric which obviated the need for the extra sheets my human had brought along anyway. You can never have too many furniture draping sheets when you travel with a hound. The flooring was of antique-looking wood that was partially covered by an assortment of Oriental rugs. I was inordinately fond of Oriental rugs. They retained scent wonderfully.

The second chamber, also paneled in wood, contained a large and luxurious looking bed with four very chewable-looking posts. If Ben decided to join us, there would be plenty of room, although he had an annoying habit of wanting to sleep on the entire bed instead of just on the edge. There was also a large mahogany wardrobe, two chests of drawers, a carved dower chest, and a vanity-desk combination.

It was a very interesting room, for other reasons too. But more about that later.

The remaining room was the bathroom which I was relieved to see featured a claw footed tub wholly unsuitable for giving me a bath. I gave the accommodation an unqualified paws up.

The luggage arrived and My Attendant Ambrose gave me one last wipe and informed my human that he would be waiting outside our door to escort us to The Chamber of Reception and Repast whenever we were ready. There was an all-day eat-a-thon in progress where our fellow guests were gathering upon arrival. The word repast immediately caught my ear. It had been several hours since my last one. I went over to the elevated feeding station I had noticed in the corner of our living room (mahogany with ceramic bowls) but it contained nothing but water. Of this I availed myself freely, as I suspected the Castle's extensive grounds would require substantial marking.

Meanwhile, my human conducted a few investigations of her own. On the vanity/desk she found an ivory and gold embossed leather booklet inscribed: The Wedding of Brooke Kovac to Percival Dudley Alden Winthrop.

Inside was the following:

Monday
    Arrival buffet in the Chamber of Repast
    Evening: Madrigal Karaoke

Tuesday
    Forest Treasure Hunt
    Sword Competition
    Archery Competition
    Renaissance Dance Class
    The Pavane
    The Almain
    The Volt
    The Gavotte
    The Courant
    The Saraband
    Evening: Masque

Wednesday
Antique Pistol Shooting Competition
Maze Hunt
Tudor Football
Evening: Games of Chance

Thursday
12 Noon: The Wedding of Brooke Kovac to Percival Dudley Alden Winthrop
The Castle Chapel, Rush Devereaux, Officiant
Wedding Feast
Evening: Wedding Celebration, Merriment, Musik, and Dance

Friday
Suit of Armor Races
Tudor Bowling
Hawking Exhibition
Pavane Dance Off
Evening: Groom's Celebratory Birthday Feast

Saturday
Pre-honeymoon Gala Departure Breakfast
Bridal Couple Departure Ceremony

There was also this on the table:

Welcome to Crackshaw Castle the finest and most unique event destination in the world! This extraordinary structure was built in the 1880s by Alaric Blicester Whitscombsbyworth, the well-known 8th Earl Crackshaw, who decided to move to the US to further his interest in the economics of the emerging energy sector. Upon his death, the Castle was sold to a fellow industrialist who was forced to sell it following the stock market crash of 1929. After a stint serving as the headquarters for a leading member of the hospitality industry, the Castle was acquired by Starlight Studios where you might recognize it as the glamorous backdrop for the studio's finest feature films. As the Golden Age of Hollywood waned, Crackshaw had several important owners, including serving as the home of a prominent member of the Saudi royal family. The Castle is currently the jewel in the crown of the Lemming Event Group, host to the most elaborate, exclusive, and atmospheric events for a discerning worldwide clientele.

When she finished this interpretive read, she opened the wardrobe and chest of drawers and groaned when she saw what they contained. There were a variety of gowns, headpieces, and other miscellaneous Tudor impedimenta as well as a gold embossed publication entitled, *Style Book for the Wedding of Brooke Kovac to Percival Dudley Alden Winthrop*, that contained instructions about what she was to wear and when.

The book also directed her to open the carved dower chest, which she had assumed was purely decorative. Instead, she found a variety of canine coats and jackets, all embroidered with RR surmounted by a gold crown and several velvet elasticized neck ruffs. There was also an array of ornamental collars and leashes that, although undeniably attractive, were not something a bloodhound should ever be walked in unless one enjoyed doing it face first. My human occasionally did this anyway, it's just that it's a lot harder with my usual equipment. And in spite of the fact that she had discouraged The Master of Revels vis-à-vis the whole hat question, there was a ruched red velvet cap with a bejeweled under strap and a gold RR on the side. On the positive side, there were a large number of generously proportioned rawhides which I carefully removed and distributed about the room in the places most like to cause my human to trip on them.

Sitting on top of my clothing there was a note in elaborate script, *"The Lady Brooke presents her compliments to The Royal Hound Rufus the Red and requests his presence in The Chamber of Reception and Repast upon arrival. She would be well pleased if The Royal Hound Rufus the Red were to be caparisoned in the crimson velvet jacket and matching hat, the wearing of which she understands might be of a very brief duration."*

My human sighed. It was going to be a long week. At least for her.

My human sighed. It was going to be a long week. At least for her.

Chapter 4

As my human set about the task of distributing our chattels in suitable locations, I alternated between snuffling, lounging, and getting in her way. Afterwards, I joined her in the bathroom where she had retired to "freshen up," which apart from the usual activity mostly consisted of her putting more goo on her face which I was just going to lick off anyway. When this exercise was completed to her satisfaction, she changed into something a tad less hairy and drool spattered, exchanged one pair of flat shoes for another pair of flat shoes—heels and hounds being antithetical constructs unless one fancies a trip to the emergency room—and brushed her glossy reddish chestnut hair, which I admired greatly since it was of a similar shade to my own.

Her toilette thus complete, I found to my dismay that it was now my turn. Out came the crimson jacket which required a bit of bribery to get me into, and then a gold leash which she clipped onto my sturdy collar, its bejeweled counterpart from the dower chest being, like my ears, for ornamental purposes only. But the final insult came when she pulled out the hat. I bayed and made a grab for it since in my experience things that look like plush toys generally are plush toys and if they are not plush toys they soon will be.

She put the hat under her arm.

We joined Ambrose who was stationed outside, monogrammed drool cloth at the ready, and off we went to The Chamber of Reception and Repast. We retraced our route to the stairs—it's a good thing my human has me, otherwise she was going to need a GPS to get back to our room—and I strained eagerly on my leash. I could smell the intoxicating odor of humans and food, my two favorite things, although not necessarily in that order.

"The Royal Hound Rufus the Red seems to know exactly where he is going," observed My Attendant with some surprise.

"He usually does, only it's generally to a pile of horse manure or someone trying to eat their lunch."

Onwards I dragged in the relentless way that indicated I was hot on the trail of something immensely desirable. We sped past multiple military displays, assorted heraldic battle flags, and elegant tapestries of hunting and hawking before I came to rest in front of a broad set of double wooden doors.

Ambrose flung them open dramatically.

"The Royal Hound Rufus the Red! And the Lady Cressida," he boomed in a stentorian voice that might even have been heard above the sound of my baying.

The place was a wall of scent. First, there was all the food at "the buffet," which resembled a buffet about as much as a Ford resembled a Ferrari. The Chamber of Reception and Repast was a large room and all along its sides were tables behind which stood attentive humans wielding a cooking show's worth of culinary implements ready to slice, dice, cook and carve every kind of meat, fish and fowl; there were fresh roasted vegetables arriving hot from the kitchen born by good-looking young men in ochre-colored doublets and hose and fetching young women in long, high waisted, ochre colored gowns worn over immaculate white, puffy, laced shirts, their hair twisted into attractive buns that were tastefully restrained by bedazzled black mesh snoods; there was a pasta station where a chef stood ready to rustle up freshly made pasta of an astonishing number of shapes and sizes. Next to the pasta station was a blini making operation with caviar and all the fixings; there were omelets of every kind waiting to be made, and smoked salmon, salads and breads in profusion and enough baked goods to make a Parisian patisserie proud. Those were just the highlights. If it was edible and expensive it was there. And if it wasn't there, it would be found.

Of less interest to me, but not necessarily to the rest of the room, was the massive bar where Dom Perignon could be quaffed along with offerings from the Châteaux of Lafitte, Latour or Pétrus. Not to be outdone, Burgundy was represented by bottles of Romanée-Conti and if Italians were more to your taste the duo of Barolo and Brunello were there to please your palate. The whites were equally as impressive, and the top shelf liquor was so top shelf that you would've needed a ladder to reach it.

And then of course, there were the people. Lots of them. Some were seated at long wooden refectory tables, and some were chatting in pairs or in groups. Most were young and attractive but there was also a smattering of the older generation scattered about, and weaving amongst them all attending to their needs were the pretty women in the ochre-colored gowns and comely young men in ochre-colored doublet and hose. And presiding over it all was a dark-haired guy of indeterminate age who zipped around like he'd had one too many lattes. He was speaking urgently into one of those headphone-mic combos popular among pop star phenoms and was trailed by a petite young woman struggling to keep up.

All this activity ceased, however, at the sound of my voice. People were either amused, confused, or terrified.

The silence was short-lived. Squeals of delight rang out from a group of exceedingly pretty and exceedingly thin young women at the far reaches of the room.

"Picture's up. Rolling. And... action!" yelled a gangly, intense-looking young man with a shock of uncombed dark hair and black glasses who, height aside, looked like he was about twelve. He was staring intently at a screen on some sort of stand as a clutch of humans wielding large cameras, one of which was pointed in my direction, sprang into action.

"Make way for The Royal Hound Rufus the Red," thundered My Attendant whose previous gig had included had played Twelfth Night's Sir Toby Belch at Shakespeare in the Park.

The crowd parted before us as we marched towards the squealers.

"Cut!" shouted the intense guy. "C camera, go tighter on the hound. A camera, I want a wider shot of the bridal party. Going again. Reset. Back to one."

Everyone looked confused. Except for My Attendant and my human whose time served in the background acting trenches meant that she knew the dreaded sound of a retake when she heard one.

We reset to one. My Attendant flung open the doors and announced me. I re-bayed as if on cue—although I generally make it a point to do nothing on cue, I was willing to make an exception for baying—and the ladies re-squealed. We advanced on the group, this time unimpeded by shouts from our director.

"Welcome to my wedding, Royal Hound Rufus the Red," proclaimed the bride while making sure that none of her attendants blocked her from the camera. She may have had questionable taste in weddings, but what was not questionable was her beauty. She was tall and willowy with a cascade of dark, softly waving hair and the kind of deep blue eyes you only see in cosmetics ads. Her bridesmaids, although all very pretty, were far less striking and far more blonde. I wondered whether she chose them for contrast.

"Ooooh, he's adorable," cooed one of the bridesmaids, as My Attendant discretely wiped my snout. "Maybe we could use him in the magazine."

"Cut. Good. Hold for stills, I want stills! Where's that photographer and the social media concierge," yelled our director looking around him.

Two much put upon looking women scurried over.

"I want shots of Brooke greeting the hound," he said. "Wait! Where's his hat. My wardrobe notes say he's supposed to have a hat." He looked accusingly at my human.

"I might be able to get it on him long enough for a few photos," she said. "But it might require some steak."

The director nodded at a minion standing by his side. "Go."

"And have them cut the pieces small," my human called out. "He won't eat them if they're too big." My human knew me well. It's what comes of routinely finding a mound of improperly sized food next to my bowl.

"Can someone fix my hair," snapped the bride.

A woman with a pink spiky coiffure rushed forward. She was wearing a tool belt of the kind usually worn by the guy who comes to fix the roof except that this one was crammed to overflowing with every grooming implement ever invented. She extracted a small comb, adjusted an imaginary stray hair, and moved a side bang one millimeter to the right. She hopped aside when the minion with the steak returned. It was mid-rare, just the way I like it. My human selected a correctly sized piece, waved it in front of my nose with one hand, ostensibly to distract me and then quickly slipped the hat over my head with the other. I of course knew exactly what she was doing and why, but when it comes to the ingesting of meaty snacks,

I like to let her think she's a dog training whiz.

"Quick," said my human to the woman with the camera, as she popped the meat into my mouth, "before he shakes his head." She stepped out of frame and Brooke stepped in and looked down at me lovingly with one eye and at the camera with the other. She was such a beauty. Too bad she knew it.

"OK, let's get a few more stills, this time with the rest of the bridal party and C camera see if you can get something usable this time."

"Is there any duck?" asked my human as she removed the hat and My Attendant wiped my face. I snuffled the bride's skirt. It was the latest number from the hot new Japanese label Baka. There had been a big spread about it in a *Marie Claire* I had recently shredded.

We did several more takes, although my favorite was a shot of me baying while an admiring semi-circle of beauties looked on. The acoustics in the dining room were excellent, so I made sure to wave my tail to reassure any alarmed onlookers of my friendly intentions. When they get to know me better, they'll appreciate that the baying I engage in when I am excited, bored, want something, or to say hello, is a mellifluous bass-baritone. On the rare occasions when I am angry, like when I smell that Scottish bastard, Wilbur the Gordon Setter who tried to assassinate me when I was a puppy, my voice drops to a menacing basso profundo.

But I digress.

When our photographic duties were fulfilled, my human removed the objectionable headwear, hopefully forever, and I towed through the crowd to where my nose had detected Ben.

He was standing and talking with his fellow groomsmen, so I surprised him by ramming my nose into his backside.

"Cress!" he cried with delight and bent over to give her a kiss on the cheek. He was tall which both my human and I liked very much. I find the shorter members of the species go down like ninepins at the merest tap. "And Rufus!" he added as he scratched me between my flews in a manner of which I highly approved. "Nice threads, my man," he chuckled. I liked Ben but he could be a real smart ass sometimes.

"That's quite a bridal party," said my human. "Brooke is looking very model-like. Is she these days?"

"No, she still works at *Me* magazine. So does one of the other bridesmaids, although which one is anyone's guess. They're Riley, Kiley, and Katie and we get them confused." Any magazine called *Me* gets my vote. No wonder Riley, Kiley or Katie thought I should appear in it. "Anyway, one of them is a PA for Giles McHurdie."

"Not the guy who tried to buy the Maldives as a present for his wife and caused a diplomatic incident?"

"The very same, But DO NOT ask her about him unless you have a couple of days to spare. The other one either does something at an art gallery or does something in fashion— she's in one and wants to do the other but I'm not sure which. Then there's Emily, the bridesmaid you haven't met. She's Brooke's first cousin who, according to Brooke, was foisted on her by her parents. Brooke says she looks like she's been eating too many of her father's pies and she can't be in the photos because she's too fat."

"Pies?"

"She's the daughter of the FOB's brother," chimed in a compact young man with dark hair who looked like he played Rugby for a living. "He's Pete of Pete's Pies, the largest pie franchise company in the country."

"I'm surprised there are only four bridesmaids," said my human. "I would have expected Brooke to have a small army of them. Also, what's with the arm candy brigade," she added looking around.

"Ah, Brooke doesn't have all that many friends and especially those that meet her decorative standards," replied Ben. "So that woman over there," he said, gesturing discretely at a whippet-thin woman of a certain age who was dressed with an impeccably casual elegance, "is Brooke's boss, Circe LaFortuna; she's brought a large contingent of models so all the photos and videos will have the right look. And Perce said they practically wet their La Perla panties at the thought of spending a week in a castle stocked with investment bankers and other wealthies. Also, Circe's one of the few older people Brooke permitted to attend. There's a strict quota on guests over forty."

"We're shocked that any of us made the cut—the decorative part, not the age part," said the compact dark-haired young man.

"Well Rush makes up for all of us, "said another groomsman of whom I immediately approved because his hair had a reddish tinge. "Brooke's got her money's worth there."

"Rush is an old acquaintance of ours from Princeton," explained Ben. "Percy and Brooke ran into him at a party, and she was so mesmerized by his looks that she tried to persuade Percy to make him a groomsman. But for once Perce grew a pair and put his foot down since it would mean booting one of us, so she persuaded Rush to get an online license from The Church of the Digitally Divine and officiate instead. Brooke said the rest of the clergymen she interviewed talked too much about God."

"Have I met Rush?" asked my human.

"No. Trust me you would have remembered if you had," said Ben. "First, he's an actor and second, he looks like one. Also, he's a loathsome toad, but that doesn't stop the ladies from dropping their knickers at the very sight of him. I'm sure he only agreed to the wedding gig because it made Perce uncomfortable. We're all taking bets on how long it'll be before Percy starts looking for a divorce lawyer. If you'd like to get in on the action, Driscoll will give you 2 to 1 on under 12 months."

"I've got a C note riding on two years at 10 to 1," said the dark-haired compact young man.

"You always were a risk taker, Barclay," (call name "Buck") said Ben. "I'm with Rufus—even money for a year."

I thumped my tail.

"Sorry Rufus," he said addressing me, "not you. Rufus, meet Rufus. Although technically he's Doctor Rufus." I nose wanded a rangy but rather wan young man who looked like he could do with a few more hours in the sack. I felt for the guy. It was bad enough being called Rufus when you're a dog but the fact that someone actually named their kid Rufus bordered on child abuse.

"I don't think that's strictly accurate," interjected Driscoll, my reddish-haired friend. "He's a radiologist."

"And not even that. He's a resident," added Barclay helpfully. "And with a name like a dog."

"It's still better than being called Barclay," said the Medical Rufus.

"I'd rather be called Barclay than Rufus. No offense old man," Barclay said turning to me. "But at least neither of us are called Percival."

"Yeah, but that's only because of the crazy great uncle with all the cash," replied the Other Rufus. If the guy'd been called Cuthbert or Marmaduke or something, poor Perce would have been called that instead. So all things considered, he probably got off easy. But speaking of cash, has anyone been to the bar? It looks like Brooke's father called up a liquor warehouse and told them to send over everything they've got that's famous and expensive."

"He probably did," said Driscoll.

"Who is he anyway? Anyone know?" asked the Other Rufus.

"He's the Knob King of the Midwest," replied Driscoll.

"That's a bit harsh, isn't it?" said the Other Rufus.

"No, he really is the Knob King of the Midwest," said Driscoll.

"He's right Rufe," Ben said. "Percy told me. He makes knobs. And then when he cornered the market in them, he moved on to dials. And now he controls a vast manufacturing empire of knobs, dials, and the precision instruments and whatnot that they're used for."

I was growing bored. The only knobs that interest me are the ones I can chew on. Also, there was a salmon at the buffet that was calling my name.

My human looked at me.

"I think Rufus and I will take a walk around the room," she said, having correctly deduced that a loud bout of boredom baying was about to commence.

"If you'd like, I can take him Lady Cressida," said My Attendant. "I know there are a lot of people eager to meet him." My human looked dubious on both counts, but having observed that Ambrose was both handy with a drool rag and seemed to know his way around a hound, she acquiesced.

"OK but try not to let him knock anyone down or poke them in the backside or snatch a squab off someone's plate. He can have whatever is on the buffet that doesn't have onions, grapes, raisins, or chocolate. And if he starts to bay put a piece of meat in his mouth; he can still bay but it makes it harder." I like to let her think that, by the way, because it encourages meat feeding behavior. It's called positive reinforcement.

I tugged at the leash, impatient to be off on my royal meet and greet.

My first stop was a gaggle of sylph-like young women, one of whom reeked of the intoxicating new Parisian perfume, *Bifteck Cru*, which according to their ads was "guaranteed to arouse male passions." They were talking animatedly to a group of young men all of whom reeked of Wall Street, guaranteed to arouse no one's passions, unless you happened to be in the market for a well-heeled boyfriend.

"The Royal Hound Rufus the Red," announced My Attendant stating the obvious.

Conversation ceased and I plunged in.

"He's so cute!" cried the ladies, caressing the length and breadth of me.

"Now that's a real dog!" exclaimed the gentlemen. It was an accolade I heard often from members of my own sex, although whether it referred to my size, my lack of frou frou-ness or my very fine and very visible pair of which I was justifiably proud, I never knew.

I moved on.

Next up was an eager young man who was talking to a young woman with a ponytail.

"So you see, our design is a state of the art middleware solution that's engineered to revolutionize the integration and orchestration of complex, distributed systems across heterogeneous environments. The product embodies a synergistic amalgamation of groundbreaking technologies that not only encompasses AI but also distributed computing, containerization, and blockchain! It's going to empower users to transcend existing integration barriers and establish an unprecedented level of agility, scalability, and security in their digital ecosystems. In short, it's a complete paradigm shift that enables seamless data flow, real-time processing, and adaptive decision-making and also…"

The unfortunate young woman with the ponytail looked like she'd rather be elsewhere. Me too.

My attention was next caught by a tall, striking figure talking to a rapt-looking female. As soon as I laid eyes on him, I knew that I would soon be nose to knee with our officiant. He was casually dressed in slacks and a blue shirt that exactly matched his eyes and there was a navy cashmere sweater slung elegantly over his shoulders, a look that's as hard to pull off for a man as a scarf is for a woman. Also, the guy, although graceful, was a hunk. The elegant duds did little to disguise that what lay underneath them was something the ladies were going to want to get their mitts on. But if his body was good, his face might even have been better. It was compelling—strong yet sensitive and full of character in a way that made him beautiful without being male model pretty. No wonder Brooke wanted him for her wedding. For a brief second his eyes left those of his spellbound listener and shot across the room and caught Brooke's. He smiled.

"Sir Rush and Lady Emily, may I present The Royal Hound Rufus the Red," said My Attendant.

I took a good look at Lady Emily, the fat bridesmaid banished from the photos. She was neither pretty nor ugly, just plain. And rather than being fat, her offense against fashion consisted of being blessed with the kind of hourglass figure that had been all the rage in the 1950s. Then to compound the horror, she was holding a plate from the buffet that had more on it than kale, lettuce, arugula, and a chickpea.

"Who's a good boy, then," crooned Rush patting me on the top of the head. I dislike being patted on the top of the head. But even worse was the fact that he didn't even smell like a toad.

Emily made a fuss over me and gave me a piece of roast chicken.

"You shouldn't feed dogs human food," admonished the officiant. And uninformed humans should keep their opinions to themselves. He might not have smelled like a toad, but he was certainly behaving like one. I wouldn't have minded if he'd hopped away. Emily, however, looked unsure.

My Attendant came to her rescue.

"By edict of The Royal Hound Rufus the Red's fair mistress Lady Cressida," trumpeted My Attendant, "it has been proclaimed that His Majesty may eat freely of the feast, excepting those items that contain onions, raisins, grapes, and chocolate. I am sure the roast chicken was much appreciated as no morsel hast passed His Highness' lips these last thirty minutes."

I was considering giving Rush a poke in the crotch when a familiar scent distracted me. I bayed to signal my desire to move on.

As I made my way through the feasting throng, I paused graciously here and there to accept tribute from the gauntlet of humans in my path. The key to a successful royal walkabout is to chat politely but briefly with one's subjects. That and to eat stuff from their plates.

When at last I got where I was going, I greeted my human's mother the way I usually did. Fortunately, there were two humans with her who caught her in time. One of them was a tall, slim, quietly dressed woman of middle age. The other was a distinguished gray-haired gentleman with a steady eye and a strong jaw.

"Yes I'm happy to see you too, Rufus" said my human's mother as she regained her balance. She turned to My Attendant. "Where's Cressida?"

"The Lady Cressida is currently engaged in social congress with her special gentleman and his friends yonder," he said, inclining his head in their direction.

"Yes, she would be," observed her mother. She turned to her companions. "By the way Anne, I don't see your sister. Are she and Aldrich here?"

"No. Eleanor said they're fly fishing in Montana, although Tucker is here."

"I think you'll find fly fishing in Montana is code for swilling cocktails in Antigua," said the distinguished-looking man cynically. "I mean, who wants to be in a drafty castle in April, let alone the rest of it," he said with a sweeping gesture around the room. "What's the matter with something nice in Nantucket in the summer." As he said this, he absent-mindedly reached into his pocket and fed me a dog biscuit.

"Now Charles, you know Brooke had wanted to get married last summer. But even so, Percy said Nantucket was a non-starter in any season, and this was the only week her wedding planner had available before Percy's birthday. Really, it could have been so much worse. Percy mentioned she originally planned to hold the wedding at Hampton Court until she decided it was too small. So at least we don't have jet lag."

"The haze of jet lag might have been an improvement. With all the nice girls Percy's met...and now having to smoke cigars with the father and hear about how many corporate jets he's got, and how much his house in Aspen costs, and the property in St. Bart's, and all the celebrities and politicians he knows. I don't know if I can make it through the week."

"I agree, Brooke's father does lack grace. But the wife isn't my cup of tea either." She turned to my human's mother. "You'll know her even before you're introduced. She wears so much jewelry she clanks when she walks and seems to have never met a designer logo she didn't love." She turned back to her husband. "But Tucker might be doing most of the heavy lifting, Charles. Katherine—that's Brooke's mother," she said to my human's mother, "claims he's become very attached to Brooke since the engagement party and he even came down early last week to help the wedding planner. I admit I was puzzled at first since being helpful has never exactly been Tucker's style, but then I noticed he attached himself to Brooke's father like a limpet."

"Ah," said her husband. "The pogo stick project."

"Sadly, I'm afraid yes." She again turned to my human's mother. "Tucker has been trying to get anyone with two coins to rub together to invest in his latest project—an electric pogo stick sharing company that he swears will be even bigger than scooters—and since Mike Kovac is conspicuously not short of cash…." Her voice trailed off. "Tucker's my nephew and I know that it's very uncharitable of me to think that way. After all, maybe he just likes the family."

"He might be a little toe rag, but I can't see even him liking that family," replied her husband tartly.

Oooh, I thought, as my human's mother massaged my neck, a toe rag. What could be better than a cloth that smells like feet! Then I remembered my disappointment with respect to the toad and decided to reserve judgement.

But as cozy as we all were, I had not yet visited the buffet. I pointed my nose thither and towed My Attendant towards the salmon. Now although I realize that there are many other fish in the sea—I should know because owing to there being a gourmet fish store in the neighborhood, I've eaten most of them—I confess to being particularly partial to salmon. Whether it's the oily richness of the fish itself or the delightful way it makes my breath smell when I breathe in my human's face, I can't say. But it's my favorite.

I was just tucking into the plate My Attendant had prepared for me when my human and Ben appeared.

"We've come to rescue you," she said to Ambrose while watching me chow down, no doubt contemplating the gas-producing consequences of my feast.

"Why don't we take Rufus for a walk," said Ben. "I want

to show you some of the grounds and I'm sure Rufus would appreciate the exercise; it'll give this gentleman a break from wiping spit."

"Excellent idea" she replied. "I could use some air. But I want to say hello to Percy first. Where is he? I haven't seen him."

"He's busy fighting with Sergio Emilio Augustus of Soho (née Steve Agostino of Flatbush) and the tailor. They don't like the fit of his doublet and they also want him to show more leg."

"Sergio Emilio Augustus of Soho?"

"Sorry. The wedding planner. You saw him earlier—the guy running around talking into his headphone. But what you saw is the tip of the iceberg; let's just say his skills wouldn't have gone amiss in the Reichstag. And should you ever think about calling him plain Sergio, I wouldn't recommend it."

We tore ourselves away from the buffet and by that, I mean that my human forcibly dragged me away from it.

"I want to get Rufus out of these clothes, get his long leash, and grab a jacket," she said.

"I'll come with you. I want to see your room. Where is it?"

"Oops. I have no idea, but it's not close. I'd better find Rufus's caretaker. He seems to know his way around."

I bayed and started dragging. For a species who seems to have taken over the planet, humans can be extraordinarily obtuse.

"No need. It looks like Rufus knows the way. Either that or we're headed to the kitchen," said Ben.

Of course I knew the way. Down corridors, up stairs,

down more corridors, up a few more stairs and down another corridor. A few lefts, a few rights and I came to a halt in front of a door.

"This could be embarrassing," said my human. She knocked on the door just in case.

Suddenly the air was filled with a deafening sound that for once wasn't me.

"WTF!" exclaimed my human above the din.

Ben sighed. "It's Tucker. He plays the bagpipes in a Scottish boy band, and he practices incessantly. My room's downstairs and a few corridors over—at least I think it is; if there was any cell service in this place I'd use my GPS—and it doesn't sound much better down there either. And it's been going on all week; he came early to help the wedding Nazi, with what or why I have no idea."

"Wait! There's no cell service?"

"Nope. A small detail that The Lemming Events Group neglects to tell you. There's a landline downstairs and Rufus—sorry, not you—claims to have found a bar somewhere outside on the property, but then he got lost and he's never been able to find it again."

"Awesome," said my human, "could this wedding get any worse?" It was probably not a question she should have asked.

She tentatively stuck her key in the door and turned the handle. It was of course The Rufus Suite.

Doubting the power of my nose was pretty insulting but I kept my opinions to myself as one human got us both ready and the other pushed on things and pulled up rugs looking for secret passages.

Chapter 5

"Oh no!" cried my human. "Ben, stop messing with those rugs and give me a hand in here."

"What's the matter?" he asked as he entered the bedroom.

She tossed him a damp towel.

"Look what Rufus has done to that wall!" She pointed to a quantity of slime with which I had decorated a section of wood paneling. For those unfamiliar, which I assume is pretty much everyone, since we bloodhounds are a rare breed, getting dried bloodhound spit off a wall requires almost as much upper body strength as taking one for a walk.

Ben got down on his knees and went to work while I continued to snuffle and snort the area like a bellows.

Then it happened.

I thwacked the panel hard with my snout and the wall swung open. My human shrieked and grabbed my indoor cloth collar before I could take off into the inky darkness.

"Who's a clever boy!" exclaimed Ben as he threw his arms around my neck.

I knew there was a reason I liked him. It's always nice to have my misdeeds appreciated.

"Stop sucking up to my dog and toss me his leash," said my human.

"Here. And don't go anywhere! I'll go grab a jacket and we'll see where it leads." His degree in architecture might not have led to untold riches, but it came handy if one was going to explore secret passageways in giant castles.

"Really?" she said. "I'm going to go plunging into a pitch-black tunnel attached to Rufus?"

"Yeah, I guess when you put it like that." He paused on his way to the door. "I wonder how Rufus knew it was there?" Probably because I am a brilliant, talented, and clever creature of dazzling intelligence. Or maybe because I can smell the air that's wafting in from under that panel.

As soon as Ben left, my human pulled that ridiculous garment off of me and swapped out the short leash Ben had tossed over for my 20-footer. Then as she noted my demeanor with the distrustful and jaundiced eye of a true bloodhound owner, she slipped my detested Gentle Leader into her pocket just in case.

There was a knock at the door and Ben reappeared holding a flashlight.

"You brought a flashlight to a wedding???"

"I thought it might be useful if I found anything, although Rufus seems to have beaten me to it. Maybe I'll have him check my room later to see if I have one too."

Enough chitchat. I bayed, eager to be off.

"Here you take Rufus," said my human. "He's even more crazed than usual and you stand a better chance of controlling him."

Famous last words.

I lunged for the opening taking Ben's arm with me.

We made our way along a dark stone passage. It was damp and dank and smelled wonderful. Ben wound the leash tightly in his hand hoping to limit my momentum while my human played the flashlight about the forbidding walls. Our passageway ended in a wider one running perpendicular to it. I had no hesitation about where we were going. I hung a hard right. At intervals we saw other passages, that like ours, fed into the main one we were on.

"Three guesses where these other passages lead to," said Ben.

"Bedrooms," replied Cressida who knew her Crackshaw history well. "I guess I'm in the adultery wing."

"I think they're all adultery wings," said Ben. "But between a hanky-panky playing earl and a bootlegger, this place must be honeycombed with these things."

"Either way, it's creepy."

"Don't worry. You have me and Rufus to protect you." Well, he was half right. "And Rufus seems to know exactly where he is going."

My human sighed and for the second time that day reminded someone that I always know exactly where I'm going, it's just that it's seldom any place you want to go. Although I was deeply offended. What about all those times she got to meet the stars of her favorite films and streaming shows who were stuffing their faces at those location catering trucks I drag her to? Nevertheless, I put these grievances aside and focused my attention on exploiting the downward slope of the passage to increase my momentum.

"We're probably heading under the castle," said Ben. "I really wish we had time to see where those other branches lead but between Brooke, the Wedding Czar and the guy who thinks he's directing a major motion picture, I'm lucky to have even this much free time. Which reminds me, I won't be overnighting with you and Rufus. Members of 'the cast' apparently have an early call time tomorrow."

"Given what Rufus has been eating, I'm not sure you'd want to stay over anyway. He's likely to produce more gas than Con Ed. But remember, I live with Rufus; I have a permanently early call time."

"Yes, but I was thinking that with all the excitement of the trip, etc., he's probably going to sleep late. And anyway, if I have to get up on Rufus time, I'll have bags under my eyes which will mean Brooke throwing a hissy which will mean she'll sic her makeup lady on me. Not a fun experience. She'll lecture me about my pores and then spackle my skin with stuff that smells like a French bordello. Or what I imagine a French bordello would smell like," he added glancing at my human. Given that she co-habitates with me, my human is tolerant of most things, but a boyfriend who hangs out in French bordellos is not one of them. "And to be honest, given the videographer's efforts to spice things up by putting cameras in odd places, I'm not sure that if I stayed over we wouldn't be starring in a porno."

"Who is he by the way? He looks a little young for Brooke to be allowing him free rein to document such a momentous an occasion."

"His name's Ethan and he's a friend of either Kiley, Riley or Katie. He graduated from NYU film school and in case you hadn't noticed, he thinks he's going to be the next Martin Scorsese. In the meantime, he does weddings to pay the rent. Not to change the subject, but Rufus seems to be pulling harder if that's possible. I'm guessing we're about to see where this leads."

Ben was indeed correct. The scent I was following was growing stronger. At least for those of us with a nose. The ground had been sloping upwards and then just around a curve I found what I was looking for. I bayed ecstatically. In front of us was a flight of stone stairs.

"Here Cress, take Rufus and give me the flashlight. It looks like there's a like a trap door up there and I'm going to need both hands." I made squeaky noises of support as Ben ascended the stairs and pushed upwards on a wooden panel. Nothing happened. He examined the area in more detail and saw a handle at one end. He put the flashlight on the top step and yanked sideways with both hands. The door slid open. He popped his head upwards.

"Very clever! OK Cress, I'll come down and go up first with Rufus." Ben took my leash and I launched myself up the steps and over the top while he reached down to chivalrously extend a hand to my human. A gentleman always helps a lady out of secret passages.

We found ourselves in a small stone structure obviously meant to evoke an abandoned mediaeval chapel. Its flooring consisted of large square tiles, several of which slid back to allow access to the tunnel below—a convenient bolt hole, no doubt, for the much-pursued Earl when attending to the less than spiritual needs of ladies linked in connubial bliss to men who happened not to be him.

"Weirdly enough, this is where I wanted to take you on our walk," said Ben as my human climbed out. "The entire wedding party was down here yesterday for another one of Ethan's endless photoshoots and I never gave much thought to these tiles, other than that they were out of period, but so much about the castle is, that they didn't register as anything particularly unusual."

We left the chapel and stepped into the sunlight of a

large forest clearing. It was a charming spot. Adjacent to the chapel there was garden in which early spring daffodils were waving in the gentle breeze. Below us there was a splendid panoramic vista and in the distance behind us we could just see the top of the castle looming above the forest.

"It's so peaceful," my human commented. "I never would have known this was here."

"A lot of the property is forest, but Tucker was out scouting locations and found this."

"He was always kind of the failure cousin so at least he's making himself useful for once instead of sponging. He would have made a great trust fund baby if he'd had one. But what was he doing scouting locations?"

"He barnacled onto Brooke at the engagement party and appointed himself bridal helper-in chief. No task too big or too small. He came down here last week with the wedding planner and his people to lend a hand and he's been buzzing around like an annoying little bee ever since. He inventoried all the rooms in the castle and suggested to Brooke and Sergio Emilio Augustus who should be housed where and which public rooms and outdoor locations would be best suited to the various wedding activities. He's definitely done his homework, but Perce told me his parents are convinced that it's only because he's trying to ingratiate himself with the family and get old Kovac to invest in his latest scheme."

"That sounds more like him. I was always glad that he was on the other side of the family and no actual blood relation. But I'm happy he found this place. It's nice to get away from everyone for a bit." There followed some canoodling which discretion, and my gentlemanly nature, forbids me from discussing.

I took care of some business and nosed about finding interesting scents. I was just about to pursue one of these further when Ben untangled himself from my human.

"As much as it pains me, we'd better get back. I'm number four on the call sheet and I'm sure there's some essential Best Man duty on the schedule that I'm supposed to be performing somewhere. We can walk back through the forest."

"Are you sure you remember the way?"

"There should be a narrow path through the trees if you know where to look. And anyway, I'm sure Rufus can find the castle."

This time he was 100% correct. I am much better at finding things than protecting things.

"Rufus, leave those daffodils alone. We're going."

"Listen," said Ben, "don't say anything about the tunnel to the guys. I'm still hoping to do some more exploring and want to surprise them as soon as all the wedding stuff is done. With any luck one of those passages leads to Buck, Dris or Rufe's room and I'd love to pop up or in or whatever and scare the hell out of them."

"My lips are sealed," said my human.

Well mine weren't and I bayed. I dragged my human to the little path and took off down its twists and turns with my nose pressed tightly to the ground inhaling the mouthwatering scent of all the humans who had trodden it before us.

The forest, by the way, was pure magic, dense with the tracery of trees above and deep earthy detritus below. Hansel and Gretel and the witch's hut would not have looked out of place. I hurtled along the twisty path occasionally stopping so abruptly to snort some intriguing scent that it was only Ben's strong arm around my human's waist that kept her from toppling over me. It was hard to say who was enjoying the walk more.

At intervals, I left the path and plunged into the

surrounding vegetation to get a better whiff of creatures who I hoped to get to know better.

"No off roading Rufus," admonished my human. "And get away from those toadstools. There's no vet down the street out here." I looked but failed to discern the presence of a single toad. I was getting seriously annoyed with this whole imaginary toad business. Nevertheless, I took my human's point. Like many bloodhounds I am an adventurous eater, a trait that has from time to time landed me in the vet's office and subject to various medical procedures that put a substantial strain on the family bank account. If vets gave out frequent flier miles, I'd be Platinum.

But I digress.

I finally shot out of the underbrush and into a clearing at the side of the castle.

"If you have time, let's go back to my room," said my human. "I didn't get a chance to show you all the stuff that they've given me to wear."

We returned to the Rufus Suite and while my humans headed into the bedroom to delve into the vagaries of Renaissance raiment, I took the opportunity to examine the door to our accommodation. It was not of the tedious knob turning variety that required thumbs and a hand, but of the handle lowering variety that required paws and a snout.

I was out the door and down the hall in a hot Tudor second. And I knew exactly where I was going. Circuitous turns and hard to fathom corridors may perplex and bedevil humans but they are no match for a bloodhound in pursuit of his prey.

Faster than I can disappear with a sock, I burst exuberantly into The Chamber of Roast Meat, Fish, and Fowl.

Chapter 6

It would be an understatement to say that my arrival in the castle's kitchen created something of a stir. Shock and awe more like, and while no one actually fainted at the sight of me it was a near thing.

The place was one vast hive of activity with a large amount of boiling, roasting and frying going on. In short, it was paradise.

Having detected the delightful scent of annoyed humans I made my way thither to see what was happening. The bride was talking to a tall gray-haired woman, although I'm not sure that talking was the most accurate description.

"No! No! No!" Brooke cried, her voice rising above the conversations of the assembled servant masses. "The crimping on these pies is a disgrace. My uncle is Pete the Pie Man, the world's leading expert on pies, and I will NOT serve him pies that look like...that look like HE" she said pointing to me, having spun around and noticed my presence, "had crimped them. I want them all redone immediately."

"But Miss Kovac, this is the way hand crimped pies look and we don't have time to redo them all before dinner," replied the gray-haired lady clearly trying to rein in her temper.

"Do NOT tell me what pies are supposed to look like! My Uncle Pete could buy and sell all of you and this castle a hundred times over from what he makes selling pies in a day. And they are not supposed to look like that. I don't know where Sergio Emilio Augustus found your catering company, but this is not the standard I am used to. Fix it!" Then she lifted a lovely looking apple specimen and placed it on the ground before me. "Here Rufus, you have it."

I gave it a preliminary sniff. It smelled pretty good, although I would have preferred it with whipped cream. Not being as much of a stickler about crimping, however, I tucked in.

While the now red-faced gray-haired lady marshalled her cooks to try to figure out how to do the impossible, Brooke continued her tour of inspection.

"I guess there are worse gigs in this place than ours," observed one of the comely servers to her companions with a nod in the caterer's direction.

"Yeah, but ours is pretty gruesome. That ad in *Backstage* has a lot to answer for. Describing it as a featured role in a weeklong run of a Renaissance immersive experience isn't exactly the most accurate of descriptions."

"I guess the tip off was at the audition being asked if I had waitressing experience," said another.

"Waitressing. Ugh! And in the world's most uncomfortable uniform. Calling it a costume doesn't make it one. And having to curtsy to the guests all the time to boot. And it's not even like there is anyone useful among them."

"Well some of the men are kind of cute, including the groom. Wonder how Bridezilla Brooke got her hooks into him."

"Why is it that nice guys who don't treat commitment like it's a trip to the gallows end up with girls like her. Maybe I'm just not mean enough."

"I've tried being mean. I've tried being nice. I've tried being selective in who I swiped right for, I tried being non-selective in who I swiped right for. Nothing works. I'm convinced that men who want relationships are just another New York City urban myth like alligators in the sewer. Let's face it ladies, New York guys are like kids in the world's largest candy shop and we're the candy."

"And speaking of which, I wonder if the super hottie who's officiating has a girlfriend."

This caused one of the group to go redder than the caterer.

"He's my ex," she spat out. "Not that he ever let me know. I met him at an audition for *Hamlet in the Bayou* and I wasted the better part of a year on him. He told me we were exclusive and that he wanted a future with me and to consider myself engaged. I even started looking at wedding stuff. Then one day he just ghosted. Well, he can't ghost here. He's going to deal with me whether he likes it or not."

I decided that I had had enough of both pie and drama, so after making the rounds of the kitchen staff to taste test some more food, I followed Brooke out the door to see what else of an interesting nature the castle had to offer.

I didn't have very far to travel.

Brooke was pinned against a wall with the officiant doing the pinning and with his mouth pressed hard against hers.

"No!" Brooke hissed, pulling away. "I told you that was a one off. I was drunk."

"I'm not sure Percy would see it that way," the

handsome young man answered smiling cheerfully "You might not need my services after all."

"You wouldn't."

"I would."

"Why?'

"I like repeat performances and besides it would be a shame to end our run so soon."

I bayed discretely and trotted past the touching scene to explore some of the other rooms. There was one that was probably a morning room and another that had a green felt table that I hopped up on to access the elevated air currents swirling about. Like most bloodhounds, I enjoy standing on tables, although I've noticed that for some unfathomable reason humans tend to find the habit objectionable.

Anyway, I picked up the wafting scent of additional humans, so I jumped down to follow it. Its source led me to a cozy room decorated with overstuffed furniture and occasional tables which I found to my disappointment were all too small to accommodate a hound of my majestic proportions. There were also two humans. One was a rather stocky, gruff looking middle-aged man whose abdomen was beginning to undergo something of an expansion. He was dressed casually, with a double G here, a medusa head there, and a horse and carriage or two strewn about. On his wrist was the obligatory heavy gold watch with the little crown. I recognized all these logos immediately because when she's not searching for 1001 ways to look younger, my human also writes the occasional menswear article for *Bro* magazine.

The other human was a young woman who was so pretty she could have been one of Brooke's bridesmaids. The man stroked her face with a hand adorned with a large ring not of the wedding variety.

"Just be patient darling," he said soothingly. "I know it's

tough. I want to be with you as much as you want to be with me. But Kathy still owns 50% of the business and it's going to take a while to figure out a way to either persuade her to give up her shares or a legal work around."

"But how long?" the pretty young woman whined. "I hate doing her PA work."

"Believe me, I have the lawyers working night and day on it. At least they should be given the size of the bills I'm getting. The only thing lawyers seem to be good at is finding more than 24 billable hours in a day. And if I had known I was going to meet you my little flower, I never would have accepted the money from her father with the proviso that she own a fifty percent stake. But I was just starting out and knob factories don't come cheap. And the interest rates at the time…"

"I don't want to talk about interest rates," she said and kissed him on the mouth.

"Not here," he said, detaching her. "And I'd better go before Kathy comes looking for me." He smelled kind of tense and as neither of them seemed inclined to pet me or feed me, I followed him out of the room where it seems I wasn't the only one who had witnessed the romantic scene.

"These things can be tricky, can't they," said Rush sympathetically. "I don't think we've had a chance to talk much."

"Brooke and her mother took care of that end of things," he replied. "You're a clergyman, right?"

"Strictly speaking no, unless you count being ordained by the Church of the Digitally Divine, but I have played them of course. I'm an actor."

"Well nice to chat with you. I've got to join the line to use the telephone, so I'll see you later."

"Yes, I'd like that. I imagine you have a lot to attend to trying to keep a wife and a wife-in-waiting happy. As I said, a tricky situation. And divorce is so expensive, especially for a man in your situation. But acting can also be a tricky and expensive situation. For instance, I've just landed a lead in play that I very much want to do but it turns out the production still needs funding. I know what with the wedding and the lawyers and everything, you have a lot of calls on your time and money, but I'd very much like to talk to you about investing. Or maybe your wife would be interested? And after that there is of course funding for the film I want to do. We have a lot to discuss."

I was impressed. This guy was the business. Pivoting seamlessly from extorting sex from the bride to money from her father. He would have made a terrific hound.

Chapter 7

I continued my exploration, wandering from ballrooms to libraries to long galleries adorned with paintings, to chambers exhibiting collections of costly bits and bobs, to elegant and cozy sitting rooms furnished both in masculine and feminine styles. In one of these a wood burning fire crackled appealingly and I decided to sleep off the exigencies of the day (and the pie) so I stretched out on the rug in front of the hearth to take a nap. I have no idea how long I was in the arms of Morpheus, but only that I had a wonderful dream in which I was seated on a throne and offered a bag of live squirrels as tribute. Periodically in the background I could hear voices asking, "What's that noise?" from which I deduced that I had been snoring, a sound that my human says makes her wish she had a pair of those headphones airport guys use to drown out the sound of jet engines.

But I digress.

Suddenly, I was rudely awakened.

"Rufus! What are you doing here?!" I would have thought that would have been obvious, even to a human but then again, they are also prone to ask, "What did you do?!" when dogs are standing in the midst of feathers and shredded pillows.

"Ben," my human called. "He's in here."

"He looks very comfortable, and no one has reported any major damage, so I'm sure it's fine to just let him wander. Except of course when he has his royal duties to attend to."

Out of the corner of my eye I could see my human looking skeptical.

She clipped a leash on me.

"And speaking of which, I'm going to take him for a quick potty walk and then I have to get both of us dressed and ready for dinner and karaoke. Rufus's manservant told me that Rufus is expected to take his meals with us."

"At the table?"

"I think there's going to be a place set for him with an elevated feeding station on the floor. At least I hope so."

When we returned to the Royal Rufus Suite, my human consulted the style book.

"OK Rufus, according to this, I'm supposed to wear the green velvet gown and the headpiece with the pearls. You're in purple tonight." At least we wouldn't be too matchy-matchy. She checked the book's instructions for how to get into her gown and how to correctly position the pearl-embellished headdress over the midpoint of her head and tuck her hair under it so only the outer locks showed. She did look exquisite if not particularly comfortable. This sad tradeoff in women's fashion made me glad to be a nudist. Although unfortunately not tonight.

When she had completed her own arrangements, she went to the dower chest and bribed me into a softly luxurious purple velvet jacket. This time my RR monogram was in pearls rather than gold embroidery and it matched the pearl-studded collar I was to wear. All of this was distressing enough, but then she dug out a ruched, green velvet ruff and slipped it over my head. It had bells.

Promptly at 7 there was a knock at the door. Dodging an obstacle course of rawhides, my human opened it. My Attendant was on bended knee with his hatted head lowered at a respectful angle.

"The presence of The Royal Hound Rufus the Red and Lady Cressida is requested forthwith in The Chamber of Libations." By this I surmised that cocktail hour was about to begin. And where there were cocktails there were also cocktail snacks. As if reading my mind, My Attendant wiped my face. This time his spit rag was purple.

I jingled up and down various corridors, descended a grand stone staircase, and trotted along more corridors until we arrived at an atmospherically lit, large wood paneled room. At one end there was a raised platform upon which were distributed a company of colorfully clad musicians with lutes and flutes, lyres and the like, playing what passed for Tudor cocktail music.

"The Royal Hound Rufus the Red. And the Lady Cressida," announced My Attendant.

'Where the f--- is C camera!" yelled a familiar voice.

Heads turned but more I suspect because of all the jingling. There was a sprinkling of guests already present, not including the bridesmaids and groomsmen. It was a stunning, if severely anachronistic sight, although I am not sure everyone appreciated looking like refugees from a big budget British costume drama. Certainly not the men. Doublets and hose were de rigeur along with velvet caps. The groomsmen's headgear had plumes. The bridesmaids, decorative at the best of times, were especially so in matching gowns of blue trimmed with gold and gold headpieces studded with what were probably faux gems. Then again, considering who was throwing this shindig it was impossible to know.

Ben detached himself from the bridal party and joined us.

"Don't," he said looking at my human who had just been about to comment after giving him the once over. Her greenish eyes sparkled with a mischievous gleam and her face was split with a grin that was as wide as the Hudson. "We were just plotting what to do to Percy when all this is over. You look gorgeous by the way. The Renaissance suits you."

In a flash, Sergio Emilio Augustus swooped in, headphone as usual firmly in place.

"No! No! No! Back!" he yelled at Ben. "Groomsmen in the center with the girls. You're spoiling my symmetry." I half expected him to stomp his foot. "Marie," he snapped, talking to the pretty dark-haired woman who seldom left his side, "don't let any of them get away!" He pronounced it MahRee, accenting the second syllable and rolling the r in the French fashion. "And where the devil is Tucker when you need him. He's supposed to be keeping an eye on them."

"I think eez trying to find zee one with zee dog's name," she replied disdainfully, adjusting her scarf.

Additional guests filtered in, the women resplendent in Renaissance finery, the men looking like they wanted to throw themselves off a high turret. There was heavy traffic at the bar. In addition, the actresses playing waitresses—a recurring role I suspect—dispersed themselves amongst the guests offering flutes of champagne and yummy-looking nibbles.

"It's Cristal, you know," said a powerfully built young man who appeared at my human's elbow. "It's $400 a bottle. And the caviar is real Beluga, none of that domestic crap." I gave him a sniff. He smelled annoying "I'm Greg, by the way, Brooke's brother."

"Nice to meet you. I'm Cressida, Percy's cousin."

"Yes, you're The Royal Hound Rufus the Red's plus one. Brooke is thrilled he could make it. It's all about creating the right atmosphere you know. And putting on a wedding that no one else will be able to top." I didn't want to point out to him that my human is always my plus one whether she knows it or not, but usually she does, and I turned instead to the server who curtsied and offered me a tasty smelling cocktail canape. The fact that I was probably ingesting a fortune's worth of foie gras made it even tastier.

"Oh, from what I've seen so far, I'm absolutely certain this wedding will be unique," replied my human. I had a feeling she said the wedding was "unique" in the same way people said I have "personality" when I was doing something obnoxious to them like poking my head into their purses or shopping bags. "Anyway, It's a lovely venue."

"Yeah, but for what it costs you'd think they'd find a way to have WiFi. And Alabama Axworthy—you know the star of *Doctor McDreamy Meets his Match Part III*—never mentioned the no WiFi thing when she recommended the place to us. We met her at St. Bart's last year and now we're like her best friends. Brooke even invited her to be a bridesmaid, and she said she really wanted to, but she'd be in Tasmania filming *The Devil Doesn't Always Wear Prada*. We're all pretty steamed about the Wi-Fi sitch. Driving thirty minutes to get service is unacceptable. I mean it's the 21st century." My human forbore from pointing out that she thought the whole point of the wedding was that it wasn't the 21st century.

"Yes, but maybe it will do us all good not to be connected for a few days," she said instead. What she really meant is that it would do her good not be able to see those pesky emails from her editor demanding the next ten non-existent ways to look younger.

"Not when you're the number two guy in a business as important as ours." Speaking as an expert in number two, I can definitely confirm that this guy was right on the money. "I shouldn't wonder if the old man doesn't have a word about making it illegal not to have WiFi when he talks to Senator Bribbage. Dad knows practically everyone in DC you know. He's even met the president a few times. Although that's the least the guy can do given all the money Dad's given him. Anyway, if we'd known about the WiFi issue, I'm sure Secretary of Defense McMinky would have loaned us a satellite uplink for the week. Dad always says what's the point in spending money if you can't call in favors." I was just debating whether to take a break from masticating a piece of poached lobster to poke the guy in the crotch but then the cavalry arrived.

"Cressida, you look lovely!" my human's mother exclaimed. "Not that you don't always look lovely of course, and I know all mothers say that about their daughters, but in your case, it happens to be true. That green really suits you."

I may have accidentally smacked the Knob Prince in the kneecaps with my tail when I said hello to her. He yelped like I had anyway.

"And you look lovely too Rufus," she said as I stood on her feet and leaned affectionately into her body, since my human stopped me from jumping on her. "The bells are a nice touch."

Further conversation was rendered impossible by a deafening blast of trumpets. I guessed that the bride and groom were about to make an entrance. Either that or the bride's father was also best friends with a crowned head of Europe.

"The Lady Brooke and Lord Percival" announced a large, costumed character with astonishing vigor as strong lights illuminated the scene. Brooke glittered in gold and it was a fair bet that the gems with which she was bedecked were not of the costume variety. And "Lord Percival" looked just as uncomfortable in his get up as the rest of the assembled men. I don't think males of the species are big fans of stockings. It probably made them pine for something comfy like a tuxedo with a tight cummerbund. And while the women looked glamorous, the men looked ridiculous. My human would have said it was a metaphor for life.

"Cut. Where's that hound!" shouted the voice of Ethan the director above the hubbub. "Somebody get me that hound!" This was new. Usually, people screamed to get me away from that hound. "He's supposed to be following the bride and groom. Is nobody capable of reading the scene breakdown!"

A harried minion appeared at our side.

"Got him," he called out.

"I want him and his loyal lady attendant behind the bridal couple so they can precess to the front of the room." As my human—or my loyal lady attendant, which I thought had a nice ring to it—and I moved behind the glorious couple, I contemplated whether playing tug of war with Brooke's train would add a more dynamic element to the scene.

"Don't you even think about it, Rufus," warned my human. The downside of having a strong bond with your human is that they always know what's on your mind.

"Going again. Cue troubadours. And… action!" We walked behind Brooke and her swain at a stately pace and made our way to the wedding party who formed a semicircle to welcome us.

"Cut! OK checking the gate. B and C cameras and photographers, mingle. I want good cameo footage."

My Attendant moved forward to tidy my face and as Percy chatted with his groomsmen and Brooke with her ladies—or at least with three of them—I noticed the officiant heading our way. He was perhaps the only man in the room who did not look ridiculous. He looked magnificent. He favored the ladies with a ravishing smile, his eyes lingering on Brooke who flushed and turned away. Not so the other ladies who stood transfixed and pinkly glowing at this dazzling display of male pulchritude.

One of the drink-bearing waitresses approached him and there was an angry, whispered exchange. Or at least she was angry. He looked complacent as he whispered his responses. There might even have been a smile playing about his wide, finely chiseled lips when all at once his face was dripping Cristal.

The waitress curtsied, "So sorry m'lord. I must have tripped." Then she took herself off towards the green baize servant's door.

"At least it's Cristal," said Rush to the bridal party with a grin. "One does so hate to have inferior brands thrown in one's face."

"Do you know her?" asked Driscoll. "Or is it part of Ethan's plan to add dramatic content to the scene."

"I know her slightly. We went out for a bit," came the response. "It wasn't serious so I can't imagine why she's so upset."

"Mingle, mingle, mingle. Ethan wants everyone out and mingling," commanded some miscellaneous minion who inserted himself into our group. "Circulate. Lots of activity." Mingling is my middle name although generally my nose mingles in places no one wants mingled with. Nevertheless, my human and I obediently made the rounds making conversation, which was mostly about me. Attending a cocktail party with an immense hound who is wearing a purple velvet jacket and bells around his neck is a natural ice breaker. I was fed, fêted, petted, and widely admired.

As we circulated, out of the corner of my droopy eye, I noticed the usually composed Brooke looking considerably less so. She was still flushed and talking adamantly and at close quarters to her brother Greg when his face transformed into an angry red. At that moment he definitely did not look like anyone I would want to meet in a dark alley. Together their eyes found the figure of the officiant who was in high spirits, gaily, if damply, entertaining his enthralled gaggle of bridesmaids. I was too far away to hear what Brooke and her brother were saying, but I had the feeling that I wasn't the only one who knew that relations between Brooke and her wedding officiant were not all that they should be.

This wedding was getting interesting.

Chapter 8

Whatever might have been going to happen was cut short by another loud fanfare and a page requesting that the distinguished company makes its way to the Chamber of Repast for that night's feast.

Tucker, who was dressed in an unbecoming shade of yellow—although to be fair is any shade of yellow really becoming—materialized at my human's side. But then again, trying to impersonate a Tudor courtier with a mic curving out from under your cap is not an easy look to pull off in any color.

"Hi Cressida. Nice to see you again. On your way to the door Ethan—that's the videographer—wants you and Rufus to do a cross in front of B camera." He pointed to a guy manning one of the Steadicams. My human stared at it warily. She had been Steadicam roadkill almost as many times as she's been mowed down by a New Yorker doing the grocery shopping.

We crossed (quickly) in front of B camera and followed the general exodus out the door and down a corridor lined with yet more menacing items of battle. Even the dining room had two suits of armor flanking it on the off chance that the diners needed defending.

The chamber was large and wood-paneled with colorful coats of arms and battle flags depending from small, ornately carved balconies on which musicians played period music with period instruments. None of that piped in rubbish here. Long tables were arranged perpendicular to the one at which the bridal party was now taking its place. My human didn't need to read the ornate script on the place cards to know where we were seated. There was a raised feeding station to the left of one of the chairs.

"Would The Royal Hound Rufus the Red prefer still or sparkling, m'lady," asked a cute server with a curtsey when we were seated.

"Still, please," said my human as she delivered my leash into the outstretched hand of My Attendant who stood behind us.

I refreshed myself with a drink—the caviar canapes had been a bit salty—while my human turned to a well-fed looking young man to her right.

"I'm Jason," he said, before she could speak. "I know who the dog is—another one of Brooke's idiotic ideas—but are you a friend of the bride or groom?"

"Neither. I'm Percy's cousin Cressida. Nice to meet you." For some reason I had the distinct impression that she was not being entirely truthful.

"Oh yes, one of the groom's people." There was something distinctly disapproving in the way he said "groom." "I'm Brooke's cousin, not that that's anything to be proud of either. She was a spoiled brat as a kid and still is. Not to mention that she and those bridesmaids of hers look like they could do with a few of Dad's pies. My dad is Brooke's Uncle Pete, of Pete's Pies," he said, indicating an even more well-fed man seated across from us, "I'm sure you've heard of him. He single-handedly built the largest pie franchise in America."

"Yes of course," said my human politely.

"What do you do for a living?" he asked.

"I'm a writer."

"I run a family office hedge fund. You've probably read about it, Pie in the Sky Investments. We're a long/short, industry agnostic investment group and mostly focus on convertible arbitrage…" The details were riveting. Especially his gleeful account of the killing he made in Luscious Lingerie, the eatable underwear company and how he launched a short attack that destroyed Teddy's Tools because the CEO refused to take a meeting with him. Who knew Wall Street could be so violent.

"… People also told me I was crazy to dabble in biotech because everyone loses their shirt. But not me. When a company goes public, I go long, because biotech companies are like babies—at first everyone is excited because they have the potential to do anything. I get out before they grow up and everyone figures out that like most kids, they're disappointments and can't do squat. And if one of them has a product that actually does make it through Phase III clinical trials, I short the stock before the company can release the results because they'll either show that the drug doesn't work, and the shares will tank or else they'll show that the drug does work but the shares tank anyway because the analysts will rip apart the data because that's what analysts like to do. And the genius part is that even if the analysts can't find anything to rip apart, the shares will crater anyway because now the company actually has to sell something and no one in the company knows how. I make a killing no matter what. See this"—he wiggled a pinky with a thick gold ring set with a large diamond—"I buy myself one of these after every kill. I have a lot of rings." He smiled like a hunter reminiscing about some especially satisfying spate of carnage. "But you have to have the brains and of course, the gut."

He definitely had the gut. Just not the kind he was thinking of. As he was talking my human's head nodded more times than a bobble head doll on a bumpy road. I'll bet she was grateful for the rudimentary acting skills she picked up as an extra, especially considering that any moment C camera or B camera or even A camera might be recording the scene for posterity. Her companion had just begun to expound upon his views on the killing to be made in distressed assets when he was interrupted.

"A toast to the happy couple, Brooke and Percy," Ben announced from the bridal table.

The room rose, drinks in hand.

"Happy my ass," my human's companion snorted. "I give it a year. A more vain and self-centered human being than Brooke Kovac never walked the earth." I guess he would know. "And she treats my beautiful sister like shit. Not that the groom's any prize either. I have no use for these snotty investment banker deal jockeys who think they're the smartest person in the room." And we all knew who that was.

"Where do you live?" he said when everyone was again seated.

"Manhattan. The Upper West Side." She glanced at me. For once I think she was hoping I would do something disgraceful that would require her immediate attention. Naturally this meant that it was incumbent upon me to be on my best behavior.

"Well, it's a convenient neighborhood for the dog I suppose but too many kids and old people for my taste. I just bought a condo in Soho. It's a penthouse with a killer 360-degree view. I'd love to show it to you some time."

"That would be lovely," (why my human's nose was not as long as mine, I have no idea), "and if I didn't have a boyfriend, I'd be happy to take you up on it."

"That's a shame, I think you're pretty. Anyway, here's my number for when you break up." Then he turned to the young woman seated on his right. "Hi, I'm Jason. Are you a friend of the bride or groom?"

My human's relief was short lived.

"I see you've met my son," said Pete the Pie Man beaming with pride. Unlike the biotech babies, his child clearly was not a disappointment. "Looks like you two got on like a house on fire. He'd be a great catch you know. And of course, he comes with all the pies you can eat," he chuckled. "Not that a girl with your figure looks like she eats many pies. Which is a shame, really. Most people think of them as fattening desserts, but actually the ancient Greeks and Romans invented them as savory meals. Very few people know that pies have a fascinating history...."

The lesson on pies and pie making was equally as compelling as the one on hedge fund investing and it continued unabated through the appetizers. As I delicately munched my own meal—roast pigeon, which I also understand makes an excellent pie—I could not help but notice that my human's wine glass was being emptied and refilled at a steady clip.

He had just begun to rail against the perfidy of the French—not that one really needed a reason—for refusing to call a pie a pie and referring to them as "en croute" instead, when his wife intervened.

"Dear, I'm sure this young lady, has heard enough about pies. Let her eat in peace."

But peace was in short supply that evening. There seemed to be a kerfuffle at the head of the table and when it ended the officiant had food on his head.

He rose to go clean up just as our main course arrived and Mrs. Pete leaned confidentially over the table.

"Have you ever been to Mexico?"

"Only to Mexico City to visit a friend from school," answered my human, happy that the conversation seemed to be taking a more general, non-pie-related turn.

"Dear, I've been simply up to my eyeballs trying to renovate our place in Cabo. You cannot believe what a nightmare it's been. No one speaks English, can you imagine? And even when they say they do, they don't. And that's just for starters..."

It would appear that the Pie Man apple had not fallen far from the tree on either side of the pedigree. At regular intervals my human excused herself from engrossing tales of the treachery of Mexican contractors and bent down to pretend to do something to me that needed doing. If she hoped for a respite, it didn't work.

The only thing that interrupted the free flow of Cabo construction ills was the momentary commotion when one of Brooke's friends had been inadvertently served a potato.

And as soon as dessert (pies!) arrived, Pete interrupted his wife to regale my human with a critique of their crimping, texture, and taste. It was saying something that "Madrigal Karaoke" was starting to look pretty good.

Its advent was heralded like so much else of significance, with a trumpet fanfare.

"It's Karaoke Time!" cried a jolly looking fellow who introduced himself as The Master of Revels. "Prithee, we must away this instant to the Chamber of Revels!"

"It was wonderful to meet you all," said my human, her nose growing another inch as she rose.

She turned to My Attendant, "The Master of Revels looks like he's having a good time," she said as she reclaimed my leash, "but I'm not sure the rest of us will."

"That's Matt. He's always having a good time," he said,

momentarily breaking character. "He and I were at Julliard together and he was a terrific Puck in Shakespeare in the Park's Midsummer Night's Dream."

We allowed ourselves to be duly herded to our next destination. The Chamber of Revels was a smaller and more intimate room and was dimly lit in a manner one would expect of a Tudor nightclub. Scattered about were tables elaborately festooned with ribbons of cloth and there was a long bar where a selection of inhibition-dissolving wines and spirits were being served. At the front of the room there was a raised stage on which several musicians and vocalists were already playing what the bravest amongst us were expected to sing. It was a stretch to try to make the karaoke equipment look Elizabethan, but an attempt had been made with some gold-trimmed velvet draping.

The soft music stopped, and a trumpet fanfare sounded signaling that Brooke, Percy, and the wedding party were to be amongst us once more.

The ubiquitous Tucker dropped anchor at my human's side.

"Brooke wants to know if The Royal Hound Rufus the Red can bay to accompany the singers. Also, Ethan wants you to move him around so he jingles."

My human explained that The Royal Hound Rufus the Red does exactly what The Royal Hound Rufus the Red wants but that she would give both her best shot.

"Distinguished Lords and Ladies, let us make merry this eve till we be parted by the lark," boomed the Master of Revels as he curvetted onto the stage. "But first, indulge we in libations to uplift the spirits."

"Madrigal Punch, m'lady," curtsied a young woman holding a tray.

"I would go easy on that if I were you," advised a deep,

melodious voice instantly recognizable as that of the extortionate Adonis of this afternoon's fun and games. He favored my human with a look that exuded both humor and charm. "It's got quite a kick, but I expect that's the point. Do you sing? I don't think we've met. I'm Rush Devereux. Our lovely bride has bestowed upon me the honor of officiating at her ceremony."

"Thanks for the warning. I'm Cressida Pennington. Percy's cousin."

"A very appropriate name for the occasion. And this is the magnificent Royal Hound Rufus the Red whom I had the privilege of meeting this afternoon. What a fine looking beast. And so well behaved. But I'm sure that's entirely down to his beautiful mistress." He flashed her a dazzling smile.

Although my human was beautiful, at least to many of us, popular opinion was strongly against the part about me being well-behaved. But I had to hand it to the guy. He was as smooth as the silk of his fine white shirt. On the other hand, it might have been less my charm or even that of my human that prompted his gallantry and more the fact that we appeared to be the focus of either A camera, B camera or perhaps even the much-maligned C camera. It was as hard to tell them apart as it was Riley, Kiley, and Katie, but as I shook my head it was only My Attendant's quick hands with the drool rag that prevented me from adding a new filter to the lens.

"Oh there you are Rush. I've been looking for you," said Emily, the "fat" bridesmaid. She put her hand proprietorially on his arm. Clearly, the officiant had had a very busy afternoon. The good humor left his face like someone had thrown a switch.

"I wish you'd stop following me," he said with annoyance. "It's bad enough that you forced me to spend the afternoon with you, but I would actually like to be able to talk to other people without your constant hovering. Don't you have bridesmaid's duties to attend to. Go!" I could see hurt and anger fight for possession of her face. And I wasn't the only one. The room had been chosen for its intimacy and excellent acoustics and at the sound of Rush's raised voice, conversation momentarily stopped. Emily fled the room followed by her brother whose choleric disposition was now on full display. He grabbed Rush roughly by the arm on his way out.

"No one talks to my sister like that! Do you understand. No one. This isn't over." And with that he dashed out.

There was a brief moment of uncomfortable silence. Then as is the way of these things everyone started talking at once and pretended that nothing had happened.

One of the decorative bridesmaids approached us.

"Oh Rush, how awful for you. That girl positively persecutes you. And she's dangerously delusional too. You're all she talked about over dinner. She thinks she's your new girlfriend. But of course, WE know that's not true." She looked at Rush the way I look at a piece of liver.

"Cressida, this is Kiley," he said making the introductions as if nothing had happened. "I do apologize that you had to see that," he said, in a voice rich with sincerity and rueful charm. "That girl's been stalking me since we met, and I'm sorry, I just lost it." Kiley didn't even glance at my human as she took Rush's muscular arm.

"Come on, let's look at music. Maybe there's a duet for us to have some fun with."

They moved off and my human took a large and therapeutic swig of Madrigal Punch.

Their place was quickly taken by my human's mother and her uncle.

"Hi Mother. Hello Uncle Charles. Are you enjoying the entertainment?"

"The music or the drama?" answered her mother raising her voice to make herself heard. The abundance of strong spirits was beginning to have its desired effect and the off-key strains of *Come Away Sweet Love*, could be heard above the conversation. Fortunately, the karaoke-ees had backup singers to carry them along. They were probably enjoying their gig about as much as the waitresses were enjoying theirs.

"I'm sorry that Percy's been monopolizing Ben," said Uncle Charles. "I think given everything, he's glad of the support. And of course, you have Rufus to keep you company." I waved my tail and looked up expectantly. He fed me a cookie and scratched me behind the ear.

"I have to admit, I thought having Rufus would be a nightmare, but between this gentleman," she said indicating My Attendant who stood ready to deploy the drool rag at a moment's notice, "and the excuse he provides to interrupt tedious conversations, he's a godsend."

"I'm happy to hear it," said Uncle Charles. "And even if this isn't our idea of a good time, between the excellent cuisine and the attentive audience, at least Rufus will enjoy himself. Oh, and I would avoid the Madrigal Punch. I think it's made up almost entirely of whichever vodka is the most expensive. I'm sure Brooke's father will tell me exactly which one and how much it costs later."

"Not necessarily, Charles," said my human's mother. "I think Anne was right and you're going to have competition for Mike's attention." She looked across the room where Tucker and Mike Kovac were in deep conversation, ignoring the madrigalia swirling about them. "On a more pleasant note, Cressida, your uncle has just been telling me he's up for a federal judgeship."

"Congratulations, Uncle Charles. It's well deserved."

Tucker, responding to the voice of his master in his earpiece, detached himself from whatever Kovacian business he had been transacting, and approached us with a purposeful stride.

"Ethan says Rufus isn't jingling enough. He wants him to circulate. And see if you can get him to bay."

We circulated as gales of laughter accompanied the increasingly inebriated madrigal singers as they were egged on by the always jovial Master of Revels. Every now and then I condescended to add my voice to theirs, which everyone seemed to find even more uproarious. It made a change from people yelling bad things at me and holding their ears.

But the winner of the circulating sweepstakes was undoubtedly Aunt Anne. She glided gracefully around the room telling anyone who was still sober enough to listen, what a wonderful concept for a wedding this was; and that Brooke is such a treasure; and how lucky Percy was to have found her.

The waitresses weren't the only actresses in the house.

Chapter 9

Our first night at the castle passed uneventfully. I found the mattress much to my liking and I hope that my appreciative snores conveyed the magnitude of my approbation. As the sun came up, I shoved my moist wrinkles and cold nose onto my human's face to apprise her of this important new development. She squealed supportively. We bloodhounds pride ourselves on being a utilitarian breed—a gym, an exercise coach, a sous chef, an interior redecorator, and most importantly, an alarm clock. We're also known for our gardening skills, although as a New Yorker, it's something I rarely get the opportunity to enjoy.

While my human was getting dressed, I as usual ran my cold wet nose along her bare flesh to chivvy her along. You would be forgiven for thinking that this signaled an urgent need to take care of business whereas what it actually signaled was an urgent need to sniff as much real estate as possible. That's not to say that once we were outside I neglected to take care of the expected business. I did. Eventually. But my first priority was to conduct an exhaustive exploration of the castle grounds, which I was overjoyed to discover included a large and fragrant shrubbery maze.

"No Rufus, we are NOT going into that maze," said my human reading my mind. "I'm hungry and we've got a busy day ahead of us." She also knew that once we were in that maze we weren't getting out of it until I chose to lead us out. That of course was the whole point, so I did what I usually did when my human starts a sentence with "No." I bayed. Fortunately, no one was sticking their heads out of windows and screaming at me, which is what usually happens when I bay at dawn o'clock. It goes without saying that my human seldom starts sentences with "No."

We returned to The Rufus Suite and while my maze-denying human took herself into the shower, I took myself out the door and into the kitchen to investigate the possibility of a pre-breakfast appetizer. As one would expect, the place was bustling with frenetic matinal activity; cooks and breakfast items flew hither and thither across the room under the close supervisory eye of the gray-haired lady whose pie crimping had not passed muster.

I was just tucking into a jam crepe when Uncle Charles walked in.

"Would it be possible to get some ice? My wife thinks she's sprained a toe." The gray-haired lady stared at him like he was Banquo's ghost. In quick succession she went white as a turnip and as red as a beet. Uncle Charles, seemingly oblivious to these color changes, ambled over to give me a scratch.

"Lucy, get the gentleman some ice," the gray-haired lady spat out with an odd emphasis on the word gentleman. As soon as the ice was produced Uncle Charles departed and as soon as I phagocytized a croissant I did likewise. I didn't want my human to get lost looking for me.

"Rufus where have you been?" demanded my human when I returned. Then she noticed the croissant crumbs on my snout. "Never mind. Stupid question."

The glories of croissant eating were soon forgotten,

however, as the odious Style Book made an unwelcome reappearance. A rustic tan leather vest was slipped over my head. My human did not fare much better and was attired in what can only be described as Renaissance Sportif.

Making a much more welcome reappearance was My Attendant and his tan drool rag who arrived to escort us to the Chamber of Repast. But when we arrived, we found our way blocked by a stately-looking fellow in possession of a large leather pouch.

"Prithee, extend thy hand and choose a hued button," requested the gentleman as he thrust the bag in front of my human. The significance of the buttons was unknown and as I downed my morning meal—a full English with kibble—the chatter amongst my fellow foragers was largely about their purpose.

We were not long kept in the dark.

"Ladies and Gentlemen, Lords and Ladies, I entreat thee, pray make thy way hence to the front of yon castle" announced our Master of Revels. He had a conspiratorial glint in his eye in the manner of someone about to spring a delightful surprise.

As we obediently assembled in front of the castle, The Master of Revels continued gleefully, "Ye shall all have drawn hued buttons whose meaning shall presently be disclosed. Ye are on the verge of a treasure quest and those with buttons of similar hue shall be your companions in this noble pursuit. Seek one another and be prepared."

"I don't understand," piped up a guy with a shock bright red hair, "is he speaking English? Were we supposed to learn a foreign language?"

"No" said someone nearby, "I think it's like what they spoke in the Dark Ages, you know like when there were Vikings and no Netflix."

"I can translate!" exclaimed a third. "I've watched every episode of *Wolf Hall*.

In the meantime, while hilarity did not exactly ensue, there were many giggles and several minutes of chaos. My human looked around in vain for anyone with a red button until she saw Ben triumphantly waving the very same.

"Well that was lucky," shouted my human over the sound of me saying hello.

"It wasn't luck; I horse traded for this button. Fortunately, it was Kiley, or at least I think it was her, who had drawn it and she wanted to be on Rush's team. Actually, all the bridesmaids did. Not sure who won or maybe it was all of them, since the teams are of four. That could be a bit of a situation since I think Rush slept with all of them. But at least it means we can be together for a while."

A man and a young woman I hadn't seen before came over to join us.

"Hi I'm Henley, Rush's sister," said the woman. "And this is my fiancé Dr. Bruce Bibble. We've got red buttons also." She was tall like her brother and although I could see the resemblance, the strong features that gave his face its striking character did not translate well to a female face. Her companion was good looking in a meticulous sort of way and although not exactly middle aged, he looked to be in its vicinity. There was a studied suavity about him that often passes for charm, and although not tall he conducted himself with the decisive and authoritative air of one who was.

The mutual Introductions completed, Henley continued, "We just got here last night. Two guests bailed at the last minute and Rush said the wedding planner was apoplectic because it messed up his numbers, so he offered us up as replacements. Plus, it was a chance to get out of the clinic for a bit."

"Yes, I believe your brother mentioned something about

it last night," Ben said.

"We'll be right back," interrupted Dr. Bruce. "Henley will need to change her shoes if we're to go traipsing about in a forest." Henley beamed at him as if he had given her the secret of life.

When they had gone, Ben turned to my human.

"Of course Rush also mentioned that his sister was a head case and under no circumstances were any of us to offer her alcohol or anything else. According to him she never met a substance she didn't try and got kicked out of boarding school for drinking and then got kicked out of St. Trinian's Country Day for both drinking and having sex with a teacher. When they finally managed to get her into The Wallis Warfield College for Women her major was drugs and tequila. Rush said she's been pretty much in and out of rehab ever since and then saw Bruce Bibble on a morning TV show and claimed to have been struck by a divine light. Not that it's an excuse, but having your mother take off in your formative years to devote herself to helicopter skiing in the Himalayas and spider ranching in Australia, is not exactly conducive to mental balance."

"What about her father?"

"Coincidentally, you actually have a bit of a connection there---Payne Devereux, was your Uncle Charles's roommate at Princeton. But he seems to have written her off pretty early as a dead loss and Rush said that he basically inherited her when their father died this year. His will left strict instructions that Henley was to be supported financially but was not to be given access to the capital in her trust fund unless Rush is convinced she's permanently clean and sober. But from the way Rush described it, Bibble appears to be her new drug of choice, and an expensive one at that. Even though they're engaged she still runs up a hefty tab at his clinic."

Any further discussion of our teammates was cut short when the Master of Revels once again commanded our attention to explain the game.

"In the dark hours, whilst the gathered company slumbered, my faiyrie minions hath been industriously dispersing engraved tokens throughout the woodland. These do contain responses to the queries presented upon the parchment thou art about to receive. Yet faiyries are mischievous, thus some tokens be true whilst others be not. It doth fall upon thee to discern. When thou hearest 'yon gong resound from the turret and the flag dost wave, return hither and the team possessing the most correct answers shall be bestowed with a crate of a cherished libation adorned with a bespoke commemorative inscription in honor of our joyful couple. And dread not becoming lost in the forest for if my mirthful minions fail to locate thee, the valiant and dauntless Royal Hound Rufus the Red shall. He hath saved many a Duke and Earl gone astray."

This was news to me unless Central Park had suddenly become a hotbed of the aristocracy. And although valiant and dauntless would not exactly have been the words I would have chosen to describe myself, I do excel at finding humans, especially those who happen to be trying to eat.

When Henley returned, she was wearing a new pair of shoes and hanging onto the arm of her fiancé. A merry minion handed us a leather pouch in which to collect the tokens and a parchment with the questions they were supposed to answer:

What is Brooke's birthday?
What is Brooke's favorite color?
What is Brooke's favorite animal?
What is Brooke's favorite movie?
Who is Brooke's favorite designer?
What is Brooke's favorite travel destination?
What is Brooke's favorite store?
What is Brooke's favorite Saturday activity?
What is Brooke's favorite streaming series?
How many pairs of shoes does Brooke have?
What sorority was Brooke in?

How did Percy and Brooke meet?
What perfume does Brooke wear?
What is Brooke's favorite flower?

"I'm sensing a theme here," observed my human. "Although I notice that there doesn't seem to be anything about her favorite food."

"Food avoidance represents a quest for perfection which will never be attained without the deep spiritual connection to all our beings that once were and will be again," pronounced Dr. Bibble. Henley was positively incandescent with pride at this new bit of wisdom. "True knowledge is self-knowledge and self-knowledge is true knowledge." My humans exchanged a look. Now I have to admit that most of what humans say that does not involve "Rufus would you like a cookie" or "Rufus do you want to go for a walk", is mostly gibberish, but Dr. Bruce may have elevated it to new heights.

"His book on the subject is on *The New York Times* best seller list," gushed his adoring acolyte. "It's called *Self-knowledge and the Path to Power and Fulfillment in Three Weeks*. If you read nothing else ever again you must read that. Of course, it can't replace the regression to progression treatments at the clinic, but I guarantee it will completely change your life."

"Also Dr. Bruce's bank account," whispered my human to Ben as he took charge of the parchment and the pouch, and we followed the others into the forest.

"How exactly does the treatment work," said Ben turning to Dr. Bruce. He was nothing if not polite.

"Well in layman's terms, I discovered during my extensive research with the shamans of the Amazon, among whom there is no mental illness" (at any moment I expected my human to jump in and point out that association is not causality, which is the kind of useful information they teach you at kennels like Stanford), "that small amounts of poisons extracted from a variety of toxic plants and venomous snakes can allow us to see and more importantly experience our pasts, including past lives and the people in them, and to understand how we came to be as we are and also to open up visions of the future that are normally inaccessible to our consciousness. It's only through transformative, regenerative regressions that lead to future progressions that we become enlightened and whole beings and can throw off the shackles that have bound and continue to bind us to whatever is holding us back from attaining the true and perfect selves that the universe ordained us to be." I listened attentively since I, too, am always looking for new ways to evade things that are holding me back. "The shamans of course don't have access to modern methods of administration so in the Amazon these mind-expanding substances are ingested. However, in my clinic we discovered that they deliver an even more potent experience when given by injection." It was pretty apparent that Dr. Bruce was not only Henley's drug of choice in and of himself but that he was also the pusher of a veritable smorgasbord of them.

"How fascinating," said my human in the same tone she used when listening to the history of pies. The only trips she likes taking tend to involve airplanes. "Are you a medical doctor?"

"Oh the medical establishment would never understand Bruce's work," declared Henley. "They're too busy pushing pills or putting patients on couches for their own financial benefit. Bruce has a doctorate in English which is why he's so good at communicating and has such a deep understanding of human nature. His thesis, *Beowulf: Why?* is a masterpiece that created a sensation at his university and the shamans even conferred a special title on him because of his special abilities." Dr. Bruce definitely had special abilities, no doubt about that, at least judging by his expensive clothes and handmade Italian shoes.

"It's true that physicians focus too closely on only a small part of the human organism and as such are often blind to the potentialities of alternative methodologies of therapeutic intervention especially as they concern the pathologic mechanisms of our inner and past consciousness and the role they play in the current state of our being," added Dr. Bruce.

"It's why we're so eager to expand across the country, so Bruce can help as many people as possible. I've been in and out of rehab clinics and therapist's offices all my life, and nothing helped because they could only treat my present self without reference to the multitude of people I was and will be. It's why we came actually. I'm hoping to persuade my brother to release the money from my trust fund so others can be helped as I was."

"Then best of luck," said Ben. "The treasure hunt might get a bit hectic, but Rush is sure to be around later today for the sword fighting and archery competitions."

"And speaking of the treasure hunt, by the sound of it, it seems we're already way behind," said my human, if for no other reason than to change the subject. She turned to her teammates. "I'm afraid you haven't drawn a team likely to win. We neither of us know Brooke very well so the treasure hunt is basically an excuse to take Rufus for a walk in the forest." I bayed to let everyone know that Rufus approved of excuses to take Rufus for a walk in the forest.

We plunged deeper into the woods as I forged ahead. From time to time, we saw flashes of metal hanging on the trees that turned out to be engraved disks with potential answers to the questions on the parchment. We heard the sounds of laughing and debate from several better-informed teams that prompted my humans to grab a few tokens for form's sake. That was when the speed at which we were traveling allowed for grabbing of any kind.

"Your dog seems to know where he is going," said Dr. Bruce. "Do you always allow him to lead you like this?"

"Life is generally easier if I do," replied my exceedingly wise human.

"Abdicating responsibility to a lower form of life is a sign of an unfulfilled destiny. It is something I can help you with. I always travel with my treatments." Now I am a peaceable hound by nature, but I wondered if it would upset my human greatly if this lower form of life were to sink his teeth into Dr. Bruce's backside.

"Where is he taking us," Henley asked with alarm. "This place gives me the creeps and there doesn't seem to be way out." She clung even more tightly to the arm of her guru.

"I wouldn't worry," Ben assured her. "In my experience Rufus never wants to go anywhere unpleasant. He's probably just tracking someone who gave him a sausage at breakfast."

There were no sausages at the end of my trail but rather a familiar location. We emerged from the forest at the faux ruined chapel and the scenic Overlook.

"Oh, it's beautiful!" exclaimed Henley as she took in the picturesque scene. "I sense that I have been here before. I think I was a medieval nun who prayed in that chapel." History was clearly not Henley's strong suit.

While the others took in the view and inhaled the spring-scented air, Ben looked longingly at the floor of the chapel. His reverie was abruptly interrupted.

"Rufus, no!" yelled my human. "Get away from those daffodils. Ben, help me drag Rufus away. He's digging up the flower bed." Too late. I had struck pay dirt. Or more precisely, its absence. Using my long nails, the cutting of which is forbidden, I scratched at something that was considerably more solid than earth.

"What's he found now?" my human wailed as Ben rushed over.

'It's made of wood, whatever it is," Ben said as he assisted me in my excavations. Henley and Dr. Bruce came over to see what was going on.

"Good boy Rufus!" exclaimed Ben as he smooshed my wrinkles in a most gratifying manner. "I can't believe it. I think he's found another one!"

"Found another what?" asked Henley.

"An entrance to a hidden tunnel. Let's see where this one leads." His eyes gleamed like mine when I spot an unattended roast chicken. Up and coming architect he might be, but at that moment Ben looked more like a young boy in an adventure comic. He tugged at the metal handle on the wooden door, and it opened to reveal a flight of stone stairs.

My human sighed. She knew when the two men in her life were determined to do something resistance was futile.

"I don't want to go down there," said Henley. "Bruce let's go back."

"Now my dear. Calm yourself." Then much to our surprise he took a syringe from his pocket and jabbed it in into Henley's unresisting arm. "In the first place, we have no idea how to go back and in the second fear is an irrelevancy in the world of our regression work. Every experience is merely a step in the journey to ultimate self-knowledge and fulfillment. With the spirits to guide us we have nothing to fear from anything on this temporal plane."

Fortunately, it wouldn't be spirits that would be guiding us.

My humans took out their phones, which they were never without in the vain hope that a bar would miraculously appear out of nowhere, and turned on the flashlights. Ben took my leash, and I led the way down. This passageway appeared to be much wider and looked to be of a newer construction than the previous one.

"See," Dr. Bruce assured his patient. "We are perfectly safe. Feel the spirits of your past and future lives enveloping and protecting us as we move forward." Meaning he, too, was curious to find out where the passage would lead.

"But what happens if this tunnel leads nowhere and we are all entombed for eternity?" Henley moaned, the drugs obviously having not yet kicked in.

"I can assure you," my human said soothingly, "Rufus is not big on being entombed for eternity. The tunnel leads somewhere. I just hope it's not into someone's bathroom."

Onwards we went for a considerable time. All idle chitchat about past lives, future lives, and eternal entombment, came to a halt when I stopped at the base of another flight of stairs. Those on this end, however, did not lead to a trap door above, but to a small landing and what looked like an actual door. It lacked a handle, so Ben pushed on it and it swung open. He started laughing.

"It figures," my human said as I dove for a box of biscuits. We were in a large pantry filled with food. Henley and Dr. Bruce joined us and Ben swung what appeared to be a row of shelves shut behind them.

"This is probably the tunnel the bootlegger dug," said Ben. "No wonder whenever the property was raided all the cops ever found was lemonade."

"Yes, I can see it all now," said Henley. "I must have been a gun moll. It explains why I've always been attracted to drop waisted dresses and those cute little pistols the ladies used. Perhaps my reaction to the tunnel was the fear I felt at getting caught."

"Exactly, my dear. You must learn to trust. We still have much work to do." He pulled a small plastic bag out of his pocket. "Have a mushroom. It will help." The guy was like a walking psychedelic pharmacy.

My human removed the box of biscuits from my mouth, and we headed into the kitchen where our sudden appearance came as a bit of a surprise.

"Rufus was hungry," said my human hastily, not wanting to explain that I had been vandalizing flower beds and discovering secret passages.

One quick smoked salmon sandwich later we were back at the front of the castle to await the appearance of the others. We joined Percy and Brooke who were chatting with the Master of Revels.

"I'm afraid we didn't do very well," said my human, as she turned in our tokens. "I realized I don't even know where you two met."

"We met at an SS party," Brooke answered. My human looked confused. She knew none of Percy's friends liked her, but she hadn't pegged Brooke as a Nazi.

"I told you not to call it that," Percy said. He turned to Cressida. "It was a party hosted for those who matched on Swipe Sideways."

"Ah," my human replied relieved.

"I still don't understand why you get annoyed when I call it the SS," Brooke responded petulantly.

Perhaps my human should take a piece of Driscoll's action after all.

Chapter 10

The teams gradually filtered out of the forest, read their answers, and delivered their tokens to the Master of Revels for verification. Not surprisingly the prize—which turned out to be four crates of Dom Pérignon with a custom label featuring a photo of the happy couple—was won by a team helmed by one of Brooke's bridesmaids. I guess at least one of them hadn't ended up on Rush's team.

We came in dead last.

It was then that the absence of Rush's team was noticed.

"Many apologies, my Lords and Ladies. I humbly confess that I bestowed the prize prematurely. Verily, one team hath not yet graced us with their presence. Mayhaps we can beseech that most esteem'd of our guests whose tracking prowess is legendary, to plunge into the depths of the forest green and retrieve them." He bowed deferentially in my direction. I of course would be happy to plunge back into the depths of the forest green and retrieve anything, but I am something of a specialist in humans. Especially those eating things I am not supposed to have.

"I'll come with you," Ben said to my human. He obviously thought she looked pretty cute in her sporty Tudor togs and I had a feeling if it were up to him, our quest would be a long one.

Back into the forest we plunged, me with my nose alternating between snorting the ground and sniffing the air, and Ben, with his arm around my human's waist, trying to slow us down. Presently we could hear voices. Well shrieks would be more like it. I took a sharp left at a fork and there was my quarry on the path just ahead of us. I inhaled deeply, lifted my nose skywards and bayed triumphantly.

I had found.

Since my baying might possibly carry even further than Tucker's bagpipes, I'm sure everyone in front of the castle also knew I had found. But what I had found was something else again.

"What the actual F!" exclaimed my human although, as usual, the language she used was considerably less ladylike. Riley and Kiley were having what is euphemistically known as a "cat fight" although what they were doing would have been a good bit more entertaining, at least to me, if it had been actual cats. It was just another example of the disappointing animal references that seem to litter human speech like so many tantalizing tidbits that promise much and deliver nothing. But at least a dog fight refers to battles between daring aviators and not silly women.

But I digress.

Riley and Kiley, never ones to shy from clichés, were going at it with the full Monty of the cat fight arsenal. There was pushing, shoving, scratching, and the pulling of hair, which I understand is traditional for combat of this kind. And they were screaming rude words at each other and claiming possession of Rush like he was a half price pair of Louboutins at a Christmas sale. Meanwhile the gentleman in question along with one of Brooke's male cousins stood by looking on with amusement.

Ben sprang into action.

"Ladies, please. Stop this immediately," he pleaded and attempted to get between them. This seemed to infuriate them even more. Ben appealed to the men.

"Don't look at us," said the Male Cousin. "I have a twenty on the one in green."

Ben would probably have had more success if he had warned the women that they were ruining their nails. However, since the situation obviously called for decisive action, I decided to do what human male chivalry could not. I leapt forward, pushed over the one not in green and sat on her. I would like to claim that it was surprisingly easy but given that she weighed practically nothing, it was not surprising at all.

The Male Cousin was exultant. "I win!" he cried.

"Absolutely not," declared Rush. "All bets are off if the ref stops the fight. What do you say, Lady Cressida. You're a neutral party." He favored her with a smile so dazzling that it nearly got the fight started again.

"I say that we help these women up and get back to the castle. The others are waiting."

And so it was. Although I noticed that Ben made sure that they were well separated on the path home.

Our arrival was greeted with relief and cheers. Naturally I was the hero of the story. If only they knew how much of one.

"Oh dear, what happened?" asked Brooke's mother as she surveyed the state of her daughter's bridesmaids. Katie, standing nearby, seemed to have no need to inquire.

"We fell," said Riley sullenly.

"What, both of you? And where were the gentlemen?" Brooke dug her elbow into her mother's ribs and shook her head.

"Verily, we may now proceed!" crowed the Master of Revels with more than a little affected mirth. "Hast thou thy precious hoard to be tallied?" They did not. The tokens had been scattered when the young women "fell." In point of fact, Riley had hit Kiley over the head with them and the tokens had been lost. "Then the results stand. Felicitations to the victors! Now hark fair ladies, as the noble gentlemen of the castle prepare their swords for combat, seeking thy favor in the name of chivalry." Which was a fancy way of saying that the sword fight was about to begin. And at least it would be the men fighting this time which would make a change. "The triumphant champion in this contest shall win the hand of the enchanting Lady Brooke and be granted the honor of leading her in the inaugural dance at this evening's Masque. Look sharp gentlemen!" He seemed to regard this last comment as worthy of a jolly laugh. I had a feeling the guy's acting career was secure.

"That's my cue," said Ben.

"Tell me you're not all expected to charge at each other with real swords," said my human with more than a tinge of alarm.

"Relax, we're using the blunted ones that they keep for film crews. But we're all expected to suit up in Tudoresque leather protective gear to make it look as real as possible. Some of us fence, so I'm sure we'll be able to put on a good show."

"Who's participating? Obviously not the women. This wedding is incredibly sexist."

"Well Tudor times tended to be like that. Also, I don't think women engaged in mortal combat in the 16th century. At least not those who weren't bridesmaids."

"I don't know, some of those Medici women seemed to do alright."

"You're correct, as usual; but as far as participants, I know for sure it's going to be me, Rufus—not you," he added as I looked up at him expectantly, "Dris, and Buck. I also think Rush signed up since he was on the fencing team at Princeton. Then there are some of the other younger guys and I heard that Brooke's brother is also going to have a go. Oh, and Percy too, of course. I haven't spoken to Brooke's brother yet, but the rest of us have agreed that we're going to let Percy win, although he's probably a good enough fencer to do that on his own."

"Be careful anyway," said my human. "I don't put anything past Buck and Driscoll." And with that, Ben kissed her on the cheek and loped off in the direction of a colorful tent that had been erected to serve as a dressing room. I bayed at his retreating back. I have entourage abandonment issues.

"And how is The Royal Hound Rufus the Red doing today?" inquired Tucker obsequiously, channeling his inner Uriah Heep and patting me on the top of my head where I do not like to be patted. "Ethan and Sergio Emilio Augustus would like The Royal Hound Rufus the Red to stand next to Brooke when she presents the winner with her hand."

"I think that can be arranged, providing Rufus doesn't decide to chase after a squirrel, a racoon, a cat, or anyone eating something he wants."

"I'm sure Rufus wouldn't do that, would you Rufus. Rufus is such a good boy, aren't you a good boy Rufus." He was cooing and using that annoying singsong voice with unnecessarily extended syllables that humans seem to think is appropriate for children and dogs. Luckily for him he oozed off to irritate someone else before I could do something unsanitary to his pants.

Not that it's saying much, but things began to look up appreciably when Uncle Charles wandered over to give me a scratch and a biscuit and not tell me I'm a good boy. I suspect as the owner of a Golden Retriever, he knew better.

"Force of habit," he explained to my human. "All my pockets have cookies for Scout." Scout might be an obedient wuss of a dog but at least he had the good sense to train his human in the basics.

"Hark, my Lords and Ladies! The contest is upon us!" the Master of Revels trumpeted. "Each round shall endure for but two minutes and the victor of each round shall face the next challenger until only one true Champion shall emerge triumphant. To commence we have Lord Jonathan of Williamsburg challenging Sir Rufus of the Upper East Side."

There was a murmur.

"Wait, the dog is fighting?" said someone off to our left. "He seemed like such a nice dog."

"No, it's the other one," her companion replied.

"Lords and Ladies, I beseech thee, grant me thy attention. Just to clarify, our combatant is not The Royal Hound Rufus the Red, but Sir Doctor Rufus."

"What another Rufus?" said a lady off to our right. "Someone named their child Rufus?!" I should have been offended, but I could only concur. Nothing that had a pulse should ever be named Rufus.

"I'm so relieved Rufus isn't going to fight," said Henley who was standing behind us talking to Tucker. Just then Dr. Bruce rolled up with a glass of something green and vile looking.

"It's time for your pre-treatment," he said handing her the glass. When she had obediently swallowed the stuff which smelled as bad as it looked, Dr. Bruce pulled a syringe out of his pocket and stuck it into her proffered arm.

"Bruce darling, I've just been talking to Tucker, the groom's cousin, who's been telling me all about his new venture. Tucker, this is my fiancé Dr. Bruce Bibble. Bruce do tell him about your work and the new clinics we want to open. I'm sure he'd love to hear about it."

"Delighted to make your acquaintance. Let me ask you this, have you ever wondered who you really are…."

"Excuse us Uncle Charles," said my human glancing behind her. "I think Rufus is badly in need of a walk." Well one of us was. A little Bibble was too much Bibble.

"I have to go in anyway," said Uncle Charles. "I'm the referee and judge."

"How do you decide who wins?"

"I've been told to score it like fencing with points for body contact. If no one makes contact I'm allowed to award points for style, although what constitutes style in this case, I have no idea."

As soon as he left to take up his judicial duties my human hustled me away just as Dr. Bruce was getting going on the importance of past life regression therapy. For my money, which as a hound is really my human's money, anyone who pats me on the head and talks baby talk to me deserves to be sentenced to an extremely long chat with Dr. Bruce.

We took up our position ready to play our part in the proceedings which I was relieved to learn did not entail Brooke awarding her actual hand to the winner but only a symbolic handkerchief. The imprecision in human speech is constantly confounding to a linguistically rigorous hound such as myself.

While we stood about waiting for the action to commence, the Master of Revels did his best to whip the onlookers into a bloodthirsty frenzy worthy of the lunchtime crowd at the Circus Maximus. In the background, Ethan was berating C camera, Sergio Emilio Augustus was talking frantically into his headphone and MahRee was adjusting her scarf. In short, it was wedding business as usual.

As the first combatants took to the field, I had to be somewhat forcibly restrained from joining them. But I am pleased to report that despite my lack of assistance, my namesake acquitted himself well and upheld the honor of we Rufuses by winning the first round amid much clapping, cheering, and baying. Following his victory, however, the champion position changed hands several times until Ben attained the honor and held it, much to the delight of my human who waved my drool rag enthusiastically in support. Only three challengers now remained—Rush, Greg, and Percy—so it looked very much like Ben would have the honor of losing to the Groom.

And it almost worked out that way.

After a hard-fought battle, Rush lunged at the last minute to score a winning point against Ben. Rush cut such a gallant and graceful figure on the field of battle it was a shame he was such a dick. And I still hadn't forgiven him for not smelling like a toad.

"Lords and Ladies, the penultimate battle is about to be joined," proclaimed the Master of Revels with his usual brio. "Our Champion Sir Rush of Chelsea is to face Lord Gregory of Terrace Park."

All eyes turned towards the two men.

Without warning Greg charged. Pure aggression animated his powerful frame. There was an explosive fury of action. The crowd fell silent, puzzled at the intensity of the combat. Rush, the cooler and more experienced of the two held his ground and fought off his opponent's relentless onslaught. Then, lithe, and athletic he lunged with a speed unexpected in so tall a man and scored a hit to the torso. Greg rushed forward, raised his sword and slashed Rush ferociously on the arm. The leather split open.

"Stop!" Uncle Charles's authoritative voice rang out. He strode forward and grabbed the sword out of Greg's hand just as it looked like he was going to strike another blow. "Are you OK Rush?"

"Yes, I'm fine. It's just a scratch. I'm sure it was just an accidental mix up with the swords." He grinned at Greg with an infuriating twinkle in his eye."

"Then we'll leave it at that," said Uncle Charles. "You are defaulted young man," he said addressing Greg. "I'm sure my son will have no problem, ceding the contest to you Rush. After all, he has a lifetime to lead his bride into ballrooms."

Everyone seemed pleased with this outcome. Or almost everyone. Brooke was as white as her brother was red.

"Let the Champion come forth and accept the token of his victory from his lady," commanded the Master of Revels.

I stood in the place of honor beside Brooke who was dressed for the occasion in an immensely flattering shade of deep purple. She handed a purple handkerchief to the victor.

It was only by dint of my superior, if highly selective, hearing that enables me to hear my human trying to sneak into the refrigerator but not her telling me to sit, that I heard Rush whisper softly to Brooke, "A token of future pleasures to come, m'lady." The captivating smile on his face caused the few ladies who he had not slept with to swoon.

"Wonder what that was about?" Ben said to my human when he had rejoined us. "It didn't look like much of an accident to me and how the devil did Greg get hold of a real sword. And why. If Rush were a gentleman he would have withdrawn and surrendered his place to Percy, but I guess a leopard doesn't change his spots."

I've sniffed the guy, and although I've never actually sniffed a leopard, I'm pretty sure he smelled even less like one than he did a toad.

As far as wildlife goes, this wedding was turning into a bust.

Chapter 11

"My Lords and Ladies," announced The Master of Revels, "ere long, luncheon shall be set forth in the Chamber of Repast. And thereafter, we have diversions that shall please both gentlewomen and gentlemen alike: the noble sport of archery, followed by a delightful lesson in courtly dance, to make ready for the Masque this eve!" Given what I've seen of gentlemen on a dance floor I'm fairly certain The Master's optimism as to their enjoyment was completely unfounded. Gentlemen appreciate dancing the way I appreciate taking a bath.

My human decided to go back to The Rufus Suite to engage in some "freshening up" of the non-makeup kind. Normally I would be in close attendance throughout this particular freshening up activity, but this was a very large castle and I had yet to scratch the surface of its possibilities.

Accordingly, I waited until my human was otherwise occupied, grabbed a rawhide in case I got bored, and slipped out the door again. I very much appreciated the design of these door handles, although I suspect they were not designed with the use to which I was putting them in mind.

I ended up in a charming little study and was just rearranging some sofa cushions preparatory to stretching out for a good chew, when Henley and her brother entered.

"Look Rush, I want to talk to you about something important."

"Let me guess, you've found a new drug or a new dealer."

"I've told you over and over that's all in the past. I don't even drink any more. I have clarity now and I've found my purpose in life. I want to help Bruce open Regression to Progression clinics around the country, maybe even around the world, and share the enlightenment and serenity that his therapeutic approach has given me with others."

"Well if it keeps you off the streets, have at it. But I don't see what it's got to do with me."

"The thing is, in order for us to realize Bruce's vision we need capital. I think I've shown that I am now responsible and sober and should have full access to the money our father left me."

Rush snorted. Speaking as one who has an excellent derisive snort that I employ whenever my human makes some ludicrous suggestion like cutting short my walk in the park because she has work to do, I can confirm that his was pretty good. Although no snort is quite as derisive as that of a displeased bloodhound, I give it a B+.

"No chance. Not sure what drugs your alleged fiancé has been injecting you with these days, but it's clearly made you delusional. The man's an absolute charlatan and the only reason I allow the trust to pay for your stay at his clinic is because it's cheaper and more convenient for me than hunting you down all the time and trying to find facilities willing to take you. And I only ever did that because leaving you to OD in the street somewhere would be bad for my career. So you're not getting a penny." Then he turned and left.

What this wedding was missing in wildlife it was certainly making up for in drama.

"Aha. Rufus! I've been looking for you," said my human brandishing a leash. "Oh, hi Henley." Then she noticed the expression of rage on her face. "I'm so sorry. Did Rufus do something to you—if he's flung drool on you or smeared his face on your clothes, I apologize."

"No, Rufus isn't to blame," she sputtered as she stalked off.

Lunch was considerably less eventful; My Attendant reappeared as was his wont when I was to be indoors and cheek by flew amongst those who might object to a little moisture flung in their direction. My human also got to meet Percy's boss and either wife number two or three, it was unclear which, who was another young woman who looked like she would have been bridesmaid material.

After lunch, Ben, who was as keen to escape from Sergio Emilio Augustus's clutches as I was our room, proposed that we take a turn about the grounds before the archery competition began.

"There's a maze on the property and I thought it'd be fun to see if Rufus can find his way out." I was pretty sure that the appeal of the maze had less to do with seeing whether I could find my way out—always supposing that I actually wanted to find my way out—and more to do with engaging in al fresco activities of an affectionate nature with my human. As a fellow male I was more than happy to indulge him in his pursuit of the female of the species, although my approach is considerably less complicated and does not involve mazes.

We made our way over to the feature in question and infiltrated the twists and turns of its high hedgerows. The mission of the bloodhound, however, is not to find the way out of mazes but to find the humans who have found their way into them. Hearing voices around the next bend, my humans came to an abrupt halt not wanting to interrupt.

"I'm telling you Bruce, he was horrible. I'd like to wipe that sneer off his face permanently. Not only did he categorically refuse to give me what is mine, which is infuriating, but he said some dreadful things about you, which was terribly hurtful."

"I'll try talking to him," Dr. Bruce replied. "I'm sure I can make him see how happy this would make you."

"He couldn't care less about my happiness or anyone else's other than his own. You and I have the power to do such great things together and to make such a difference in the world that it's grotesquely unfair that this one selfish and revolting individual should stand in the way."

"What would happen if he wasn't around? After all accidents happen so your father must have made a provision for that."

"Oh, in that case the management of the trust and decisions about its capital would be transferred to Percy's father, Charles. They were college roommates and he was daddy's best friend. I'm sure he would be more reasonable. But then anyone except Rush would be. I hope someone shoots him with an arrow!" The fury in her voice was palpable.

"You never know my dear, we must trust to our past and future life's guides. Things often have a habit of working out even if we can't see our way. Just out of curiosity, what happens if both your brother and Percy's father aren't around?"

"I'm not sure but the management of the trust would probably revert to the bank."

My humans started to drag me backwards hoping to quietly backtrack and bumped into Tucker.

"Oh hello," he said cheerfully. I stepped aside before he could pat me on the head again. "Well that was quite a convo we overheard, wasn't it? I've been trying to map the maze for a scene Ethan wants to do. Do you think those two would be willing to do it again for the camera? Ethan says his film needs a more dramatic through line and he's always looking for additional cinema verité content."

"I don't think they meant for anyone to overhear, so it might be a bit awkward to ask," said Ben diplomatically.

"I suppose you're right. Ethan says all the good stuff happens when there are no cameras around, so he couldn't believe his luck with this morning's sword fight. Although he says it would have looked better if there had been more blood. On another note, no pun intended, I hope I am not disturbing either of you with my bagpipe practice. I try to get some time in in the afternoons. My band has a big concert coming up at Hamish's House of Haggis."

"Oh no not at all," lied my human. Lying was becoming as habit forming as one of Dr. Bruce's injections. "We must be off; we were going to see if Rufus can find the way out."

As there were no additional humans in the maze to find, I acquiesced since I smelled a crowd gathering in the vicinity of this morning's sword fight.

"My Lords and Ladies," announced the Master of Revels following a trill of the trumpets, "we are on the brink of beholding our ensuing contest, one in which we earnestly entreat all to partake, regardless of their skill level. For in archery, as in love," here he bestowed a beatific smile upon Brooke and Percy, who stood in proximity, "we can never foretell when a wayward arrow may find its mark."

I think after this morning's unpleasant incident, the "lords and ladies" of the castle were eager for some light entertainment and the fun of watching everyone try to even hit a target, let alone score points, did not disappoint. As might be expected, there was a great disparity in skill level. The men were a mixed bag, with some shots flying wildly well over the targets while a few others, including the ones shot by my namesake, Rufus, actually scoring points. But in an unexpected development, the two top scorers of the men's competition were the Father of the Bride and his brother The Pie Man.

"Pete and I used to go deer hunting with bow and arrow as boys," the Knob King explained to some of the surprised guests. He had just edged out his sibling, which given the satisfaction of one and the glowering of the other, was probably not an uncommon state of affairs.

There was a brief pause as the target was chivalrously moved up for the fairer sex.

When the competition resumed, its highlight was undoubtedly watching the spectacle of Riley, Kiley, and Katie attempting to even pull back the strings of the bow. Their arrows landed not far from their well-shod feet.

My human handed off my leash to My Attendant and did considerable better. But just as was the case with the men, the winner of the women's competition emerged from an unexpected quarter. It was Henley. Whether this was due to the power of Dr. Bruce's potions or the fact that one of the many schools she had been in and out of taught archery, was unknown. She herself attributed it to the fact that she had been a skilled Native American princess famed for her prowess at the hunt. But at least she hadn't used her brother as a target.

Following her triumph, she joined her beloved who appeared to be engaged in a rather good-humored conversation with Uncle Charles. I advanced to extract a cookie. Since I had a rather high opinion of Uncle Charles owing to his sagacity in keeping himself well supplied with biscuits for random canine supplicants, I was pretty sure he wasn't listening to a discourse on Regression to Progression therapy. I was right.

"Your fiancé and I were just comparing notes on our various disastrous dance experiences and the lack of enthusiasm with which we are anticipating this evening's entertainment," said Uncle Charles addressing Henley.

"I do hope we can be partners for one of them. Father told me stories about what the two of you got up to at cotillion and it will be like having a part of him back. I miss him so much and you were such a good friend to him."

I wasn't able to linger. Dance class required a less sporty costume for my human so we went back to The Rufus Suite so she could change. I know she was looking forward to the class, although I suspect she would have enjoyed it even more if Ben were scheduled to be present. The wedding party and the family had received private tutelage earlier in the week as befitted the stars of the show. What she did not enjoy, however, was the sound of bagpipes, which was once more shattering the peace of the castle. I can only say that if you've never heard *Stairway to Heaven* on the bagpipes, count yourself lucky.

Since I had no formal role in the dancing, I was mercifully relieved of my leather jacket and hopped up on the bed for a well-earned snooze.

I had an excellent dream in which I had successfully brought down a massive squirrel, an accomplishment that has sadly eluded me in real life despite numerous attempts. Greatly refreshed, I had a stretch, and a drink and decided to take a stroll to see if anything of an entertaining or edible nature was going on. We hounds are inveterate busybodies and delight in sticking our noses, literally and figuratively, into places where they are least wanted.

I grabbed a rawhide—I was determined to distribute as many of them as possible around the castle in case the opportunity for a chew presented itself—and took myself off down the stairs and onto the main floor. Behind one large set of double doors, I could smell a large congregation of humans and could hear the intermittent strains of music that was a lot more to my and everyone else's liking than that being played on bagpipes. As usual C camera was being chewed out for its multiple misdeeds and Sergio Emilio Augustus was calling for

MahRee who was no doubt off somewhere adjusting her scarf.

I gave it a miss and decided to explore some of the rooms towards the back of the castle where I had detected the odor of humans intermingled with that of food. Always a winning combination.

I dropped my rawhide at the door of a cozy, chintzy, overstuffed looking room, obviously designed with the castle's lady guests in mind. It was sunny and cheerful which was more than could be said for its occupants.

Brooke and her mother were sitting at a table with all the traditional fixings of English tea laid out on a three-tiered cake stand before them. None of it had been touched.

"…you know all I've ever wanted is for you to be happy Brooke," said the Mother of the Bride, although given that her slacks were Prada, her shoes Gucci, her belt Versace, her blouse Valentino, and she flashed gold and diamonds wherever gold and diamonds could be flashed, she clearly had wanted a good deal more.

"Oh hello Rufus," interrupted Brooke. I eyed the cake stand and I debated whether I should begin with a scone with clotted cream, a smoked salmon and caviar sandwich or a slice of lemon cake. In the end I decided to respect tradition and poked my nose at the sandwiches. I hate to see food go to waste. Brooke took the hint and began handing them over at regular intervals. She turned back to her mother, "I wonder how he stays so slim. Have you seen what he can put away?"

The Mother of the Bride sighed. "A good metabolism is a gift few of us are blessed with. But maybe he takes something. I'll ask Cressida. But as I was saying, I worry about this marriage. I really wish you had listened to me and asked Percival to sign a prenup. Then you'd know if he was after your money, which to be frank, I've always suspected he was. Not that he isn't a nice boy, but I just can't see how he is going to support you. He works in a *bank*." She said it in a way that made it clear that she harbored distinctly unfavorable views of the remunerative potential of these institutions.

"Yes, but he's an investment banker. It's not like the regular kind."

"Do you know what an investment banker does then?

"No. No one does. I just know that they make a lot of money and that the banks are different than the ones where they have the ATMs."

"Even so, he just shuffles money. Maybe he shuffles more of it, but he still shuffles it. That's different than owning factories and employing people and selling actual things. When people used to ask me what your father did, I could tell them that he made knobs and then sold them to people who made things that use knobs. Besides, if Percy's is doing so well, why does he live in one room in a decrepit old building that looks like it should have been torn down years ago."

"It's a loft, not a room. And Tribeca is one of the most expensive neighborhoods in New York City precisely because everyone likes those old buildings. And anyway, his family has money. I told you that after the wedding and his birthday he's supposed to come into an inheritance from some old will. It's why we had to get married now instead of waiting until June."

"I think that's just a story he told you to get his hands on your money sooner. People will tell you all kinds of things when they want your money. And I hardly think it's likely that his family has money. I won't even go into the fact that they fly commercial, but have you seen the state of them. The mother is positively *shabby*."

She said it like it was a class A felony.

"She seems to own almost no jewelry and looks like she shops at Goodwill. I will admit that she's a lovely woman and seems greatly appreciative of my style advice and is very much in awe of the splendor and tastefulness of the wedding arrangements. And of course, she positively worships you. But all this indicates to me is a serious lack of funds, which is not surprising since the father also dresses like he's broke. His law firm clearly must not be doing very well. I mean they are nice looking people, so at least your children probably won't be ugly, but children cost money and I just don't see how that's going to happen without our help. I will not have my grandchildren growing up in a single room in a dangerous old building. I wish you'd at least talk to Percy about our offer."

"I promise I will, but not until after the wedding. I might have a bit more leverage then if he's very opposed. But I can't think Greg is going to be very pleased at the idea of having a brother-in-law join the firm. You know how bad tempered and difficult he can be sometimes. And I'm not sure Daddy will like the idea so much either." I was happy to see that familial discord did not cause Brooke to neglect her hostess duties. She smeared a scone with clotted cream and offered it to me.

"You leave your father and brother to me. I own half that company, so I have some leverage of my own. But the sooner we can get it settled the better for all of us. At least if Percy's after your money your father will make him work for it."

I had just finished polishing off a slice of lemon cake when a waitress/actress entered, executed a deep curtsy and eyeing the empty cake stand asked if m'ladies would like another brought in. She had an amazed look on her face since I'm not sure anyone had seen Brooke eat anything. I indicated in the negative by hopping up on a comfy looking couch and settling in for a post snack nap.

All things considered. It had been a very successful afternoon despite being prevented from participating in the sword fight or chasing after errant arrows. I had had a lovely afternoon tea, interesting conversation, and now I was ensconced on a comfy and overstuffed chintz settee.

Chapter 12

"Oh there you are Rufus. Come on, it's time for a walk." My human clipped a leash onto my collar and I placed my paws on her shoulder and gave her face a good wash. "Somebody's been feeding you again," she sighed as I belched English tea fumes in her face. She was also all too aware of the principle that what goes in must come out.

It was a very productive walk.

As soon as we returned to The Rufus Suite, I was dismayed to see the repugnant style book make another unwelcome appearance. This time my jacket was of an extremely vibrant shade of yellow and my RR cipher was set in stones of green, which matched those on my collar. It was still a little matchy-matchy for my taste but at least they had again resisted the temptation to have my human's clothes match mine. This evening, her gown was of an appealing shade of burgundy as was the trailing cloth of her headdress. The only concession to the fact that we were a pair were the green stones in her headdress that echoed the ones on my jacket and collar.

While my human went into the bathroom to do those various and mysterious things to her face that human females are wont to do, I contemplated what might be on this evening's menu. The good thing about productive walks is that they create space in one's digestive apparatus for additional supplies.

Ambrose knocked on our door promptly at 7 and we made our eye-catching entrance into The Chamber of Libations where cocktail hour was once again alive with troubadours and trumpets. My human grabbed herself a strong drink and we went off to circulate lest we be rebuked by our director for dereliction of our mingling duty. She had just begun to explain to one of my many admirers why having a bloodhound is a bad idea if one intends to have either a bank account or a life, when this afternoon's archery champion descended upon us.

"Hi, I'm Mike Kovac, Brooke's father," he said extending a hand. "I haven't had a chance to thank you for bringing Rufus. I hope the plane was comfortable enough for him." Before my human could politely assent, he continued, "My daughter had her heart set on his being here and I make sure she always gets what she wants. Apart from my business, she's the most important thing in my life; I told Percival that if he ever hurt my daughter in any way, he would live to regret it. In fact, anyone who hurts my daughter will live to regret it. But I suppose that's the special bond between fathers and daughters."

Now although I always enjoy meeting a man who has his priorities straight and threatens the groom even before the wedding, and to his relatives to boot, not everyone was a fan of the Knob King's priorities. A sulky black cloud overshadowed the lovely face of Mike Kovac's PA who seemed to take her role as his right hand quite literally.

My human took another sip of her drink.

"I'm sure Percy and Brooke will be very happy together and yes, Rufus enjoyed the plane very much. It was very kind of you to think of it. This is a wonderful wedding and is absolutely something that Brooke will always remember. I know I will."

"As I said, nothing is too good for my girl. And if my brother's daughter Emily ever manages to hook a man, my brother will have a tough time topping it, no matter how many pies he sells." There seemed no gracious response to this snippet of sibling rivalry, so my human just nodded and smiled and bent down to adjust my collar that didn't need adjusting. She was saved by the trumpet as it were, and we were quickly hustled away to play our part in the procession into dinner.

The good news was that the individual sitting to my human's right was neither of the hedge fund nor pie making persuasion but was one of Percy's genial office friends. The bad news was that across from her sat the petulant PA. My human chatted happily with Percy's friend with nary a distressed asset involved while I munched my way even more happily through the salmon carpaccio. The sulky PA was silent although from time to time she shot a look down the table at her boss and smiled brilliantly in case he happened to look her way. It was like having to maintain a perfect stack in the show ring on the off chance the judge happened to look your way.

Tonight's main course was a hearty beef wellington, which was a relief. As much as I enjoy salmon carpaccio it wasn't very filling, and I needed sustenance. I had had a busy day plunging through forests, discovering secret tunnels, and breaking up cat fights that had nothing to do with cats. I had just been reflecting on whether the consistency of the duxelles was quite right, when my train of thought was interrupted by an exclamation of pain from further down the table.

"Beg pardon, m'lord," curtsied the officiant's culinary nemesis. "Did I accidentally jab you with this steak knife?" He held his arm and for the first time he seemed to lose his temper. He glared at her and hissed something. But getting stabbed at least made a change from having food and drink dumped on his head and didn't require as many changes of clothing.

"That guy better watch himself," said the PA ominously. "That girl isn't the only enemy he's made in this castle and Mike—I mean my boss Mr. Kovac—has a way of dealing with those who cross him in ways that are very unpleasant." Since Mike Kovac wasn't one of Rush's female conquests, my human was naturally perplexed. But good manners prevented her from pursuing the matter further.

"Do you enjoy working for Mr. Kovac?" she inquired. "He's so successful I imagine he must keep you very busy."

"Oh yes," she purred, "he keeps me very busy. He's ruthless of course, which is SO attractive in man, but he has a gentle side too. Although there are some people who don't appreciate him enough." She looked down the table and scowled at the Mother of the Bride.

My human took a swig of wine and bent down to adjust my collar.

When she poked her head above the table again, Percy's friend asked her where she lived, and they conversed amicably about the merits of various New York City neighborhoods. The rest of the meal passed pleasantly with no further collar adjustments needed. I appreciated being able to finish my beef wellington in peace.

When everyone had finished eating the trumpets once more gave voice to signal that an announcement concerning this evening's revelry was about to be made.

"My Lords and Ladies, the Masque is nigh to commence," proclaimed our Master of Revels. "For those among you who may deem this night's festivities ill-named, take solace, for we have a most extraordinary diversion in store to astonish and delight. But ere that, we must all adjourn to The Anteroom of the Grand Chambre of the Masque."

All of which was a fancy way of saying that in contrast to its name, a Masque is simply a night of dancing, pageantry, and entertainment, rather than some courtly Halloween spectacle.

As we made our way down the hallway leading to the Antechamber, I noticed that an urgent sidebar seemed to be underway. Brooke and her brother had cornered Tucker and the bride looked to be in the early stages of a major meltdown.

"Brooke does not want to dance with Rush," snarled Greg. "He insulted her and I don't want that slime bucket anywhere near my sister unless it's to marry her."

"I just can't bring myself to touch him. Even by the hand. The thought of it makes me physically sick." She shuddered as she spoke.

"But we don't want to make a scene," Greg continued, "so we think it would be best if you spoke with Ethan and Sergio Emilio Augustus and suggested that it would be more fitting if Brooke led off the dancing with her bridegroom."

"What did he do?" asked Tucker.

"It's not something we're prepared to discuss, but he threatened to ruin Brooke's life."

"Well that's not nothing, and I can ask, but once Ethan has assigned his roles, he's pretty hard to shift."

Meanwhile, those of us not involved in personnel disputes entered the small room—small being a relative term in Crackshaw Castle—where the partners for the first dance were pairing off.

Since it had been previously determined that it was unlikely that I could be taught to dance since I couldn't be taught to do anything else, my leash was handed over to Ambrose. The plan was for me to lead the company into the Grand Chamber of the Masque and then make myself scarce on the sidelines.

"Do NOT let him participate, no matter how much he

insists," admonished my human sternly as she gave Ambrose my leash. "He can be very persuasive when he wants something." That's one way of putting it given the physicality of my persuasive tactics.

When Brooke and Greg finally entered the antechamber one look at her shaken face and Greg's angry one told me that Tucker's assessment of the director's intransigence had proved correct.

Ah, at last, the lovely bride and my most magnificent partner," declared Rush bowing gallantly. "A cut on the arm is but a small price to pay for the honor of your hand." His charming smile had just the barest malicious twitch to it. "May it be the first dance of many."

I took my place in front of them. The opening bars of the music of the stately Pavane were our cue. The doors separating the chambers were flung open by liveried pages and we entered the room at a measured pace. As the pairs took up their positions, I moved to the side of the room to watch the (mostly) graceful figures separate, cross, and rejoin, in a carefully choreographed pattern. Rush's eyes seldom left the ashen face of his partner's. And the eyes of Greg seldom left those of Rush.

I for one am pleased to say that I mostly behaved myself, except during some of the livelier numbers in which I was convinced that the presence of a dashing hound would add an unexpected element of fun to the festivities. In this I was sadly restrained by the strong arm of My Attendant and the beady eye of my human.

An intermission was announced, and servers circulated with various refreshing beverages; I noticed that Rush placed as much distance as possible between himself and his accident-prone nemesis. I guess he was running out of dry doublets. It had also probably occurred to him that it might not be the wisest of ideas to drink anything she offered him from her tray. And speaking of trays, it looked very much like the sulky PA might have availed herself the offerings of one too many of them. She appeared to be more than a little overserved and had cornered Tucker and seemed to be treating him to a litany of her woes.

My human and Ben came over to where I was standing, and I greeted them enthusiastically. I am happy to report that The Grand Chamber of the Masque has excellent acoustics.

"Mayhap The Royal Hound Rufus the Red would appreciate a bit of fresh air," suggested My Attendant. "I noticed his Grace hath availed himself rather freely of his water bowl this evening."

"I'm sure he would very much appreciate that," replied my human. "And even if he doesn't, everyone else will."

Exeunt The Royal Hound Rufus the Red.

The ballroom—for such was its usual appellation—had French doors at one end and it was out of these we exited into the fresh night air. I poked about around the corner and was just watering some shrubbery when I heard voices from out front. No doubt I wasn't the only one who required some air, although I hoped not for the same purpose.

"Ah, Rush," said Uncle Charles. "How have you been? I'm sorry not to have been more in touch after the funeral. I feel your father's loss terribly so I can only imagine how difficult it must be for you and Henley. But at least she looks like she's finally landed on her feet. I was talking to her fiancé, and he seems to be a nice fellow and a good influence on her."

"Don't you believe it. He's after her money to expand his clinics and if he asks you for any, don't give it to him. But on a happier note, I hear congratulations are in order. Your wife told me that you are being considered for a federal judgeship."

"She shouldn't have said anything. Nothing is final."

"I'm sure you will sail through the process. Although

before he died, my father did tell me what happened at Princeton. He felt very guilty about it you know and when he became ill, he said he wanted to get it off his chest."

"Yes, I feel guilty about it as well. We were young and unbelievably foolish. I don't know what he told you, but when the school found out we were selling drugs, even though it was never the hard stuff, it was panic, not malice, on our parts that made us tell the Dean that it was the poor girl who was Payne's girlfriend at the time who was responsible. Of course, both our families had had a long association with the University and the girl was a scholarship student, so it was all too easy and probably much more convenient for the Dean to put the blame on her. I never knew what happened to her after she was expelled, and I am ashamed to admit that neither your father nor I ever tried to find out."

"Still, that's the kind of thing that you don't want being raked up by the media. Especially for someone in the legal profession with a judgeship in the offing."

"Yes, but we were exonerated. Wrongly, it is true, but there it is."

"Sadly, it wouldn't matter. Given how things stand these days and how much social media controls public opinion, once someone gets their teeth into a good scandal, well…you know how it goes. And then there's your family. Percy's career is looking so promising and all. But since I'm the only other person who knows the truth, as long as I don't say anything, no one's the wiser. But still, it does trouble my conscience. I mean, I'm OK at the moment, but it's impossible to say how I'll feel about it in the future. But when that happens, I'm sure we can come to some arrangement." It was all said in the pleasantest and most sympathetic of tones, but the threat it implied was hard to ignore.

I was very fond of the biscuit-bearing Uncle Charles, so I bayed in a low register to signify my displeasure. If My Attendant had been listening to the conversation, he didn't let on. I'm not sure he even heard since tonight, he too was wearing a headphone and was most likely listening to a cacophony of Sergio Emilio Augustus and Ethan yelling orders to their unfortunate staffs.

"We're wanted for the next scene, Rufus," he informed me. I walked about a bit to identify a suitable spot for a final leg lift and when we rounded the corner to the French doors, the area was empty. It's a good thing to or else Rush might have found himself minus a piece of his posterior.

"M'lords and Ladies," boomed the Master of Revels, as a camera drew in for a tight shot, "I trust ye have all partaken heartily of refreshment, for we are now prepared for a competition of opulent rewards, fashioned to divert, enchant, and regale. Ladies, if it please thee, repair to The Antechamber, where all shall be revealed."

He waited until the ladies were safely out of earshot, before gathering the gentlemen in a conspiratorial circle around him at the far reaches of the room.

"M'lords, surely, ye are not ignorant of the meager esteem the fairer sex holds for our gentlemanly powers of observation regarding the particulars of their form and attire. Now, ye shall have an opportunity to ascertain whether these notions be true or no. I beseech thee, draw near, M'lords, and from yon pouch, procure a parchment inscribed with the name of one of the fairer sex gracing our assembly. The ladies shall shortly return to us, their visages concealed by masks of glorious gold, for what would a Masque be without the name'ed article? In turn, each gentleman shall endeavor to discern the identity of the lady whose name he hath drawn amongst their company. Upon making such determination, he shall stand beside her. Should two gentlemen claim the same lady, they shall both take their place at her side. When the exercise concludes, each gentleman, in his own turn, shall reveal whom he doth suspect his chosen lady to be, whereupon she shall remove her mask and unveil her countenance. Each gentleman shall thereby win, for his chosen lady, a pair of diamond earrings for her comely ears, and for himself, a timepiece of exquisite craftsmanship for his wrist."

My Attendant moved me at a discrete distance lest I influence the contest. Of course it was a ridiculous game for those of us with a sense of smell. All humans smell as different from each other as lime from limburger.

When the drawing of parchments was complete, the Antechamber doors opened and a steadycam operator emerged walking backwards to capture the re-entry of the ladies. Each had a rigid gold mask of an antique looking design covering their face with only small slits for the eyes and ventilation holes so they could breathe.

The men studied them closely. No man was eager to make a mistake that cost a lady a pair of diamond earrings, and for any gentleman who had drawn a wife or a girlfriend the cost of a mistake was likely to be much higher. Some men moved confidently to take their place next to their choice and others less so. When at last every man had selected a lady, they one by one read out the names on their parchments. As each lady revealed herself, there was laughter for some and relief for others.

But no one elicited more mirth than my human since next to her stood yet another Rufus. I pulled My Attendant over to where they stood.

"I guess you just can't get away from us Rufuses," said Dr. Rufus.

"How did you know it was me," asked my human. "Unless anyone drew a wife or a girlfriend who they had watched get dressed, I would have thought that the lack of attention men pay to women's clothes would have made the choice difficult."

"That's true," said The Other Rufus, "but as physicians we are trained to be observant. Also, I noticed that the ornaments on your headband always seem to match those on Rufus' jacket. So it was really pretty easy."

We were interrupted by a commotion that for once did not involve a waitress. Rush had drawn his sister but had selected another lady.

"You did that on purpose, you bastard," Henley shrieked.

"You'd only have pawned the diamonds anyway, if not to buy drugs, then for your gold-digging fiancé."

"Don't you dare talk about Bruce like that. You know nothing about anything." She slapped him hard on the face. Rush grabbed her arm as she was about to repeat the performance and Dr. Bruce rushed forward to intervene.

I thought that it would be a dereliction of my Royal Houndly duties not to distract everyone and break the tension. So I bayed and poked The Other Rufus hard in the crotch. This caused the room to look away from the fratricidal drama unfolding and to chuckle. Even Dr. Rufus. Fortunately, he was wearing a codpiece. If there is one thing a Rufus will not tolerate is having his human stolen by another Rufus.

Ben arrived just in the nick of time to spare The Other Rufus some more of my comic relief.

"Come on Cress, let's give everyone's ears a break and take Rufus to the billiard room. Or I guess I should say the Chamber of Small Balls and Long Sticks. No, that doesn't sound right. And the less Rufus hears about balls, the better. Anyway, there are always after dinner drinks in there and I could use one. Katie or Kiley or Riley are out for my blood. I cost one of them a pair of earrings. They're tough enough to tell apart even without masks."

I approved of this plan. I like rooms with sticks and balls.

When we arrived, my humans helped themselves to the promised restorative spirits and I hopped up on the soft green felt for a quick snooze.

"Rufus, get off of there immediately!" ordered my human, as I made myself comfortable. I did not get off there immediately. Ben lifted me off so I sat on my human instead. Or at least the part of me that fit.

"How are things among the bridesmaids, these days?" asked my human while taking a sip of something potent looking. "It can't exactly be a jolly group given the bad blood between Riley, Kiley, and Emily."

"You left one out. It turns out our Rush has been at it with Katie too. She's just been more secretive about it than the others. She thinks it gives her an advantage."

"On the plus side, Ethan wanted drama. He can hardly complain now, although I don't think that Brooke is going to be much of fan of his production."

"Yes, about that. I understand from Tucker that Ethan's hoping to quietly peddle the director's cut as a bold wedding exposé."

"He may get more than he bargained for. If I were Rush, I wouldn't be too happy about having any of the ladies holding pistols tomorrow morning."

"Or a tray of drinks," said Ben.

"Your friend Rush certainly seems to have a way with the ladies."

"More like he has his way with the ladies. And he's not my friend. In fact, I'm not sure he even had any at Princeton. At least any who were male. And the pistols are still much better than the original plan. Brooke had been opposed to the pistols because the weapon is of a slightly later period. Tucker told me she had originally wanted a jousting competition, but this was vetoed on the grounds of practicality. A lot of us know how to ride, but few of us were willing to do it wearing armor and charging at each other with pointy sticks. She was very unhappy about this, but was forced to relent when even her father said no. If you hadn't noticed, it's a word that she doesn't hear very often, especially from her father."

Personally, I would have enjoyed the horses. As a hunting hound, I am a greater lover of all things equine, particularly the large fragrant snacks they so considerately leave behind. But I soon fell into a peaceful snooze while my humans undertook various pursuits that they were forced to abandon when some of the other guests entered to put the table to a use that wasn't as a bloodhound bed.

I was soon tucked up in the real thing, however, snoring gently in my human's ear, kicking her with my feet, and looking forward to seeing what excitement tomorrow would bring.

Chapter 13

The day that dawned was distinctly colder and cloudier than the previous ones, much like the atmosphere inside the castle. Conversations were more subdued and, in the case of Brooke's bridesmaids, wholly absent. Nonetheless, after my human consulted the day's style guide, I was pleased to see that I was once again to be outfitted in the sporty leathers that betokened something physical was on the agenda.

"My Lords and Ladies," declared the Master of Revels after that morning's repast, "let us away to the Field of Battle, where a fresh trial of martial prowess is about to begin." Even he sounded a little less hearty than usual, perhaps also alarmed at the thought of pistols in the hands of some of the more assertive members of our less than merry company.

Guests donned period cloaks for warmth, as a chilly wind whipped around the outside of the castle. Several of the ladies had the hoods up against the increasingly brisk conditions and the air smelled different too. You didn't have to be a meteorologist (or a bloodhound) to sense that a change of weather was upon us.

Relief rippled through the crowd as soon as the nature of today's competition was revealed. Rather than something reminiscent of the Wild West, there was a table with a single antique-looking pistol on it. Standing next to it was a knowledgeable gentleman who was to load a ball into its barrel and explain to each competitor how to sight it and fire it. Everyone had only one chance to hit the target—a padded dummy in the shape of a knight with a coat of arms over its heart. As each contestant stepped up to the table, Rush discreetly maneuvered himself behind someone else. Especially if the shooter was a woman.

Despite both the dampening of the weather and the guests' spirits, nearly everyone took a turn. And although it was not nearly as entertaining as the archery competition, I did my best to look interested as I pondered the question of whether that stuffed knight might have a squeaker inside. This happy thought was interrupted by Tucker.

"Brooke and Ethan would like Rufus in the scene where she presents the prizes," I was extremely annoyed that he referred to me as just plain Rufus as if I were merely The Other One.

The slight was soon forgotten, however, when I perceived that gentlemen's winner was none other than Uncle Charles. Who knew that in addition to his biscuit feeding abilities he was such a marksman. The lady's winner was also a surprise. That honor went to Emily who clearly relished the fact that for once Brooke could not shoo her away from the camera. Each winner received a velvet lined, engraved wooden box that contained a Les Baer pistol for Uncle Charles and a lightweight Rohrbaugh for Emily.

"Congratulations," my human said to Emily, when she had retrieved me from my duties as Royal Hound. "Where did you learn to shoot, or was it just a lucky hit?"

"Not a lucky hit at all. I learned to shoot as a teenager. Daddy insisted on it. He said he and Jason won't always be there to protect me and it was important for me to always have a gun handy and not be afraid to use it. But I'm sure you must have one too. Daddy says New York is a very dangerous place." My human, being too well-mannered to debate the point, fell back on her usual response when anyone mentioned the often-exaggerated dangers of our beloved city.

"I have Rufus to protect me, so I never worry," she replied. Nothing is quite as satisfying as being admired for qualities that one doesn't possess. Like being well-behaved.

I was just about to drag my human over to disembowel that stuffed knight when the Master of Revels once again commanded our attention. He seemed to have picked up a bit of steam as he announced our next amusement.

"My Lords and Ladies, as thrilling as our contest of pistol marksmanship hath been, I assure thee that our next diversion shall be even more so." This seemed more than a little optimistic. On the other hand, I'm sure that there were many amongst us who were relieved that the pistol shooting hadn't been thrilling at all.

"Let us away to the maze," he chortled, "where each gentleman shall be afforded the opportunity to rescue a lost damsel in distress."

We all obediently assembled near the entrance to the maze in a way that adhered to Ethan's strict sense of photographic aesthetics. Off to one side there now stood a large and antique-looking clock that was incongruously attached to a digital timer. I guess precision timing wasn't a thing amongst the Tudors.

"I do hereby proclaim the commencement of the Contest of the Maze," thundered the Master of Revels. "Our esteemed Sir Tucker shall guide a lady into a location deep within the labyrinth following which each gentleman shall draw a coin from a sack. He who draws the gilded coin shall be the lady's champion. The fortunate gentleman must then embark on the noble endeavor of rescuing the fair maiden whilst yon clock measures the fleetness of this feat. Upon fulfillment of this heroic act, the lady and her champion shall be granted the lofty privilege of being escorted to yonder throne by The Royal Hound Rufus the Red." Here he gestured towards two elaborate and elevated thrones that had been erected. "The twain shall remain upon them until they be deposed by a swifter pair. And to the victors a truly extraordinary reward awaits. Each shall receive a repast for two at the most coveted table in the City of New York—La Connerie—the fabulous and impossible to get into all seaweed restaurant recently opened by the third cousin of Alain Ducasse."

"Ooooh," whispered someone behind me. "I hear it is even more fabulous than his previous one where diners had to escape a room in order to eat!"

Although I was naturally disappointed at not being allowed to compete since I most certainly would have won, I don't think I would have been much of a fan of the prize. In my opinion seaweed is only acceptable when wrapped around large piece of salmon sushi.

"Now, let us ascertain the alacrity with which our champions may rescue their fair ladies. Sir Tucker, I beseech thee, guide Lady Brooke to a concealed recess within the labyrinth."

Brooke came forward and Tucker, his map in hand, walked into the maze accompanied by A Camera. This act completed, the gentlemen plunged their hands into a proffered pouch and drew coins. Rush drew the gold one. The bride may have been rich and skinny, but she certainly wasn't lucky. He smiled mischievously at Percy who was looking less and less happy about his bride's choice of officiant.

Greg grabbed his arm.

"Give the coin to Percy," he hissed audibly.

"I think not, my friend. He'll have plenty of time with her soon enough and remember sharing is caring." He detached Greg's arm and entered the maze as The Master of

Revels pressed the button to start the clock.

He was gone a considerable amount of time.

"Maybe we should send Rufus in after them," suggested one of Percy's friends to his Plus One.

"I didn't know they studied mazes in medical school," she replied.

"No, not that one. The good one."

I liked the way this conversation was heading and was already planning what I would do when I found Rush, but sadly the pair emerged before I could act. Brooke looked upset and disheveled, Rush looked complacent and composed. I had a feeling that the prospects for Ethan's director's cut had gone up astronomically. She avoided Percy's eye as she and Rush took their places on the throne.

Greg's face looked as threatening as the weather. Jason came up to him and the cousins could be observed deep in conversation as they stared malevolently at the Officiant ensconced elegantly on his throne holding Brooke's unwilling hand.

Next up was Katie and her rescuer Percy. They logged a decent time, but it wasn't hard to beat the one Rush had put up. Nevertheless, Percy looked eager to get Brooke off the seat next to Rush.

My human was the next damsel in distress and her rescuer was Pete the Pie man. Their time was considerably over that of Percy and Katie.

"What happened?" Ben asked my human after she had emerged. "It took you forever and you were just in the maze yesterday."

"Oh we would have been out ages ago but Pete begged me to delay. He's afraid if he won his wife would make him go to the restaurant. She likes feeling that she's part of the celebrity scene."

My human's mother followed her daughter; the Other Rufus drew the gold coin.

"It's important to keep the Rufus's in the family," he joked to my human after he led her mother out after somewhat of an extended stay.

"Given the prize, I'm afraid I prevailed upon Dr. Rufus to dawdle a bit," she explained.

"There might be a lot of that going around," said my human. "Except maybe among Riley, Kiley and Katie. They look like they might appreciate a hearty meal of seaweed."

The next lady in was Brooke's mother with Driscoll as her hero.

"We might actually have to send Rufus in for this one," said Ben. "Driscoll couldn't find his way out of a paper bag, let alone a maze. It's why we never let him drive unless we want to end up in the opposite direction to the one in which we had planned to go." My human glanced at me; she was all too familiar with going in the opposite direction to the one in which she had planned to go. What can I say? It's a bloodhound thing. Anyway, Driscoll did not disappoint. True to form, he was well over the winning time, and when he and an annoyed Mother of the Bride eventually made it out, it appeared that Kathy Kovac had been Driscoll's rescuer rather than the other way around.

"I think I might have to adjust my odds," he said when he rejoined our little group. "Madame Kovac was distinctly unhappy with my maze navigating skills and she wasn't shy about telling me. And somehow, I don't think the apple has fallen very far from that particular bad-tempered tree."

Mrs. Pete the Pie Man was the next lady to enter the maze and when Ben drew the gold coin, the Pie Man could be observed whispering urgently in Ben's ear. He might also have tried to press a few twenties into Ben's hand. They didn't win.

The Petulant PA was next and when Greg drew the gold coin, his father's aggressively confident demeanor for once came a bit undone.

"The Knob King seems a bit jumpy," observed Driscoll to my humans. "Look at him pacing back and forth and checking the clock. Wonder what that's about?" I of course knew what that was about, but we hounds are nothing if not discrete. My pendulous lips were sealed.

When the pair finally emerged, Mike Kovac studied his son's face for any sign of emotion and seemed relieved when he found none.

Henley was next up, but Tucker had a bit of a job pulling her away from where she and Dr. Bruce were again chatting animatedly with Uncle Charles. They seemed to have taken quite a shine to him lately. When Tucker was finally able to detach her and lead her into the maze, Brooke's father drew the honor of being her champion.

They seemed to be another rather dilatory pair.

"I wonder what's taking them so long?" asked Ben rather rhetorically.

"Maybe she's having another past life regression and is waiting for a Minotaur," suggested my human.

"I'll bet she's hitting him up for money for her charlatan fiancé's bogus business," interjected Rush who had sauntered over. "He's got more than enough of it to waste if this wedding is anything to go by, so it does seem a shame not to relieve him of some of it."

I guess he would know.

Then he drifted off to try to find a woman he hadn't

slept with yet.

When Henley and the Father of the Bride did finally come out, Henley had a dreamy rather than mercenary look about her, so it appeared that the knob billions were safe. At least from her.

The next lady was the young, pretty wife of Percy's boss and her husband drew the gold coin.

"Isn't that like an etiquette violation or something?" asked Driscoll.

"But a wholly appropriate one," said Ben. "Percy tells me that his boss rescued her from an impoverished life as an art dealer at the Betrugerin Galleries. You know the gallery in Soho where they make a fortune selling that garbage by Szemét."

"Even if you don't like his work, Ben, I'm sure if it's selling it's not garbage," chastised my human's mother who had joined us.

"No, Mrs. Pennington, it's literally garbage. Although technically he calls it *L'art de Poubelle*. He coats a canvas with glue and then drags a trash bin in from the street and dumps it on top. And for patrons of the arts who can afford custom pieces, he'll come to your home and dump your own personal garbage on top of the canvas. I'm told he accepts very few of those commissions though, and you have to have connections to even get your garbage in the running."

"In that case, Rufus is a disciple," said my human "I wonder if they'd be interested in some of his creations. For a hefty fee I could let him loose in someone's apartment wearing a beret."

I bayed at the very mention of me wearing a beret, although I have to admit that I found the rest of the concept intriguing. My ability to turn garbage into smaller pieces of garbage and to turn things that weren't previously garbage into things that are, is legendary.

The humans continued to chat and I continued to escort. Pairs went in and out of the maze and the throne changed hands several more times.

In the end the winning pair was Uncle Charles and Riley, although Uncle Charles gallantly gave her his share of the prize.

"She looks like someone who would enjoy a seaweed fine dining experience," he said as he joined us.

"My Lords and Ladies, let us be of good cheer and repair to the Chamber of Repast, for our midday banquet doth await us. And whilst we can't promise any seaweed, I am confident that this omission shall be overlooked by this most gracious assembly."

This was excellent news as I was peckish and eager to fuel up for this afternoon's activities which I hoped would be more exciting than the Maze Hunt.

I should have been careful what I wished for.

Chapter 14

A noisy trumpet fanfare rocked the large dining room to announce the arrival of Brooke and Percy while I thrust a chunk of my face into my water bowl to cleanse my palate for what I hoped would be a fortifying lunch. I was not disappointed. There was an excellent squab with a side of wild rice and a tasty ragout of wild mushrooms. But although the music played, and the guests munched, the mood in the room continued to be subdued. Everyone seemed to be aware that, weather aside, things were not as they should be on the day before a wedding, especially one that had cost the GNP of a small nation. There was, as they say, an atmosphere.

I had no sooner belched my final post-prandial belch when the Master of Revels took to the floor. But rather than tell us how much fun we were going to have playing Tudor Football, he made an announcement of a different kind.

"My Lords and Ladies, it hath become evident that the weather conditions are not propitious for our planned outdoor diversions. But even so let us be of good cheer and seek entertainment within. Our current abode abounds with opportunities for amusement. Be it your inclination to behold the numerous splendid paintings and tapestries gracing our castle's many chambers, or to partake of billiards or board games, or to explore the vast library, or to peruse the armory, or to admire the botanical wonders in the conservatory, or to relax with the many fine wines and spirits at thy disposal, or simply to lose thyself in the splendor of thy surroundings, the choice is thine. We will regather in customary fashion for our libations when the clock striketh seven."

Ben appeared at my human's side with a speed worthy of Usain Bolt. He looked happier than he had since our arrival. Being relieved of his duties as Percy's liege man of life and limb, however temporary, clearly agreed with him.

"Let's change and take Rufus out to go potty and then we can explore the castle."

In the first place, I can't tell you how much I object to my very necessary and copious eliminatory activities being referred to as "going potty" as if I were a toddler in need of toilet training. Second, it was apparent even to my human, that exploring the castle was an architectural euphemism for hunting for things of a more hidden and subterranean nature.

We went upstairs and much to my annoyance, my human decided to leave my jacket on since it was getting quite cold outside. Now it is true that my human forced me to wear a coat last winter owing to the fact that the people in our neighborhood berated her for taking me out with only my natural coat of thick, dense fur to protect me. But that doesn't mean I have to like it. While my human was changing her clothes, I calculated the best place to leave a rawhide for her to trip on.

Before we even left the room, it was abundantly clear how at least one Crackshawrian was going to spend the afternoon. An enthusiastic bagpipe rendition of *White Wedding* assaulted our ears, and its dulcet tones followed us all the way to the front door. Bagpipes were as hard to get away from as a bloodhound who wanted your bagel.

We met Ben met in the entry hall and when he pulled open the front door, we were buffeted by a blast of frosty air that was more like the Arctic in winter than spring in Pennsylvania.

"Look at Rufus's ears; it looks like he's going to fly!" laughed Ben as the wind lofted my ears to the horizontal. Since comments of this kind were right up there with, "Why don't you put a saddle on him," I favored him with one of my more derisive looks. We bloodhounds have extremely expressive faces and are not above using them to put our humans in their place. Nevertheless, I am not a wholly unreasonable hound, and although I myself greatly enjoy a bit of brisk weather, my humans made it clear that given their lack of a suitable wardrobe, it was not a taste they shared. For once I humored them and took care of business with commendable rapidity.

"I think I'll leave Rufus in the room," my human said once we were back in the warmth. "Otherwise, we'll just end up going where he's going."

I thought this was an excellent idea.

After she had departed, I waited a suitable interval and selected a fresh bone and made my way to the Morning Room to see if anyone was eating tea instead of drinking it. Kathy Kovac was sitting alone on a chintz settee with a cup on the coffee table in front of her and a copy of *Me* magazine in her lap. Although there was no cake stand full of goodies this time, I did spy a small plate of some tasty-looking vanilla biscuits that looked ripe for the cadging. Being able to persuade humans to relinquish things that they wish to retain is one of my many talents, so getting a human to relinquish something they don't, is puppy's play.

When I had wiped the last crumb from my snout, I picked up my bone and lay down in front of the fire for a toasty chew. I hadn't been at it very long when a new scent wended its way into my nostrils and I lifted my head.

"Hi Mom. Escaping everyone for a bit? I can go if you want," said Greg.

"No, sit down. I was trying to have a nap but it's impossible with those bagpipes playing. At least they're not quite as loud in this room. Tucker's been so helpful you know that I haven't had the heart to ask him to stop. Poor boy is so proud of them and told me he chose that room specifically for its acoustics. Anyway, I'm glad you're here Greg. There's something important I wanted to talk to you about, but I haven't had the chance."

"It sounds serious. There's nothing the matter with you or Dad is there?"

"No, nothing like that but it is serious. I know how close you've always been to Brooke and that you would want what's best for her, so please keep that in mind and hear me out. Percy's probably a nice boy and Brooke seems very happy with him, but I'm afraid that after the newlywed glow wears off, she'll see that he's not going to be able to give her what she needs. She's never had to worry, or for that matter, even think about money, and I really don't believe that Percy fully appreciates the expectations of a girl like Brooke. I mean he works in a bank and judging by the appearance of his family, he comes from a very financially disadvantaged background."

Personally, I thought this was even more hilarious the second time around. I'm pretty sure my human's family could be described as many things, but financially disadvantaged is not one of them.

"We can of course just offer him money, but no young man likes to be thought of as not being able to support his wife. In any case, that probably wouldn't be a good thing for their marriage and it's not really a long-term solution, is it? It's why I'd like your support when I talk to your dad about offering Percy a position with the firm."

If Madame Kovac had thought this would go down well, she was very much mistaken. Greg flushed and took on the look of an angry bull who has just spotted a guy waving a red flag.

"I'm sorry Mom, but the answer is no. It's a terrible idea. As someone who is Dad's second in command who'll be running the business one day, I don't have the time or the patience to babysit some clueless Ivy League brother-in-law. Have you any idea how much time and effort it takes to learn about knobs? Not to mention dials. And then there's all the precision equipment they go into and all the delicate relationships we've built up in DC. I mean Percy seems like a nice guy, but I really don't think he has the foggiest notion about business. And it would be terrible not just for the business, but also for my relationship with Brooke. You know he's going to go crying to her every time he's unhappy about something. If you think Percy would object to having some extra cash, why don't you just give it to Brooke? He'd never have to know. Married people keep secrets from each other all the time."

Out of the mouths of Knob Princes....

"I strongly disagree Greg. I've spoken to Brooke about it and she's going to talk to Percy after the wedding and then I'm going to talk to your father. If I'm being honest, I've always thought that Percy is after her money and at least this way we can keep an eye on him. I never thought that you'd go against your own mother on something that's so important to our family." She sounded annoyed, and the volume of her voice made it clear that her son wasn't the only one who lacked patience.

"This isn't about family. It's about business. And if you speak to Dad about it, I will let him know in no uncertain terms how bad an idea it is." His voice, too, had increased in volume.

"Really Greg. You're acting like a child..."

Just then my human's mother and her sister-in-law entered the room.

"Oh, I'm so sorry, "Aunt Anne said and reversed course.

"No, please come in. I was just leaving," said Greg. He turned towards his mother and glared. "Why don't you see what Percy's mom has to say before you go taking a wrecking ball to the business." And with that he stormed out.

"I must apologize for my son. He has a terrible temper. Takes after his father like that."

"We didn't mean to intrude," Aunt Anne said.

"It's OK, have a seat. Greg and I were just discussing an idea I had for Brooke and Percy. As I'm sure you can appreciate, marriage puts a financial strain on a young man and that's especially true when children start arriving. So, I thought a wonderful way to help the young couple would be to have my husband offer Percy a job. You know, a real one," she added in a manner that suggested she was pleased with the tactful way this was put.

Aunt Anne looked at her and paused for a moment to gather her thoughts. I might just have detected a twitch of a smile on the face of my human's mother.

"Why that's so generous and so thoughtful of you Kathy," Aunt Anne replied. "But you know, Percival has rather a good job that he enjoys, and his prospects are excellent. But it's lovely of you to have thought of it."

"Yes, but that job is in a bank. I'm not sure you realize that there is serious money in knobs. It would be a chance to secure Percy's future. And of course, Brooke's. I am proud to say she has never wanted for anything, and I think that life on a bank salary might be difficult for her to adjust to. And marriage is always an adjustment even without worrying about money."

"I understand your concern but I'm sure your fears are groundless," said Aunt Anne. "Christopher Penrose & Sons is America's oldest investment bank and their people do quite well. So please put your mind at rest. Not that he needs it, but Percival is also due to come into some family money from my late uncle after his marriage."

The Mother of the Bride looked skeptical.

"Yes, Brooke did mention something about that. I'm sure you think your son has plenty of money but where money is concerned, it's all relative isn't it?" Here she looked pointedly at Anne's well-worn cashmere sweater and plain black slacks. "I mean to a young man living on the street in India, twenty dollars is a fortune."

My human's mother broke out in a sudden fit of coughing that required her to place her hand over her mouth. I think comparing an investment banker to an Indian street urchin was just too much for her.

"Oh, Anne, I forgot," said my human's mother between coughs, "there's a lovely oleander I wanted to show you in the conservatory. I know how much you love gardening. Perhaps you'd like to join us, Kathy?"

"No thank you. I don't have to do my own gardening. We have people for that. But I hope you'll think about what I've said. Brooke will be speaking to Percy about it after the dust from the wedding settles."

I followed the ladies out.

"Are you going to warn Percy?" asked my human's mother.

"No. He's made this particular bed all by himself so he can lie on it. What do you think Rufus?" she asked giving me a scratch on the neck. I think that I hope she had cookies in her pocket.

The conservatory was another eye-catching room, replete with decorative furniture and a wide assortment of plants, including a luxurious oleander. Although it would have been a lot nicer had the skies not been so dark and had the ladies decided to order the kind of tea that came with three tiers of snacks.

"I'd better go check on Charles," said Aunt Anne after they sat for a while. "He wasn't feeling well, and I've asked Rufus to look in on him." I put my head in her lap. "Sorry, Rufus, I meant the Other One." I decided to go with her and check on

Uncle Charles anyway. If one Rufus was good, two were better.

"Oh dear," she said when we walked in. It was unclear whether she was referring to the bagpipe rendition of *Purple Haze* or the unpleasant sounds coming from the bathroom.

"Where's Rufus," Anne asked the pale figure with his head bent over the toilet. I was of course right there, seriously concerned for the welfare of Uncle Charles. People who freely dispense snacks are not to be taken for granted.

"He went to look for Dr. Bruce."

"But he's not a real doctor."

"I know but Rufus thinks I might have ingested a poisonous mushroom and since Dr. Bruce specializes in hallucinogens, he thinks he might have some atropine which could help."

And with that he resumed vomiting.

Chapter 15

I left him to it and went back downstairs. Nothing exceptionally interesting seemed to be going on, so I decided to stand by the massive front door and inhale the delicious odors of fresh forest air seeping in from under it. It was most annoying that it didn't have one of those convenient handles I could open.

I was just contemplating whether another visit to the kitchen would be in order, but in light of the fact that they might have just poisoned someone, I decided to give it a miss.

I was just contemplating my next course of action when I saw Barclay approach; I waved my tail.

"Hiya Rufus. Would you like to go out?" I smacked him with my tail and made loud snorting noises at the bottom of the door to signify that, yes, Rufus did indeed want to go out. He wrenched open the door and out I flew before anyone who knew anything about bloodhounds could stop me.

This next bit, I only heard about later, since I myself was out and about annoying as many fauna and flora of the forest as possible. At least initially. But we'll get to that.

At first no one realized I was missing, but after eyeing the increasingly inclement weather my human proposed to Ben that they abandon their seemingly futile hunt for more secret passages and take me out for a walk. Armed with my long leash they went in search of me, never a quick or easy process given the size of the searchable real estate involved. They wandered about calling my name until they poked their heads into the billiard room where Percy and his other groomsmen were having a game.

"Oh are you looking for Rufus?" asked Barclay. "He was standing by the door, so I let him out about an hour ago. Isn't he back yet?"

I would like to suggest to those who believe that hell hath no fury like a woman scorned that they acquaint themselves with hell hath no fury like a woman whose hound some idiot hath allowed to escape. It might alter their views on the subject.

The words that escaped my human's mouth were even less printable than usual, but they got the point across. Namely that I would never be back. At least not willingly. One of the downsides of the powerful bloodhound nose, apart from the fact hiding anything from us is about as easy as hiding an elephant with a dishtowel, is that it's dangerous to let us off leash. Once we pick up a scent we take off, oblivious to the hazards posed by roads, traffic, or anything else. Alarmed at the potential loss of so honored a guest, the billiard players scattered like picnickers in a hailstorm to don whatever outerwear they possessed to help in the hunt for yours truly. Off into the forest they all ran, shouting my name as went.

Meanwhile, I had been innocently amusing myself in the frosty sylvan glades when I flared my nostrils to inhale the intoxicating scent of eau de raccoon when I smelled something completely different instead. Something that should not have been there. I galloped down the wooded paths with whippet-like speed, as fast as my four legs could carry me and dashed out of the forest and into the clearing with the deracinated daffodils.

And there he was.

The good thing about having a deep chest and an exceptionally healthy pair of lungs is that my voice might possibly carry even further than Tucker's bagpipes. I bayed as loudly as it is possible for me to bay, to which anyone who has ever tried to eat a pizza in my presence can attest, is loud enough to shatter an eardrum. So acoustically robust were my efforts that I was certain that even the minimally effective ears of humans would be able to hear me. And eventually they did.

My human and Ben were the first to emerge from the forest and I rushed forward with undimmed enthusiasm to greet them. To her credit, my human did not scream when she looked beyond my head and saw what had drawn me to the spot. Instead, she mechanically clipped a leash on me and then stood staring and immobile like a street mime waiting for a tip.

Ben shouted for the others.

"I guess now we know why Rufus was baying," said my human when she had recovered the power of speech. "I was always worried he'd find a dead body in Central Park one day. But here?"

My rescuers gathered round and gazed at my find. Rush lay sprawled on the ground before us with an arrow protruding theatrically from his torso. It was right below the bullet hole in his chest and above the sword stuck in his stomach. He also had a kitchen knife jammed into his neck. And just for good measure, a syringe protruded from his arm pinning a note.

"Holy F….! What the hell happened," exclaimed Barclay.

"It looks like he's dead," said the Other Rufus.

"I guess even a radiologist can diagnose that," said

Driscoll, never short of snark. "But it appears that Colonel Mustard is missing a few items."

"What killed him?" asked Percy. "And how long has he been dead?"

"I'm a radiologist, not Hercule Poirot," replied the Other Rufus.

"I don't suppose it's possible that he died of natural causes?" asked Barclay. The others shot him a look. "OK, maybe not. But then maybe lots of people did it. Like in *Murder on the Orient Express*."

"Whatever killed him, the police pathologist will have to figure out. Just don't touch anything," said the Other Rufus.

"Yes, we've watched cop shows too," said Percy.

"I mean, I know he was a snake, but he didn't deserve this," said Ben. I looked behind me just in case. Toads and toe rags were one thing, but I draw the line at snakes.

"What does the note say? Maybe it will tell us who did it?" suggested Barclay who seemed to be as ignorant of the behavior of criminals as he was of bloodhounds. The Medical Rufus bent over the body.

"It says 'Meet me at the Overlook. We have a lot to discuss.' And the letters have been cut out from a newspaper."

"Who reads newspapers these days," said Barclay.

"Well, my father for one," replied Percy.

"And I saw Brooke's father with a *Wall Street Journal*," added Driscoll. "Maybe he killed Rush to stop the wedding."

"Seems a bit extreme," said Percy.

"But isn't the person who found the body usually the

killer?" asked Barclay. All eyes turned towards me.

"Nah, there are no teeth marks," said Driscoll. "And apart from the fact that I saw Rush pat Rufus on the top of the head, I don't think Rufus has a strong enough motive."

"I think there are better candidates," said the Other Rufus, obviously motivated by the desire to defend the honor of us Rufuses. "I think for the moment the more important question is what to do next. Buck, why don't you go back to the castle and call the police; the rest of us will wait here. The less tramping back and forth the better."

Barclay was clearly reluctant to relinquish his role as theorist in chief, but he did as he was told.

While they stood about trying not to turn into popsicles, everyone's thoughts turned to the obvious subject.

"Not to be an ass, but maybe there is some truth to Buck's theory," said Driscoll. "Not the Rufus one, but Henley and Mike Kovac both seem to be handy with a bow and arrow. And then there was Greg and the sword incident plus the syringe-happy Dr. Bruce. Emily is a good shot and Rush treated her pretty badly. Although there seems to be no gun. I wonder if that's significant."

The merits of these theories were bandied back and forth as we awaited Barclay and the boys in blue. Fortunately, no one brought up the fact that if this were a mystery novel the culprit would be the one least likely to have done it. Which would once again be me.

After an extended wait, things took a distinctly undesirable turn, however, when instead of the expected platoon of police the only thing to emerge from the forest was Barclay carrying a large garbage bag.

"You don't think Buck is going to suggest that we stuff Rush into a garbage bag, do you?" asked Percy. "Rush was kind of garbage, but even so...."

All eyes turned speculatively towards the athletic young man as he advanced against the blowing snow that had begun to fall.

"I've got some bad news. The police in East Snodsburgh—that's the nearest town with an actual police department—say a blizzard is on the way and given the distance, they can't send anyone out until they're sure they'll be able to get back."

"What are we supposed to do now?" asked Ben. "We can't just leave him here—he'll be buried."

"Yes, about that," said Barclay. "I told them about what we'd found. First, if anyone has a phone, we need to take detailed pictures and videos of the body and the crime scene. I brought rubber gloves from the kitchen, and a bunch of plastic bags and tape. Also, a couple of sheets. They said to remove each item from the body, bag it separately and then seal the bag with tape. Personally, I think we should leave that bit to Rufus." I wagged my tail. We Rufus's have a very participatory nature. "When we've done that, they suggested that we use a sheet to carry the body back to the castle and store it somewhere cold."

"I don't think the caterer will let you put Rush in her meat locker," said Driscoll.

"The wine cellar might be a better idea," said Ben. "It's likely to be cool and more importantly, to be locked. We don't want anyone tampering with the evidence."

We got to work. Or more accurately, the guys got to work. My human moved me away under the guise of my efforts being surplus to requirements but really because she had no desire to take pictures of dead bodies nor to see weapons being extracted from them, even one as handsome as Rush.

"We need Rufus," called Ben.

"I'm right here," said the Other Rufus with a puzzled look on his face.

"No, the useful one," said Ben.

My human brought me over to where Rush lay and handed my leash to Ben. It was clear they were taking their documentary duties with the utmost seriousness. Ben had me stand exactly as they had found me—baying over the body. I was photographed from all angles virtually guaranteeing that one of them would be the money shot for the media.

When they finished photographing and videoing everything from every conceivable angle—where is C camera when you need it—the Other Rufus donned the kitchen gloves in the manner of one about to perform open heart surgery. He carefully removed each item, placed it in a bag and taped it shut before placing it in the garbage bag.

That task completed, the guys then began discussing the tricky logistics of how to get a dead body onto a sheet in winds that threatened to transform it into a kite.

"Cress, I'm sorry," Ben called, "but we need you over here." My squeamish human was not particularly happy about this turn of events, but she was as eager as everyone else to get back to the castle and into the warmth. Everyone except for me that is. Just as I enjoy smells that humans find revolting, I enjoy weather that makes them want to hibernate.

"If you can get Rufus to sit on one corner of the sheet and you stand on the other—you can turn your back—then Buck and Percy can stand on the other two corners and the three of us will lift Rush onto the sheet." My human muscled me into place.

"Rufus, sit."

I bayed.

"Really Rufus?" she fumed as she fished around in her

coat pocket for a cookie. Having cookies or bits thereof, stuffed into the pockets of all your clothing is helpful when you have a regular dog but when you have a bloodhound, it's essential.

After being suitably compensated for my trouble, I sat. In point of fact, I would have sat anyway given the circumstances, but if you don't ask, you don't get.

As soon as the four corners were secure, the three men lifted.

Driscoll groaned.

"Jesus, he's heavy. I definitely need to be spending more time in the gym."

"Seriously, Dris, it takes a dead body to inspire you to go the gym?' said Ben.

"There's a second sheet in the bag," said Barclay when Rush had been transferred, "I suggest we place it over him and then four of us can carry him with the top sheet and the bottom sheet twisted together. It will keep the snow off of him and also cover him up in case we run into anyone."

"Exactly who were you expecting to meet out here in the middle of a snowstorm?" asked Driscoll.

"I think he means when we get back to the castle," said Percy. "Anyway, let's each see if we can each carry a corner and Dris, you can be the relief man or help out where needed."

"We'd better make tracks; no pun intended," said Barclay. "The snow's really starting to come down and it's getting hard to see."

"Yes, but we have Rufus," said Ben.

"I'm in the same boat. I can't see well in this snow either," observed the Superfluous One.

"Not you," said Ben. "There's only one of us who doesn't need to see to know where he's going."

"Yeah, but what happens if he wants to go in search of a squirrel instead of taking us back to the castle?" asked Driscoll.

"He hasn't eaten since lunch" replied Ben. "At least as far as we know; he might have caught something in the forest." I appreciated Ben's vote of confidence in my hunting skills. I did nearly get a vole but thundering along at 125 pounds has a tendency to alert snack animals to your presence.

"Yes, but lunch was only a few hours ago," said Driscoll.

"Exactly," said Ben.

"Brooke told me he polished off an entire afternoon tea yesterday, and it was even earlier than it is now," said Percy.

My human and I were put in charge of the evidence bag and the guys lifted their burden and fell in behind me. I do so love an entourage. It was at least some recompense for Rush being a merely metaphorical toad. I moved forward at a brisk pace. All this talk of afternoon tea was making my stomach rumble.

"Speaking of Brooke," said the Other Rufus straining under his burden, "Buck, did you tell her or Henley about what happened."

"Nope. I didn't run into either of them and I thought it was more important to get back here as soon as I could. Also, as a medical man, you're used to delivering bad news to the relatives of the patients you've killed, so I think the news would be better coming from you."

"I haven't killed anyone. At least not since I became a radiologist. But you're right. I'll talk to Henley and Percy can talk to Brooke and then I'll see if that idiot Sergio Emilio

Augustus can figure out how to get everyone together in the Great Hall of the Cocktails so I can tell everyone else. But after Henley, I need to check on your father Percy, and make sure he wasn't the first victim. He's very ill, although I do expect him to recover."

"I hadn't thought of that," said Percy. "You don't think someone tried to kill him also?"

"I don't know. But no one else got sick from lunch, so it'll be something for the police to investigate."

"Whenever they get here, that is," said Barclay. "The guy I spoke to didn't sound too optimistic about it being anytime soon and I can't say I blame him."

We made slow progress. And by we, I meant the humans. All my attempts to bound ahead and disport myself in the deepening snow were met by the appearance of The Heinous Gentle Leader which was waved in my face in a most disconcerting way. Unfortunately, cookies weren't the only thing my human kept in all her pockets.

"You OK up there Cress," Ben shouted above the sound of the wind.

"Yes, but I'm cold, wet, and my shoes are shot. But if anyone can get us out of here fast, it would be Rufus in search of afternoon tea."

It was my Balto moment.

Chapter 16

We had just cleared the forest's edge when, after singing my praises lavishly, the men looked at each other questioningly.

"Now what?" asked Barclay. "I mean barging through the front door of a castle full of convivial guests expecting a wedding carrying the corpse of the guy who was supposed to perform the ceremony is going to be a bit awkward, isn't it?"

"Also, does anyone actually know where the wine cellar is?" asked Driscoll. Everyone shook their heads.

"OK," said Ben, "in that case I think we should take Rush to one of the rooms near the kitchen. I'll go ask the caterer if she knows where the wine cellar is and if there's a key. I'll tell her Sergio Emilio Augustus asked me to look for Chateau something or other or that Ethan wants to shoot a scene down there."

"Make sure it's a good year of Chateau something or other otherwise she'll get suspicious," said Driscoll. Ben favored him with a look like the one I give my human when she suggests that the fish store might be out of salmon.

"Anyone have any better ideas?" Ben said. My human touched him on the arm and pulled him aside.

"What about taking the body through the pantry," she whispered. "That tunnel might be colder than the wine cellar."

"I did think of that. But since there's a murderer loose and we don't want anyone to know where the body is or to mess with it, I think the wine cellar is safer because it probably has a lock. Also, there's no way to get Rush down to the tunnel without letting a bunch of other people know that it exists and, in the circumstances, the fewer people who know anything about any of those tunnels the better. It'll be one of the first things I tell the police."

"Sorry," said Ben to the others, when they returned to the fold. "Boy-girl stuff. OK let's get going and hope that we don't run into anyone."

We proceeded as stealthily as it is possible to proceed when one is carrying a corpse in a sheet. Although at least the snow would hide us from anyone casually looking out of the window.

Ben pulled out his phone, found the "key to the kingdom" and the front door clicked open. It's nice to have a castle with all the mod cons. But as soon as he pushed it open, all bets of sneaking quietly into the castle were immediately off.

Brooke was standing in the entry hall. And she didn't look happy.

"Where the hell have you been! Sergio Emilio Augustus is frantic. We've been looking everywhere for you. Well not you Cressida, but the rest of you. And you all look a mess which means I'll hear about it from Ethan also. And what on earth are you carrying? We have plenty of firewood."

Thinking there was no time like the present and hoping to avoid the attention her raised voice would attract, Percy spoke up.

"I'm afraid Rush has met with an accident. Well not an accident exactly. He's been murdered. Possibly several times. The police have been notified but they can't get here until the weather improves. As soon as we secure the body, Rufus is going to speak with Henley and I'm going to speak to Sergio Emilio Augustus and your father about getting everyone else together to let them know."

"But that's impossible. Rush is supposed to marry us tomorrow."

"Well, he's not available," piped up Driscoll.

"Then what are we going to do!" exclaimed Brooke. "We need to find someone else in the castle who can marry us. We can ask after you tell them about Rush." The humans stared at her with a variety of strange expressions on their faces. When it came to bad behavior Brooke was clearly an overachiever.

"I think you're just in shock. It's a lot to take in," said Percy. "We are obviously not getting married tomorrow."

"You're right. There probably isn't anyone else here who can perform the ceremony. I'll tell Sergio Emilio Augustus to have his people reach out to the local churches to find a minister or something and maybe we can do it the day after tomorrow. It'll wreak havoc with the schedule and the money you said you were supposed to come into though."

"No, Brooke. We are not getting married this week. And after what's happened, certainly not here. The money's not important."

If Rush's demise failed shock her, Percy's last statement certainly did.

"I don't see how you can possibly say that. And you might not care about money, but my father certainly will, after all he's spent on this wedding. It simply can't all go to waste just because Rush got himself killed. After all, murders happen every day and the world doesn't come to an end. There has to be a way."

"No, there isn't. There is a murderer somewhere in this castle and given what happened to my father, Rush might not be his only victim. Or his last."

"Now you are just being difficult. I'm sorry about your father but it doesn't mean someone tried to kill him. Old people get sick all the time. And probably some angry woman killed Rush."

"This gives an entirely new meaning to 'out of the mouths of babes'" whispered Driscoll to Ben.

Brooke paused as she thought about the ramifications of what she had just said. "Although not Riley, Kiley, or Katie, of course. But there are plenty of other angry women. And anyway, I know for a fact that they couldn't have killed him because they're playing cribbage in the Games Room to see who gets him. I guess I should tell them that they can stop."

"And speaking of stopping," observed Barclay, "someone should probably tell Tucker to." Even down here the painful strains of *Jumpin' Jack Flash* were clearly audible.

"I'll do it," said Ben. "As soon as we finish dealing with Rush, I'm going to escort Cressida back to her room and he's just down the hall."

"There's no need to come with me. I have Rufus."

"No, I'm going to check on Percy's father after this," said the Other One.

"She means the dog," replied Ben. Then he glanced at my happy, slobbery face. "All the same I think I would feel better if I came with you. I'm also moving into your room. We should all try not to be alone until the police arrive."

"Don't even think about it," said Brooke to Percy. "You are absolutely not moving in with me. I don't want you to see my dress. In spite of how negative you're being, I still think I'll need it. Anyway, I'm off to let my girls know that they don't have to fight about Rush anymore. A least now maybe they'll look happy in the photos again."

Percy, however, looked anything but happy. Whatever he was thinking, the task at hand was once again uppermost in his and everyone else's mind. Especially mine. A visit to the kitchen under any circumstances, even homicide-related ones was bound to be a rewarding experience. Given the hour, cocktail nibbles and dinner prep should be well underway, although I made a mental note not to accept anything with mushrooms in it. You never know.

Our less than merry little band trundled off towards the kitchen in silence and much to everyone's relief without encountering anyone else. The guys deposited Rush behind a sofa in a nearby room.

"Here take Rufus," said my human. "It will look more like nothing is wrong and I'm sure he could use a snack." I could always use a snack, especially after finding dead bodies and leading a pack of clueless humans through a dense forest in a blinding snowstorm.

While Ben confabbed with the caterer, I was petted, fêted, and snacked in a way I found most gratifying.

"OK, let's go" said Ben after we had returned to the others. "The caterer gave me a key. Apparently, the key to the kingdom doesn't include the alcoholic parts. This might not be the only key, but it's at least something."

We plodded down several hallways and came to a halt in front of a green baize door. Behind it lay another, significantly less opulently decorated hallway off of which stood another door. Ben unlocked it revealing a steep flight of stone stairs.

"Cress, why don't you wait up here with Rufus," said Ben. "There's no one around so you should be safe. Even with Rufus."

"What should we do with the killer's bag of tricks?" asked Driscoll.

"Why don't you hide it in the wine cellar near the body," said my human. "And if anyone —even Henley—asks us where the body is, we can just say that it's in a safe place until the police arrive."

"Good idea," said Driscoll. "I'll carry the bag; the rest of you can carry Rush," This suggestion surprised no one. And no one was inclined to tell him to stop being a girl because no one wanted to be on the wrong side of my human's tongue again. She's generally a calm person—she has to be to live with me—but when she lets loose, she has reduced many a brave lad to a quivering blancmange. Having a large vocabulary is an asset.

The guys had now begun to bicker about the best way to get Rush down the stairs without either dropping him or falling. Those at the feet accused those at the head of moving too fast and those at the head accused those at the feet of moving too slow. Things were at an impasse until Barclay took charge. He had captained an eight at Harvard and began to rhythmically call out each step like the strokes of a coxed four on the Charles.

Once Rush and the murderer's goodies had been safely stowed and locked, the men came back upstairs and began to discuss who should do what and with whom.

"I need to check on your father, Percy. Buck can come with me," said Radiological Rufus. "Then we can go find Henley and break the news to her."

"Somehow I don't think she's going to be terribly upset," said Ben, "assuming of course that she didn't kill him. She and Rush apparently had a serious falling out over the money in her trust. Anyway, Cress and I will go tell Tucker to cease and desist playing what he thinks passes for music and then we'll go down to Great Hall and wait for everyone else."

"Dris and I will go find Sergio Emilio Augustus and Mike Kovac and tell them what happened," said Percy. "Then we'll help them try to get everyone to the Great Hall so Rufus can make his announcement about Rush."

"Let's hope Brooke was wrong about her father being upset about the money," said Driscoll. "I know he's going to be your father-in-law and all that Perce, but there's something about him that makes me think he's got a short fuse and a long memory."

"I agree," replied Percy, "but it's not as if I killed Rush myself to cost him the money he's thrown away on this ridiculous wedding. For the record, I wanted a quiet wedding in Nantucket, but Brooke and her family shot me down."

"I think we got away lightly," said my human to Ben after everyone had dispersed to their various assignments. "I don't envy the others. Telling Tucker to stop playing bagpipes is hardly in the same league as telling Rush's next of kin that he's dead."

"Or informing Brooke's father that he's just poured a small fortune down the drain. I agree with Driscoll. I don't think he is going to like it at all, and from what I've seen, he'll especially not like not being in a situation that he can't control."

"You know I keep thinking of that conversation we overheard in the maze. Rush is dead and Uncle Charles has probably been poisoned. Rufus doesn't seem to think he's in immediate danger, but he did say that without identifying the cause of the symptoms he can't know for sure."

"Well hopefully everyone else is hale and hearty and the announcement that the police have been called will act as a deterrent in case he has other victims in mind."

"Or she," added my human.

Conversation ceased when Ben pounded on Tucker's door. Somehow, I had a feeling this was not all that unusual of an occurrence.

The "music" stopped, and Tucker opened the door.

"Sorry am I disturbing you?" That would be an understatement, but ever the gentlemen Ben refrained from comment.

"Something very unfortunate has happened and if you could go down to the Great Hall—the Chamber of Libations—as soon as you can, there will be an announcement."

"What's happened? Is Brooke OK? Don't tell me Ethan doesn't like her dress."

"Yes, she's fine. Or at least fine-ish. But Rufus will tell everyone more."

Tucker looked down at me.

"Oh, the doctor one. OK. I'll be right down."

That chore completed, we proceeded in blessedly bagpipeless silence to the Rufus Suite where my human changed out of her wet clothes while I engaged in a lively game of tug of war with the towel Ben was trying to dry me with.

When they left to move Ben's stuff into our room, I picked up a rawhide, eager to see how our fellow wedding comrades were faring.

I found the Other Rufus in the music room talking to

Henley and Dr. Bruce. Although calling him Dr. Bruce is a misnomer since he's no more a doctor than I am a chihuahua.

"So we don't really know much about what happened. The police surgeon will be able to tell you more when the police are able to get here. Do you have any questions?"

"No," said Henley with a smile on her face. "He's really dead, right? I mean you're sure about that?"

"Oh, yes, it's the one thing we are actually sure about. And again, I'm sorry for your loss."

"Trust me, it's no loss," she replied. "Quite the opposite in fact."

"How is the groom's father doing?" asked Dr. Bruce.

"He's about the same, but at least he's no worse. Do you have any atropine by the way?"

"No, sorry. I used the last of it."

"That's too bad. Oh, until the police get here, we think it would be a good idea not to be alone. Just a precaution. I'll be in the Great Hall if you need me."

As soon as he made his exit, Henley threw her arms around Dr. Bruce and gave a long, lingering kiss. I have no idea why when humans do this it's a good thing, but when I do this they scream and run for the mouthwash.

I picked up my bone and went to see how Percy and Driscoll were doing with their assignment.

They were with Mike Kovac and Sergio Emilio Augustus in the library. The latter gentleman was pacing up and down like a cat whose breakfast is late and talking furiously into his headphone. I dropped my bone and went over to nose wand the Knob King's trousers. They were damp.

"I just can't say how sorry I am Mike," Percy was saying. "I know how much time, effort, and money have gone into the planning of this…this extraordinary occasion."

"Can't be helped. And you've nothing to apologize for, it's not your fault that the guy got himself whacked. What did you do with the body by the way? You didn't leave it out there did you?"

"No, the police told us to photograph it and bring it indoors."

"Where is it then?"

"Somewhere safe. Don't worry, Brooke and the guests won't stumble upon it. We also think it would be a good idea if people stick together as much as possible until the police get here."

"That seems unnecessary, and it'll worry the women. It's hardly likely that one of Brooke's guests is a homicidal maniac. Rush probably just pissed off one of the staff. And it's a good thing I made sure there's plenty of food and booze. All top shelf stuff. Nothing like it to ride out a blizzard."

He seemed remarkably composed for a guy who's just lost a considerable chunk of change.

Chapter 17

"...that's about all we know at the moment," concluded The Other Rufus speaking to the castle's inhabitants. "There's plenty of food and drink and I'm sure the catering staff will do their best to carry on and until the police arrive, I suggest that if possible no one be on their own, staff included. And please lock your doors at night." He looked out from the raised platform that had so recently hosted Elizabethan cocktail musicians.

There was a shocked silence in the crowded room. Riley, Kiley, and Katie, having been alerted to the catastrophe in mid-cribbage were all in black. Brooke had a peeved look on her pretty face and seemed to still be remonstrating, albeit at a whisper this time, with Percy. Mike stood by his wife and his PA and looked unexpectedly calm.

Tucker hovered near Ethan and his crew and looked theatrically shocked. Perhaps he was hoping for a featured role in this gripping new thriller; one could practically see the directorial wheels turning in the filmmaker's head as he evaluated the many possibilities of this unexpected gift from the film making gods.

When the Other Rufus had finished his remarks, he handed the karaoke mic over to Mike Kovac who seemed impatient to address the crowd and resume his rightful role as the man in charge. He held up his hand for silence. His audience held up their phones for social media.

"We are all of course deeply shocked and upset by what has happened" (although truth be told he looked neither) "but I have been informed by my future son-in-law and his able-bodied groomsmen that the police will be here as soon as the weather permits. In the meantime, let's be clear. If whoever did this dares to try again with my family or my guests, they will not live to regret it." As he said this, he opened his jacket to reveal a holster.

There was a loud murmur.

"On a more practical note, there is plenty of food and drink, all of course of the highest quality", here he indicated the abundantly stocked bars on either side of the room, "and as dinner is going to be delayed a bit, I've asked the catering staff to put out trays of hors d'oeuvres. I have also spoken with the facilities staff, and they have assured me that the property is prepared for weather-related emergencies of this kind and that there are backup generators in case the power goes out. We're snowbound and conditions are dangerous outside so please stay indoors."

"Conditions might not be safe indoors either," quipped Driscoll, "but it's hard to imagine that there are any weapons left. I suppose there's still a rope or cracking someone on the skull with a wrench or a lead pipe, but those would seem to present some practical difficulties, although…"

"Seriously Dris, put a sock in it," said Ben. At the mention of socks my ears perked up but this desirable article seemed not to be in evidence. "Make yourself useful and get Cress and me some drinks. I'll have a Scotch."

"A gin and tonic for me, please," said my human.

"Are you sure you don't want A Rufus?" asked Ben.

"A Rufus?" said Driscoll. "I don't think I've heard of that one."

"It's a glass of gin," replied my human. "And a G&T will be fine."

Meanwhile the room crackled with conversation.

"Do you think this is part of the entertainment?" asked a cheerful young woman with spectacles. "Like one of those murder game things. Maybe if we guess the killer, we'll win a vacation or something."

"I hope so. I could use a vacation," said her companion.

"Didn't you just come back from the Galapagos?" said another of the chatty throng.

"That was weeks ago, and it doesn't count. My parents made me go because they thought it would be educational. No booze, lots of animals. And anyway, I need to get away; my boss is driving me crazy. He's giving me work to do."

Their expressions of commiseration to this outrage were lost when my human's mother hastily arrived.

"Are you alright, Cressida? Thank goodness you have Rufus to protect you. And you too, of course, Ben." I was touched by her reluctance to abandon her view of me as a fierce guard dog. "No one seems to have any idea of exactly what happened or even who found the body."

I bayed.

"Tell me he didn't..."

"He did," said my human. "It was probably his dream come true. But I was with Ben and the boys, so I'm fine. Or as fine as one can be when your dog finds a dead body."

"I'm staying with Cressida until all this is cleared up," said Ben. "Why don't I ask the staff to put a bed in the sitting room for you."

"That's very kind of you Ben, but if you just walk me to my door later, I'll lock myself in and I'll be perfectly safe. My windows are already locked so there's no way into my room."

"I'll just check over your room tonight when we take you back if that's OK." said Ben.

"Good evening, Mrs. Pennington," said Percy as he joined the group.

"How's Brooke?" asked Barclay. "Has she accepted the fact that she is not going to be Mrs. Percival Dudley Alden Winthrop this week."

"I tried to tell her that it's in bad taste to start asking the guests if anyone is licensed to officiate at a wedding because someone murdered the previous one, but she insists that I'm wrong and that we should carry on as planned because no one really knew Rush anyway. Fortunately, Tucker had more luck with her. He told her that she absolutely shouldn't get married here, even if she can find someone else to perform the ceremony, because she deserves to have a wedding that people will remember because of how beautiful she looked and not because someone was murdered. Also, that since Riley, Kiley, and Katie, are refusing to get out of their black clothes, it would mess up the photos. He was very persuasive. Now at least she's thinking about it."

Before anyone could comment, Driscoll returned with a Rufus and Tonic for my human and a Macallan for Ben.

"Good madam, how dost thee," inquired Driscoll of my human's mother, "wouldest thou desire a beverage from yon bar?" I'll bet my human deeply regretted mentioning to him that her father had taught Shakespeare at Yale.

"Thank you, yes. I think I could use a drink. A glass of

white wine would be much appreciated."

"Once more unto the breach…" and he disappeared barwards with a bow and a flourish.

"I'm so sorry Percy. This must all be a terrible shock," said Percy's boss who hove up with his young, white-faced wife clinging to his arm.

"It's like that movie," she wailed, "the one where those people are trapped in a castle on an island and get murdered one by one."

"I think you're thinking of *Ten Little Indians*," said Barclay, "but given that there are a lot more than ten of us, I wouldn't worry; it would take a murderer ages to kill us all."

"Very true," observed Driscoll who had returned with both a glass of Montrachet and The Other Rufus in tow. "There is quite a lot of debate over by the bar about which ten of us would get killed first. Sergio Emilio Augustus and Ethan are in the lead but I think that's just wishful thinking on everyone's part."

"Come on Annabel, let's get another drink," said Percy's boss with a frown at Barclay and Driscoll.

"I don't think your boss likes us Percy," said Driscoll.

"Well personally I'm glad you're all here," said my human's mother. "And especially that we have a man of science to take charge."

"Not to contradict, Mrs. Pennington, but I think you'll find that medicine isn't science," said Barclay.

"And radiology isn't medicine," added Driscoll.

"So you keep telling me. Which reminds me that I should go check up on Mr. Winthrop again," said the Other Rufus. "You can come with me, Buck."

After they left, a large young man appeared behind my human.

"Lady...I mean Ms. Cressida, I just wanted to let you know that we've made special arrangements to take care of Rufus's lavatorial needs in this weather"

It took my human a minute to realize that the figure in jeans and a sweater rather than doublet and hose was none other than My Attendant.

"The groundskeeper says that given the direction of the wind, the best chance of getting Rufus out is using a side door by the kitchen. He's left some boots and warm clothing for you and your young man. They probably won't fit very well but they are at least better suited to the weather than what you've probably got. He also recommends making sure you have other people with you to stand inside by the door in case you fall or get into trouble. It's dangerous weather to be out in without backup. And I've left a pile of towels for Rufus. Then as far as dinner is concerned, I've been asked to let you know that there aren't going to be any place cards so everyone can sit where they like; as soon as you're seated, we'll bring over Rufus's feeding station. Just remember to leave a seat next to you open. I'll be available if you need anything and the rest of the staff too. We're all very fond of Rufus and want to make sure he isn't too upset by everything that's happened."

He was doing such a nice job scratching my ears that I didn't have the heart to tell him that I was probably the only one who wasn't. It's not every day I get to hunt unleashed and unfettered in a forest and then on top of that find a dead body. It was even better than the time I dragged my human into the lake in Central Park and she got two fines because we were both "swimming."

Chapter 18

When the humans had finished swilling their drinks, we filed into the room formerly known as the Chamber of Repast which stripped of its anachronistic claptrap, was once again just a large, conventional dining room. My dinner companions consisted of my human and her mother, and the groomsmen, minus Barclay and the Other Rufus who were still with Uncle Charles. There were no trumpets and the nuptial dais had been removed. Percy sat just upwind of us with Brooke, her family, and the bridesmaids, black clad and lugubrious, with the exception of Emily who was not lugubrious at all and who, with her mother, was in the protective custody of her brother and father. As the rest of the guests dribbled in, the room was soon filled with loud top shelf induced chatter. The initial shock had passed and now the question on everyone's mind was whodunnit and why.

As instructed, my human left the chair to her right vacant, but as soon as we sat down it was claimed by the Other Rufus who had just returned from his medical duties.

"Sorry, that's Rufus's place," said a server dressed in black. The rest of the servers were also dressed in black; but they weren't in mourning; they were from New York.

"Yes, I know. I'm Rufus."

"But you're the wrong Rufus," she said as she pointedly removed the chair and replaced it with my feeding station.

"Am I ever the right Rufus?" lamented my namesake as he took a seat next to my human's mother. It was a rhetorical question since the answer was an obvious one.

The serving staff may have been unrecognizable when out of costume, but they remained efficient as always and even remembered that I preferred my water still. The Master of Revels was nowhere to be seen, but I noticed some discrete camera work being directed from the sidelines.

"How is my brother?" inquired my human's mother of the Wrong Rufus.

"He's still pretty much the same but I'm hoping he'll be over the worst of it by tomorrow. Depending on how he does overnight, I'd like to see if he can hold down some bouillon in the morning. If you're available, I propose that we both go to the kitchen and prepare it, or anything he's able to eat and drink, until we can be sure he's not a target. Your sister-in-law hasn't wanted to leave his side, which given what happened to Rush, is a good thing, so I think it's best that she should continue to stay with him for the time being."

The idea was well received. Also well received, at least by me, was the delectable dinner that made its way into my bowl.

"Why don't you ask Cressida to help her mother in the kitchen instead," suggested Barclay, "then you'd be free to help us snoop around and hunt for clues."

"No!" This was said simultaneously by Ben and my human's mother.

"I love my daughter but watching her try to chop an onion would bring tears to your eyes for an entirely different reason," she said. "I'm not sure my brother's stomach could take it."

"And on the subject of hunting for clues," said the Other Rufus, "let's find a quiet spot after dinner. I want to talk to you all about something." I was all ears, but he didn't elaborate.

The rest of dinner proceeded deliciously and without incident. The guys were pretty pumped with respect to the whole clue hunting thing, but they had the good manners to try to rein in their enthusiasm given that the deceased's sister was also in the room. She was, as usual, accompanied by Dr. Bruce but the affianced couple were making very little attempt to keep their elation under wraps. After they had finished their dinner, they stopped by with smiles on their faces to ask after Uncle Charles in whose health they now seemed to take a keen interest.

When they had departed, probably in search of the past life regression of Lucretia Borgia, they were replaced by Percy and a sulky-looking Brooke.

"How is my father?" he asked.

"Stable," replied our medical man.

"See, I told you he was OK. You'd have heard if he wasn't," grumbled Brooke.

"Can I see him?"

"I was going to ask the same thing," said my human's mother.

"I'd prefer not," responded the Other Rufus, "if there's any change, I will of course let you both know."

"Well then, I actually think I'll go to my room," said my

human's mother.

"I'll come with you, Aunt Elizabeth," said Percy. A black cloud descended even further over Brooke's brow.

"You're supposed to be protecting me. I'm sure one of your friends can go with your aunt."

"You have your brother and father, and they look like they are more than up to the task."

"It's not the same thing."

Here Ben interrupted.

"Don't worry about it; If we're on the buddy system, Buck and I can take Mrs. Pennington to her room and then we can both come back down here together."

"See," said Brooke.

"No," said Percy. It was clear from the expression on her face that she disliked this word almost as much as I did. It was also clear that it was not a word she was used to hearing from her husband to be. "She's my aunt, not Ben's or Buck's" He turned to Ben. "But I take your point about traveling in pairs. We'll go together." Brooke spun on her stilettos and stalked off in a huff.

"Don't get started until I get back," Ben said as he rose from his chair. Percy looked perplexed.

"Rufus—no not you" he said addressing me as I shoved my ears forward with an expression of alert enthusiasm— "wants to talk to us about something privately." I wondered why no one ever wants me to talk to them, privately or otherwise.

"Am I invited?" asked Percy.

"Yes. That is, if you're able," said Ben, as he shot a look

at Brooke who appeared to be in the process of venting to her family.

"I'm able," said Percy.

"Looks like we might have a second murder on our hands," observed Driscoll glancing down the table where Brooke's father and brother were glaring at Percy with homicidal expressions on their faces.

"They are looking rather thuggish," said Barclay.

"You mean more than usual?" asked Driscoll.

"I admit, they're not exactly what I had in mind as in laws, but we'll be in New York, and they'll be back in Ohio," said Percy.

"Anyway, Cress can you and Rufus come with us?" asked Ben. "No, not you Other Rufus."

"Good idea. He hates waiting around and as soon as you leave, he'll just bay and make a nuisance of himself until you come back." My human might know me well, but I had an inkling that Ben was not asking out of consideration for my feelings.

The reason for my presence became apparent as soon as we reached the door of my human's mother's room.

"I think it would be a good idea if we came in and had a look around just to make sure it's safe," said Ben.

"Oh I'm sure it will be," replied my human's mother. "I'm on the third floor and there's no balcony or anything so no risk of intruders." The penny dropped for my human.

"Ben's right Mother," she said. "I'd feel better if we look around."

And by we, she meant me.

It was a large and luxuriously appointed room. I always appreciate fine décor, particularly with respect to cushy chairs that are ideally proportioned to accommodate the ample bloodhound bottom and capacious couches that are both long and deep and not upholstered in any offensively scratchy fabric. If you haven't guessed by now, I am a delicate flower.

But I digress.

I got to work. Ben considerately moved aside the carpets and I snuffled the floor and then my human led me along the perimeter of the room paying special attention to walls and baseboards and around and over to the wall of closets. Here she stopped and let me inspect them at my leisure. There was nothing of interest, which was good news for her but bad news for me. Ben wasn't the only one who was keen to find those tunnels. Finally, for forms sake she had me look under the bed.

"All clear," she said and gave me a scratch under the chin.

"I told you it would be," said my human's mother. "But I suppose if anything had been amiss, Rufus would have let us know. He must be a great comfort to you living alone." I'm not sure bloodhounds can be described as being a great comfort in any circumstances, but I take my compliments where I can get them; I wagged my tail and nearly obliterated a bit of chinoiserie carelessly placed on an occasional table.

We said good night.

"Who knew that Rufus would actually be useful for once," commented my human. I would have resented it if she hadn't been right. Unless you were looking for fast moving rodents, a dead body, or secret passageways, I pride myself on being purely and inconveniently ornamental.

"What were you looking for," asked Percy who had been watching from the doorway.

"Nothing special," said my human, "just generally making sure the room is safe. But while we're at it, I know the Other Rufus wouldn't approve, but given everything, I'd like this Rufus to take a look at your father's room too, Percy. If you can go in first and let your parents know. Just tell them I want to see how they are."

I liked this game. We bloodhounds are incorrigible busybodies and normally it's something I get reprimanded for, so it's nice to hear, "Go be a busybody, Rufus."

Percy knocked on Uncle Charles's door and announced himself through the door.

"Percy, what's happened. Is anything else the matter?" asked Aunt Anne as she opened it.

"No, no. Everything's fine. Well apart from Rush, that is. Cressida just wanted to see if she could come in for a few minutes and see how you're getting on and if there's anything she can do to help." If Aunt Anne was puzzled, she was too polite to say anything, especially when my human and I entered the room together and she dropped my leash. First of course, I went to see how Uncle Charles was. He was propped up in bed looking as white as the sheets under him. He gave my neck a feeble scratch, but at least he was alive. I then perambulated about the room sniffing this and that while my human made the appropriate inquiries and kept a close eye on me. She casually picked up my leash and walked me around the perimeter of the room.

"Is he looking for anything in particular?" Aunt Anne asked.

"No, you know Rufus; probably just any bits of cookies Uncle Charles may have dropped. Please let Mother and I know if there is anything we can do for you. She might be by tomorrow if Rufus says it's OK. He won't be happy about my visit, but I just felt I had to pop in anyway."

Which was completely true, just not for the obvious

reason. And it was a good thing we did too. There was an air current drifting in from a section of paneling at the far end of the room and I began snorting like a pig with a truffle. I was just about to give the panel a good shove when my human hastily dragged me away.

"I can feel a draft over here Ben," said my human to her partner in crime prevention. This presented something of a conundrum. Neither one had thought past just having me check the room. They had no actual plan of what to do if I actually found something. "I don't think a draft is healthy for Uncle Charles in his condition," she said pointedly.

"No you're right. These old, warped panels are probably letting air in from somewhere," said Ben with an architectural mendacity that rivaled my human's with respect to hedge funds and house renos.

"What should we do?" asked my human. It was obvious that Uncle Charles was in no condition to change rooms even if an excuse could be concocted for such a thing.

They both looked around the room.

"Mrs. Winthrop, would you mind if we moved that small settee against this wall? It should block the draft and I'm sure Dr. Rufus wouldn't want Mr. Winthrop catching cold in his weakened state." The actual Rufus wouldn't want that either. Or something worse.

"I don't feel a draft, but by all means if you think it's a good idea, please go ahead," replied Aunt Anne.

Ben took one end, and my human took the other and together they repositioned the settee. At least if anyone wanted to harm Uncle Charles it wouldn't be that way.

Afterwards we returned to the dining room, where speculation among my entourage was running rampant about what the Other Rufus wanted to tell them.

I would say they were frothing at the mouth, but I'm the only one allowed to do that.

Chapter 19

We wandered about the castle looking for a room that was a) empty and b) abundantly stocked with alcohol.

Ben let the others go ahead and held my human back by the arm.

"Look Cress, I trust the guys and all that, but as I said before, I think the police should be the first ones to hear about the tunnels. That way there's no danger of us being overheard—I wouldn't put it past that weasel Ethan to have hidden cameras and mics everywhere—and also then there's no danger of the others saying anything to anyone else. Percy might want to tell Brooke and Dris, well is Dris. He's about as discrete as a town crier."

"Seems a shame not to let them in on it, but you're right, it's safer all around." Meanwhile I could barely contain my excitement at the prospect of there being a weasel in the castle. I was still smarting from the escape of that vole.

When we caught up to the others they were standing in front of a snug, masculine-looking lair, heavy on leather, wood, and booze. Decanters of cognac and port—all vintage and probably costing a month's rent—were arrayed on silver salvers. Should these not be to your liking, there was also a wide selection of eaux de vie and liqueurs ready to get the job done. The only thing missing were the smoking jackets and cigars.

When everyone was settled with the drink of their choice, and I was settled on the lap of my choice, all eyes turned expectantly to the Other Rufus.

"The floor is yours Rufie," said Driscoll.

"Call me that again and you'll be joining Rush."

"I'm only trying not to confuse the corpse-finding Rufus. And besides you never minded when we were boys together," replied Driscoll.

"I didn't mind a lot of things when we were boys together. Including you. And no one wants a doctor called Rufie."

"This doctor thing seems to be going to your head. I don't think the computer you sit in front of looking at pictures cares what you're called."

"The corpse-finding Rufus doesn't like bickering," said my human. "If you don't stop it, he'll bay. So unless you want to call attention to our location, let's just hear what Dr. Rufus has to say."

"Thank you, Cressida. Well as sick as he is, Perce, your father is first and foremost a lawyer. When I saw him this evening, he suggested that since it's unlikely that the police will get here tomorrow, that we try to get them up to speed as quickly as possible when they do arrive. He proposes that we ask everyone where they were on Wednesday afternoon to give them a snapshot of everyone's movements and also that it would seem less like an inquisition if there are only two of us—one to ask the questions and the other to take notes. He thinks that way we're more likely to get useful information and that knowing everyone's whereabouts will speed up the police investigation."

"Let me guess, my father wants to be the one asking the questions," said Percy.

"Yes, that was the general idea, but I don't think that's wise either medically or frankly for safety reasons since he might be a potential victim. Although it's hard to see what he and Rush had in common that would make them both targets; but you never know."

"I think I should do the questioning," said Driscoll. "I spent most of college watching detective shows and everyone knows I have a mind like a steel trap."

"That would be news to your professors," said the Other Rufus, "and you lack sufficient gravitas, to put it mildly. Percy, it can't be you because you'll need to be with Brooke. Buck…well what can I say. I see your talents as being more physical than intellectual." It was a polite way of saying he thought Barclay had been hit on the head one too many times with an oar. "Cressida, you've only just got here, so aren't as familiar with some of the actors."

"He means suspects," said Driscoll. "Sorry Perce, I know they'll soon be your family, but apart from us and your father, everyone is fair game. Although maybe not the women."

Before my human could jump in with a rogue's gallery of murderous females, Barclay beat her to it.

"Oh, I don't know about that. Emily looks pretty capable. And she's a crack shot."

"Yes, but there's also the arrow and the sword," said Driscoll. "That might take some strength."

"They probably said the same thing about Lizzie Borden," replied Barclay. "And anyway, we don't know what killed him."

"I still think they all did it, like in *Murder on the Orient Express*," said Driscoll.

"That only happens in books," said Barclay. "But maybe the killer was just being really thorough. Anyway, I still don't think we can rule out the women. Maybe Henley had a past life regression about being a Viking Warrior Princess or Boadicea or something."

"Wait, you know who Boadicea is?" exclaimed Percy.

"Old Haverstraw of sophomore Latin has a lot to answer for," replied Barclay.

"Well, he certainly didn't appreciate it the time you showed up for class naked except for a bedsheet," said Percy.

"It was a toga. And I was just trying to demonstrate my commitment to the subject."

"I think he would have been more impressed if you had ever learned to conjugate a verb."

It was nice to see that I wasn't the only one who digresses.

"Anyway, I was about to say that I volunteer to take notes," said the Other Rufus. "I have experience looking at patients while they are talking and typing at the same time."

"Patients? What patients? You don't have patients, you have pictures," said Driscoll.

"As I was saying," continued the Other Rufus looking snappishly at his adversary, "I can do the note taking and I think Ben should ask the questions. He has a much more logical mind than either of you two."

"I disagree," said Driscoll. "I think I'd make an excellent

grand inquisitor; I'm sure I had a past life in Spain."

"It's comments like that that would turn the whole thing into a circus, Dris," said the Other Rufus.

"OK, but as soon as you know who the prime suspects are, maybe Buck and I can trap them into doing something incriminating."

"I wouldn't recommend it. People who try to trap murder suspects into doing something incriminating usually end up dead," said the Other Rufus.

"Well maybe we can just tail them and see if we can overhear them saying something incriminating," said Barclay clearly itching to take an active part in the investigation.

"And speaking of overhearing," said my human, "I think Ben mentioned that Henley and Rush had an argument about releasing the money in her trust; well Ben and I overheard her telling Dr. Bruce about it when we were exploring the maze the other day. She wants to use the money to expand his business. I'm afraid the management of the trust now falls to your father, Percy and given what happened to him, Rufus is right. We should all be very careful about what we do and say and to whom." We Rufuses are always right.

"Then we're agreed," said the Other Rufus. "Tomorrow, I'll see if we can get everyone together at breakfast and I'll make an announcement about the interviews. We can use the library and I suggest we start with the wedding party and the guests. I'm sorry Percy, but that will mean Brooke and her family too. Maybe you can ask Tucker to help with that. He seems to have a good relationship with them. And while you're at it you might mention that he should continue the moratorium on bagpipe playing."

"Good idea about Tucker," said Percy. "I'm not sure I'm exactly flavor of the month with Brooke or her family right now. But we might want to talk to that waitress sooner rather than later. You know the one who stabbed Rush with a steak knife. And maybe the caterer because of what happened to my father. Maybe she saw something, knows something, or can shed some light on what happened."

"I wouldn't do that if I were you," said my human. "If you announce what you're going to do ahead of time and anyone has anything to hide, it will give them time to fabricate a story. It's much better to capitalize on the element of surprise. I can approach whoever you want to speak to and tell them Dr. Rufus wants to see them in the library. I'll make it sound completely innocuous, and they'll probably just think it's something health related. Meanwhile, one of you two," here she indicated Barclay and Driscoll, "can lurk outside the library door and stop anyone from interrupting. Whichever of you is not standing guard can come with me to look for people to send to the library."

"An ambush! I love it!" exclaimed Barclay.

"You're right, the surprise element does make a lot more sense," said the Other Rufus, shooting a daggerish look at the increasingly buoyant Barclay.

They all still looked very much like the prep school boys they had once been, cooking up some thrilling after-hours caper in a dorm room.

"OK then, gentlemen we have a plan," said Ben. "Drink up. Cress and I need your help in the kitchen." At the mention of this sacred precinct, my ears shot up. "We're going to try to get Rufus outside to relieve himself and I need you all to stand by in case we get buried. After that, we can go upstairs as a group and drop everyone off as we go. I've moved in with Cress, so if you need me, that's where I'll be."

I love how strongly the masculine urge to protect the female asserts itself when danger threatens. Dead bodies aside, my human is not exactly a shrinking violet—she handles me after all—but with a murderer on the loose, even she could see the advantage of a gaggle of young, protective males rallying round. And if she couldn't, I could.

We headed to the side door of the kitchen where, as promised, there was a table piled high with mismatched toggery. It looked like North Face was having a rummage sale. My human began trying stuff on while the sartorial peanut gallery offered unhelpful advice. By the time she was done she looked like a cross between a clown and a Lilliputian who had raided Gulliver's closet. Driscoll pulled out his phone.

"No Driscoll!" she cried.

"Yes Driscoll!" cried everyone else.

Meanwhile I snorted the air under the door like I was doing a line and bayed to remind everyone that the purpose of the exercise was not embarrassing social media photos. The wind was howling and although I pride myself on being a snowdog—watching my human try to stay upright while attached to me is a well-known Upper West Side spectator sport—I had a feeling our visit outside was going to be uncharacteristically brief.

There was a large shovel propped conspicuously next to the door and Ben used it to reduce the height of a snow drift blocking our way. The three of us hurled ourselves into the raging storm and by the time we returned, I looked like the abominable snowhound. But we had accomplished our mission.

"We'll take this stuff with us for tomorrow," Ben said as my human ineffectually attacked me with towels. "Buck, get us a garbage bag from wherever you got the other one, then we'll drop you all off."

"Well it's been a day," said my human when we finally returned to The Rufus Suite. She locked the door and dragged a chair in front of it, although I had a feeling it wasn't so much that she was worried about someone getting in as about someone getting out.

"Ben help me get something in front of that panel in the wall. I will not have Rufus go exploring in the middle of the night." Harumph. Humans are such killjoys.

In spite of this, I always enjoy having extra company at night. The more warm bodies the better. But sleep was not exactly the first thing on Ben's mind.

"Really Ben, now? We're snowed in in a remote castle with a murderer. Is there anything that affects you?"

"No. Plus you're hot when you're sleuthing, and it will take our minds off of things for a bit."

Or more than a bit.

In the interests of male solidarity, I took myself off to the sofa until things got less active and it was safe to return to snore in everyone's ear.

Chapter 20

Bright and early the next morning I gave my human's face its customary thorough wash, being especially careful to jab her with the pointy bristles for which my snout is justifiably famous. And while this is always delightful, I admit that I do sometimes like to change things up by thrusting a drooly stuffie in her face and squeaking it relentlessly instead. No sense getting into a rut.

Anyway, although it was early, I'm not sure bright was exactly the word I would choose to describe the day. When my human finally summoned up the energy to roll out of bed—all the while muttering foul imprecations since it's not all that easy to resume slumber when one's face is under attack by wet wrinkles and pointy bristles—she pushed back the curtains and saw with dismay that it was still dark and still snowing.

With one human up and on the hoof, I was now able to turn my attention on the other.

"Jesus, Rufus, stop! What time is it anyway?" Since I neither wear a watch nor carry a phone my only answer to the question was that it was time to get up and go out.

"Don't ask," replied my human. I know from experience that checking the time in the morning generally has a tendency to depress her. "Do you think we should wake the others to help with the walk?"

"And risk another homicide on our hands? No. Anyway, there should be someone in the kitchen starting the prep work for breakfast; they'd hear us if we yell for help. If there's no one in the kitchen, I'll pound on Buck's door; he's less of a sloth than Dris."

While my humans tidied themselves and prepared for the perils of the impending walk, I commandeered a fluffy pillow and went back to sleep. This appeared to annoy them somehow.

The cobbled together clothing my human threw on was just as ludicrous this morning as it was last night. Ben had to take charge of my leash—one of the short ones for some reason—because she was afraid she might trip in the super-size boots she was wearing. Her fears were not unfounded. As I might have mentioned, even without clown boots, I admit to being a bit of a handful on snowy mornings. It's why all her boots are equipped with the kinds of crampons usually used for scaling K2.

But I digress.

As Ben had predicted, there were already a few prep cooks up and at it under the supervisory eye of the formidable looking caterer. He alerted them to our presence and pushed open the side door. The wind had died down but even on the lee side of the storm, the drifts were piled high. He handed my leash to my human and went to work with the shovel to carve out an eliminatory space for yours truly. A few extended leg lifts and poop circles later, we were all back inside and upstairs, safe and sound.

My humans headed into the bathroom and since they seemed to be spending an inordinate amount of time grooming each other and whatnot in the shower, I did briefly consider whether I should take a turn about the castle, but as my absence might delay breakfast, I settled for eviscerating a stuffie and beginning work on a new bone instead.

When my humans were at last clean and presentable and in their own clothes—or any clothes, we went to collect the others. The upside of someone getting murdered is that the dreaded royal wardrobe chest remained firmly shut.

We picked up Barclay and Driscoll, although not Percy who had apparently persuaded Brooke to let him guard her person, and then went to the Other Rufus's room. There was a note on the door informing us that he was with Uncle Charles. If anyone was still asleep by the time we picked up my human's mother, my joyous greeting would have ensured that they were no longer so.

Murder or no murder, breakfast was, as usual, a stellar affair. I've never been one to be able to decide between sweet and savory, so I went with both. Meanwhile my humans mainlined coffee and gave me the evil eye.

I was just working my way through a vertiginous stack of buttermilk pancakes when the Other Rufus joined us.

"Mr. Winthrop is looking better this morning," he said, much to everyone's relief. "I think he might even be up to trying some clear broth. Mrs. Pennington, perhaps after breakfast we can go and prepare a tray."

Tucker trickled by just as a Wyke cheddar cheese omelet was being offloaded into my bowl.

"Dr. Rufus, I was wondering if you'd like me to take attendance to make sure all the guests are present," he said.

"He means alive," interjected Driscoll.

"Or alive-ish," said Barclay as he too sucked down some coffee. "Recent events have not exactly been conducive to getting a good night's sleep."

"Thanks Tucker, that's an excellent idea," said the Other Rufus who now seemed to be in charge of insuring that the castle's inhabitants remained in a state of ongoing viability.

As soon as sufficient levels of calories and caffeine had been ingested, the Other Rufus and my human's mother departed to the nether regions of the kitchen to prepare a restorative soup in which poison did not feature in the recipe. Barclay and Driscoll decided to go to the library to await the start of the day's entertainment and Ben and my human decided to return to the room to "freshen up." I knew they hadn't been together for a couple of weeks but even so, this seemed like an excessive amount of freshening up.

In normal circumstances, the post-matinal meal portion of my day would consist of the sacred Morning Nap, but today there was much to be done. I passed on supervising the broth making in the kitchen and opted instead to accompany my humans back to the room to retrieve the bone I had started during this early morning's freshening up. I took it with me to the library, as those already in residence lacked sufficient appeal.

"Look Dris, it's Rufus! He's come to help," declared Barclay as I trotted in carrying my bone du jour. "I wonder if he can sniff out when people are lying?" Only when they tell me a real whopper, like what's behind their back isn't the nail clipper.

"He'll probably be a lot more useful than Regular Rufus," replied Driscoll, still peeved at having been denied his role as inquisitor. They gave me a scratch and then they resumed the game they had been playing which consisted of competing to see how few of the books on the shelves they had each read.

Barclay had racked up several impressive zeros when they were interrupted by the arrival of my humans followed by the less useful Rufus and his more useful laptop.

"How's Uncle Charles?" asked my human. "Is my mother still with him?"

"He's weak but we were able to get some fluids and broth down him. He was still trying to persuade me that he should join us but I told him that it was out of the question. And yes, your mother is with him. I'll send one of these clowns," he said looking at Barclay and Driscoll, "to check on them at regular intervals, maybe with some board games or cards or something to keep them occupied. Meantime, I want to see if my laptop will print on this printer. It'll be more secure than using the library desktop. He turned on the printer, loaded it with paper from the pack on the desk, and plugged in the printer cable from the desktop. In due course the welcome whoosh of a printer in action was heard.

"Success! Good, that also means we can use those couches over there which is much less formal than me sitting behind a desk."

"I've been thinking," said my human. This was a surprise. I don't believe her recent activities came under that heading, but then again women are supposed to be good at multi-tasking. "Although we can't be sure of who else knew about the clearing where we found Rush, we definitely know those who did: the wedding party and all the people who planned, filmed, and helped with the photoshoots. Also, during the scavenger hunt Ben and I and Henley and Bruce ended up there. Can you think of anyone else?"

"Not offhand," said Ben, "except that as a bridesmaid Emily was there and she might easily have spoken to her family about it. We don't know about the musicians or the servers or the castle staff—any one of them could have gone exploring or overheard the wedding party or the planners talking about it. But since it's unlikely they had any connection to Rush, they're probably not high on the list of suspects anyway."

"Also," said my human, "I suggest you guys make sure to ask everyone if they saw Rush that afternoon. I only remember seeing him at lunch. Ben and I were exploring the castle, but we didn't run into him." You didn't have to be Sherlock Holmes to know that the only kind of "exploring" Ben was interested in was the kind with walls that swung open. "Did anyone see him after lunch?"

"Dris and I were shooting pool," said Barclay, "and I don't think I saw anyone. Except of course, Rufus when I was passing through the hall to see if any of the rooms had beer in them."

"You did? I didn't see you, I was in the library catching up on some journal articles," said the Superfluous Rufus.

"Not you. The Real Rufus. That's when I saw him by the door and let him out." My human shot him an evil look. "Which actually turned out to be good thing," he said brightly glancing at her, "because if I hadn't, Rush would still be out there under six feet of snow."

"As for me," said the Other Rufus, "I was still here reading when Mrs. Winthrop found me and told me that Mr. Winthrop was feeling under the weather and asked me to take a look at him. We didn't see Rush as I recall. And right after that I went with all of you to search for the much more popular Rufus."

"I think that's part of the problem," said Driscoll. "if you don't know you're supposed to notice someone, you don't. Plus this place has more rooms than Brooke has shoes, so the odds of running into anyone anywhere aren't all that great."

"I wouldn't be too sure about the shoes part, but as much as it pains me to say it, for once Dris is right," said the Other Rufus. "And not just about the inside of this place, but the outside as well. Lunch ended about 1-ish and we found the body around 4. I'm not making any guesses about time of death, especially in light of the cold weather, but we didn't see anyone in the forest when we were looking for Rufus or on our way to the Overlook..." My human was about to say something, but caught herself in time, "...which may not mean anything given the size and density of the forest, so we basically need everyone's movements from lunch until we found Rush's body."

"Who should we start with?" asked Barclay, like a frisky border collie eager to have his way with some sheep.

"Why don't you start with someone easy, kind of like a practice run, before you move on to the more serious suspects," suggested my human. "My mother for instance; and at least we know where to find her."

"Also, I'm aware it's not something that any of us want to consider," said Ben, "especially since he might also be a victim, but Rufe you didn't see Mr. Winthrop until shortly before we gathered to go look for Rufus, so we should probably find out where he was between lunch and when you saw him."

"That reminds me," said Barclay. "The night of the Masque, I saw Mr. Winthrop go out onto the terrace and Rush followed him. Mr. Winthrop looked pretty upset when he came back in."

"Then I propose that Cressida, Buck, and I go to Mr. Winthrop's room, "said the Other Rufus, "and Cressida can ask her mother and Mrs. Winthrop to come to the library. Buck, you and Cressida can escort them down and Ben can speak with the ladies on his own. I don't think there is much harm in talking to them together since we're really more interested in who they saw than if they nipped out to the clearing and topped Rush. In the meantime, I can speak to Mr. Winthrop alone and ask him where he was after lunch. Maybe I'll also see if I can get him to tell me anything about the night of the Masque. Dris, you stand guard by the library door and ask people not to go in. Tell them I'm talking to someone about a medical problem or something. Get creative. Although not too creative," he added noting the gleam in Driscoll's eye.

So there it was: Barclay was a retriever, Dris a centurion, the Other Rufus, a scribe, Ben an inquisitor, and my human a messenger. Everyone had an assignment except for me. I was tempted to remain where I was and continue working on my rawhide, but the more I thought about it, I too was curious about what Uncle Charles had been up to after lunch.

Looking longingly at my rawhide, I rose and followed my human, Barclay, and Other Rufus out the door.

The free-range Rufus policy had distinct advantages.

Chapter 21

My human knocked on Uncle Charles's door.

"Who is it?"

'It's me, Aunt Anne," said my human. "And both Rufuses."

Aunt Anne unlocked the door and we went in. Uncle Charles looked better today, although clearly not up to full biscuit dispensing strength. He was sitting in a chair talking to my human's mother. I poked at the edges of that irritating settee that had been moved last night while my human explained the purpose of her visit.

"Mother, Ben would like to speak with you and Aunt Anne in the library. Rufus will stay with you, Uncle Charles, until they return."

"Is anything wrong?" asked my human's mother anxiously.

"No, not at all. We're just following up on Uncle

Charles's suggestion that we give the police a head start by finding out where everyone was yesterday afternoon."

"I really think I should go down to the library," said Uncle Charles. "Ben is an intelligent boy but he's not a lawyer."

"We do understand that Sir, but I would really feel more comfortable if you stayed where you are. You're still very weak and there is no guarantee that the symptoms won't return."

"Listen to the doctor Charles," said my human's mother. "I'm sure Ben will do very well. He's bright and capable and perhaps it might even be less off putting if he's doing the questioning." Uncle Charles was as reluctant to abandon his inquisitorial role as I was to abandon my bone.

"Rufus, are you coming?" asked my human.

"No, I'm going to stay and examine Charles," said the Other One.

"Oh, sorry, I meant him," she said pointing in my direction. I hopped up on that problematic settee and lay down in a determined manner. "It looks like you are going to have both Rufuses, Uncle Charles," said my human.

"You don't have to stay, you know," said Uncle Charles to the Other Rufus. "I have Rufus to protect me." I thumped my tail. I have to say I am flattered by everyone's confidence in my protection abilities. It made me wonder if just annoying an intruder to death would qualify. Humans seem to find being bayed at, drooled on, and knocked down and sat upon very inconvenient. So much so that it serves as a litmus test for my human's dates. It goes without saying that Ben passed with flying colors. He thought it was funny, although to be fair, he was too big to knock down, so I had to content myself with merely sitting on him and digging my elbows into his squishy bits.

But I digress.

"I wanted to stay behind because I also wanted to speak with you," said the Other Rufus, when everyone had gone. "We thought we'd give the police not just as complete a picture as possible of everyone's movements as you suggested, but also find out who they saw or spoke with yesterday afternoon. Rush especially."

"I'm happy to see you are being thorough. It never does to make assumptions about anything or anyone. As far as yesterday, after the announcement about the cancellation of the afternoon's activities, Anne said she wanted to use the free time to show my sister some especially fine pieces of furniture. The castle is very much like a museum, and it's a shame that none of us really have had the time to appreciate It properly. As for myself, I came back to the room to get some papers with the intention of going to the library to read them. But as I was coming down, I noticed Tucker going up, and I unfortunately knew what that meant; I made a detour to the Tapestry Room which is in the opposite wing from his room. I don't think I ran into Rush, but I may have seen a few of Percy's friends from Christopher Penrose. I'm not sure I know exactly what time it was that I started to feel ill, but I thought I just needed some fresh air, so I came upstairs for a jacket, and went out. I ran into Anne and Elizabeth and mentioned that I wasn't feeling well, and Anne said she'd ask you to check up on me. Anyway, I was out front for a while and then realized I was going to be sick, so I came back up here. I believe that's everything."

"Thanks, that's very complete. I think the problem is no one was paying much attention to who we saw or didn't see. None of us, for instance can remember seeing Rush after lunch but we can't be certain. Percy says you and Rush's father were at Princeton together. Did you know Rush well?"

Some color came into his white face.

"Not as an adult and frankly I'm not sure his father would be very pleased with how he turned out. We had a very unpleasant conversation at the Masque and if that was anything to go by, it's not surprising that he ended up as he did."

"If it's personal, I don't mean to pry, but the police will ask," said the Other Rufus. This part, I obviously knew about but was curious to see how Uncle Charles handled it.

"Yes, it was intensely personal and involved something that happened a long time ago involving Rush's father and myself. No one, not even my family knows about the incident, and I would prefer to keep it that way, but I can tell you that Rush knew about it and seemed to be threatening to blackmail me. As I say, I obviously never really knew him and perhaps he said the wrong thing to the wrong person. I guess I should have realized he wasn't the charming young boy I knew after that appalling scene with Emily."

I was happy that Uncle Charles had decided to come clean. Or cleanish—just like me after a bath—even though it now gave him a motive. But so many other people did as well, that I was losing track.

"He did seem to have a talent for making enemies," said the Other Rufus. "I know Percy was very unhappy that Brooke seemed so taken with him and even more so when she asked him to officiate at the wedding. But then again, weddings do belong to the bride."

After that the conversation became far more general, i.e., boring, so I decided to return to the library where that bone was calling my name. Usually when I hear my name being called, I head in the opposite direction, but I make an exception for bones in the early stages of destruction. I went to the door and made a squeaking noise that resembles a rusty hinge; it's the sound I make when I want something but am too polite to bay. I could have opened the door myself of course, but why do something yourself when you can get someone else to do it for you.

The Extra Rufus opened the door and with a genial wave of my tail I was off to the library.

Driscoll was standing by the door, and he opened it as soon as I appeared, since the rule about no one entering the library did not apply to me. But then again, rules seldom do, however much my human might beg to differ.

"Can you give me a minute Anne," said my human's mother. "There is something I want to discuss with Ben."

"Yes, of course. I'll be outside when you're ready."

"Is this about Cressida?" asked Ben when she had gone.

"No actually. It's about our visit to the Morning Room yesterday afternoon. I know Anne didn't want to say precisely what Kathy and her son had been arguing about nor what was said during our subsequent conversation with her because it is almost certainly irrelevant, but just in case it somehow isn't, I thought you should know."

"I appreciate that. Although we are focusing on giving the police information about everyone's movements, you never know what will be useful. It's really for them to decide."

"Good, but I'd appreciate it if this goes no further since Anne has no intention of telling Percy; it appears that the Kovacs think he has no money," Ben's mouth twitched with amusement, "and Kathy wants him to quit his poorly paid investment banking job and go into the knob business instead." This brought smiles to both their faces. "Needless to say, I had so much trouble controlling myself that I suddenly found that I had important things to show Anne in the conservatory. So that's where it ended. Again, I can't think of how this has anything to do with Rush's death, but Greg was very angry about it when we saw him, and Kathy did mention that both her son and her husband have bad tempers."

"Thank you, Mrs. Pennington. I think we'll just mention the temper part and not the rest of the conversation. The police will be taking statements from everyone, so I'll leave the details to them."

Ben walked her to the door and then stuck his head out.

"Please escort these ladies back to Mr. Winthrop's room," he said to the tag team of retrievers, "and send Rufus back down. Then go find me someone else to interrogate."

"It looks like Sergio Emilio Augustus isn't the only one who's channeling his inner Teutonic dictator," said my human.

As soon as Ben returned, I abandoned my bone and dropped my head in his lap, sensing that he would appreciate the opportunity to scratch me while he waited.

A short while later, the door opened, and the Duplicate Rufus returned to his post.

"Anything illuminating at your end?" he asked as he sat down and opened his laptop.

Ben summarized what he had learned from Aunt Anne and my human's mother, omitting as requested, the specifics of their chat with Kathy Kovac and just that Greg was angry when they saw him.

"Well, it's hardly news that the Kovac men have a temper," said the Other Rufus. "Any guy who packs a pistol to his daughter's wedding is not likely to be much of a pacificist. And as for Kovac junior, I somehow don't buy the fact that he accidentally acquired a real sword and just happened to use it to slice Rush's arm. There was definitely something at work there, but I doubt anyone is going to tell us what." He then briefed Ben on what he had learned from Uncle Charles.

"And the Rushian plot thickens," commented my human's beloved. "Unfortunately, we have only Mr. Winthrop's word for it that he was reading papers in the Tapestry Room. I very much fear that our short list is going to turn out to be the people in the castle who didn't want to murder Rush."

And speaking of which, their cozy sleuthist chat was interrupted by the stormy entrance of Hurricane Brooke.

"Cressida said you wanted to talk to me," snapped Brooke in a tone of voice that made it abundantly clear that the reverse was very far from true. Recent events had done little to improve her temperament.

"Yes, thanks," said Ben. "Mr. Winthrop suggested that it might accelerate the police investigation if we provide them with a summary of where everyone was after lunch on Wednesday. I know all of this must be very difficult for you," said Ben diplomatically, "and I can't tell you how much we appreciate you taking the time."

"Difficult doesn't even begin to cover it. I'm furious. This should have been my wedding day and probably still could have been if I'd gotten any support at all. It's not like Rush," she spat out his name like it was a cookie with too many calories, "was family or related to anyone. Or at least anyone except that freak sister of his and she doesn't seem to mind what happened to him one bit. In fact, maybe she and that guy who sticks needles in her arm, killed him themselves. Anyway, the point is no one cares that he's dead and I'm sure we could have found someone else to perform the ceremony. Daddy could easily have helicoptered someone in before the weather got too bad if Percy hadn't said no and spoiled everything."

"You have my condolences," said Ben, but the irony was lost on her. "If you could just think back to Wednesday after lunch and let us know where you were it would be very helpful."

For the first time she hesitated and looked a bit uneasy.

"Yes, after lunch I went to my room to try on my dress; you know the one I am not going to get to wear today that Armand d'Arnaqueur, the exclusive French couturier flew in from Paris to design especially for me. It cost more money than what either of you make in a year combined. I was worried that it wouldn't fit after everything that I've eaten this week." The fact that no one could remember seeing her eat anything was completely beside the point. "Then Greg stopped by to…" here she wavered, "to help me rehearse my vows. That's where we were. We didn't leave."

"I see," said Ben. "But we met you in the hall, when we were bringing in the…you know, Rush, so you must have left." She shifted what she had of a body as she processed this inconvenient fact.

"Oh yes, I forgot. One of Sergio Emilio Augustus's people knocked on the door and said it was time for a quick run through, but no one could find Percy or any of you people, so I went looking for you myself. That's what I was doing when I met you."

"And did you hear anything? said Ben.

"You mean apart from those horrible bagpipes? Like what exactly?"

"Like a gunshot," replied Ben.

"No."

"OK, thanks again," said Ben. "That's very helpful."

"Whatever," she said sulkily, and got up to lick her nuptial wounds elsewhere.

Chapter 22

Ben gave her a few minutes and then also headed for the exit, narrowly escaping face planting in the Aubusson after an unanticipated encounter with one of my rawhide rejects. He stuck his head out the door.

"OK Buck, time for you and Cress to find us our next victim."

"That's a particularly poor choice of words," remarked my human.

"Yes!" agreed Driscoll brightly. "It's like something I would say."

"Blame it on Rufus waking me up at dark o'clock this morning. BTW, as soon as you see one person leave, feel free to scamper off and find someone else, although in this case you might want to scamper off in the direction of Greg. I have a funny feeling Brooke will be looking for him also."

"Sounds like a story there," said my human.

"Let's just hope it's one that doesn't end with us following in Rush's footsteps," said Driscoll.

"Don't worry. If anyone tries to murder you—at least without provocation—just shout and I'll send Rufus to save you," said Ben. I wagged my tail and tried to look fierce. But if anyone really did try to murder Driscoll, you'd find me somewhere sensible, like under the couch. Nevertheless, Driscoll did have a point. In books people who messed with murderers usually came to a bad end. Then again, whoever discovers the body is usually the killer.

Ben rejoined the Other Rufus, this time being careful to pick his way cautiously through my boneyard.

"What did you make of Brooke?" said the Other Rufus. "I wonder what she was doing that she didn't want us to know about?"

"Or what Greg was doing. The two of them have been thick as thieves lately. Let's hope our amateur bloodhounds get to Greg before she does." I was glad he had the good sense to use the word amateur since Barclay and my human were about as much like bloodhounds as I was like The Sugar Plum Fairy.

Ben, however, got his wish. When the door opened it was a belligerent Greg Kovac who bulldozed his way into the room.

"What's this about? Cressida said Rufus wanted to see me." Then he softened a bit. "Have you found someone to marry Percy and my sister?"

"Unfortunately, not," said Ben, and then explained the reason for the summons.

"I don't see what business it is of yours," he responded.

"No, you're absolutely right, it isn't," replied Ben, employing the tact he used when dealing with a client who wanted a 20,000 sq. foot house built on a 15,000 sq. foot lot. "But Mr. Winthrop is of the opinion that giving the police a preliminary idea of where everyone was on Wednesday afternoon will speed up the investigation and get us all out of here sooner. I'm sure a busy and important man like yourself has a lot to attend to." He exuded sincerity like I exuded hound stink.

"You got that right. Sacrificing time for Brooke's wedding was one thing but sacrificing it to find out who rid the world of that piece of shit Rush is another."

"I gathered from the sword fight that you didn't much care for him," said Ben.

"That was a total accident," said Greg combatively. "Although Rush was…rude to my sister. And in my kind of family, we take care of our women." The implication being that in Ben and the Other Rufus's kind of family they didn't. "Anyway," he continued quickly changing the subject, "after lunch I went to have a closer look at the weapons in the armory. Then I was going to play some pool but when I passed by the Morning Room I saw my mother sitting alone so I went in to see if she was OK. We talked for a while," here his face flushed a bit, "and then I just kind of wandered around the castle thinking. After that I went to my room to do some work."

"Do you remember meeting anyone?" asked Ben.

"Not to talk to. I may have passed a few of Brooke's friends from Pilates or something; if I had known I was going to be interrogated I would have taken notes," he replied sarcastically. "Although now that I think about it, when I was crossing the entry hall, I did see that Bruce character come in with Rush's crazy sister. She looked even more nuts than usual and barely able to walk; he had to practically carry her up the stairs."

"And did you happen to hear anything that sounded like a gunshot?"

"Not that I can recall. And even if I had, I'd have assumed it was hunters somewhere and paid no attention."

"Thank you. You've been very helpful," said Ben.

"I hope not. And now if there's nothing else," he sneered, "unlike some people, I have work to do."

And on that pleasant note, he took his leave.

"Well, he's a class act," said Ben. "Still, that's interesting about Bruce and Henley. But as far as Brooke and her brother, one of them is lying, but I'm not sure which or why."

"Apart from the obvious that is," said his fellow sleuth. Further discussion of the matter was cut short by the sequential entrance of several more guests, none of whom had anything illuminating to say, with the possible exception of one of Percy's friends who thought he saw Rush leave shortly after lunch but wasn't really sure and didn't remember the exact time.

"Not that the time really matters," said the Other Rufus when he and Ben were once again alone, "but I was hoping that Rush might have told someone about the note he received."

"Yes, but we can only assume that the note was the reason Rush went to the Overlook; we actually have no evidence that it wasn't put there after he was dead to mislead us," said Ben.

"You mean to mislead the police. Remember, we're only here to gather information, not to solve the case," said the Other Rufus.

"I know, but it's hard not to try. Dris is probably laying odds as we speak. And think of the story Cress could write."

"Whether we solve the case or not, the big winner in all

of this is Ethan; I'm sure we'll all be signing movie release forms in the not-too-distant future. And I pity whichever member of the constabulary has to wade through all his footage."

Speculation about the creative possibilities of the killing came to a halt when the door swung open and Pete the Pie Man lumbered in like a bear who had been disporting himself rather too freely amongst the salmon.

"I was told you wanted to see me?" he looked from one to the other with a guarded expression on his face. Ben once again explained their mission and prudently emphasized that the idea and rationale had emanated from Uncle Charles. He definitely knew how to read the room.

"I see," Pete said, "in that case, after lunch I went straight to the phone. We're soft releasing a new pie in select urban markets. It's vegan and gluten free and it's got kale, quinoa, algae, brussels sprouts, some weird berries, and a whole lot of stuff I've never heard of. Tastes like shit of course, but Marketing says it'll go gangbusters. Me, I'm an old-fashioned apple pie man myself, but if you want to make a buck in this business you gotta move with the times and sell whatever crap people want to put in their stomachs. Anyway, after my phone call I went to that long room, you know, the one with the paintings of women on the walls, to look over some marketing materials for the campaign."

"All the rooms have paintings of women on the walls. Was it one of the rooms with the naked ones or the clothed ones?" said Ben.

"Oh definitely the clothed ones. Not that I really looked; art's more my wife's thing, and she disapproves of naked people in paintings." I looked up from my bone. Now while I am far from an art connoisseur—although I did once chew up a very fine etching that my human didn't think I could reach— I was pretty sure that kind of let out most of the Renaissance and much of what came after. But I'm hardly objective in the matter, since I'm convinced that humans only cover up the good bits to prevent me from getting at them.

But I digress.

"I think you might have been in the Ladies Gallery," said Ben. "Did you see anyone or talk to anyone after lunch?"

"Just the folks in line for the phone. As I said, as soon as I had finished lunch, I made a beeline for it, so I think only that older guy—the one with the young wife—was ahead of me. He moved fast but I guess he needs to keep in shape, if you know what I mean. But I still can't believe that with all the money my brother forked out for this shindig there's no cell service. What a f--- up," he cackled. "Mike couldn't even persuade one of his Pentagon buddies that he brags so much about to give him a satellite uplink. Can't wait for my Emily to get married. Then he'll see what a real wedding looks like. Anyway, I was still in the room with the paintings of the women when one of those stuck-up asses with the headphones told me to go to that drinks place with the silly name."

"Thanks, that's great. I'm sure it will help get us out of here sooner when the police arrive. So you didn't see Rush or see anyone speak with him after lunch?"

"No. For the record, I'm not sorry that c---s------ is dead. He got what he deserved, treating Emily like that. From what I've seen, all these Ivy League boys are just entitled pieces of trash." He seemed not to have noticed that he was talking to two of them. Tact, like gluten-free pies, was clearly not his strong suit.

"One last question, did you hear anything that resembled a gunshot?"

"No."

"Well thanks again. The police will want to speak with everyone when they arrive, but this will help speed the process." With that the Pie Man rose and made his way to the door with a rotund self-satisfied swagger, undoubtedly reviewing the colossal cockup of his brother's arrangements in his head.

"Correct me if I'm wrong, but didn't his son go to Wharton?" asked the Other Rufus after he left.

"I guess no one broke it to him that U. Penn is an Ivy," said Ben. "And not to speak ill of the still very much living, but from what Cress said, Jason would be a frontrunner in the entitled trash sweepstakes."

"Hedgies usually are," said the Other Rufus.

My head popped up. A hedgie in the castle! This was exciting news since I collected stuffed hedgehogs the way Napoleon collected countries. And such was my devotion to them that no sooner had one met the fate of most stuffies in my care than I dragged my human out to the nearest pet store to purchase another. It was the least she could do for me for protecting her from marauding squirrels. Nevertheless, the idea of coming snout to snout with the genuine article filled me with indescribable joy.

But sadly, when the door opened it wasn't a hedgehog, stuffed or unstuffed, that appeared but Pete's better half.

"That nice young lady with the giant dog said you wanted to see me. Has someone else been murdered? It's what you get for holding a wedding in castle with dangerous weapons all over the place. Gives people ideas. When Emily gets married it will be somewhere normal like on one of those private islands where celebrities go. There won't be any weapons and I'm sure no one will get killed."

"Please sit down, Mrs. Kovac," said Ben. "No, nothing new has happened. We're just trying to get an idea of everyone's movements on Wednesday afternoon to help the police when they arrive."

"Do you know when that will be? I'm having nightmares

about what's going on at the house in Cabo. You can't possibly imagine what a horror show it's been. Nothing's ever done on time or correctly, and the veining in the marble they used is completely the wrong shade. And now there's some nonsense about permits that have to be applied for before an extension can be built. I could just go on and on." And she looked as though she might. But suddenly she paused and looked at Ben. "Someone said you're an architect. Do you speak Spanish? I could see if I can get that contractor on the phone, and you can talk to him. I'd pay you of course. Whatever you want to charge is fine."

"I'm very sorry you are having such trouble, Mrs. Kovac, but unfortunately I don't speak Spanish so I'm afraid I wouldn't be of much use."

Ben absolutely did speak Spanish. I happen to know this because he gets chatty with all the food delivery guys who bring New York City's finest Mexican restaurants into my human's living room and into my food bowl. I may not be a connoisseur of art, but I definitely know my way around an enchilada.

"Do you remember where you were after lunch yesterday?" Ben continued smoothly.

"Yes, I went to my room to make some more notes about the house, not that any of that matters since those people don't seem to understand anything I say. All they want to do is sell you on local this and local that—ugly tiles, bricks, and pottery. If I wanted to live in a Mexican restaurant, I would have bought one." Pity. Some of us dream about living in a Mexican restaurant. Still, one's person fantasy is another's fiasco. "After I finished making notes, I went to look at the rooms in the east wing to see if there were any paintings that I could buy that had the right colors in them for my design scheme. Pete always says I have an eye for art. Then I noticed a painting with a waterfall, and it gave me an idea for the shower wall in the spa room. I was on my way back to my room to add it to my notes when I ran into one of those wedding planner people who told me to go the place where we have the cocktails."

"Did you meet anyone or speak to anyone?"

"I don't think so. But I was very absorbed in the art. There's a painting where the sky is the perfect shade of blue for one of my powder rooms."

"One last question," said Ben. "Did you happen to hear anything that sounded like a gunshot."

"No, but that reminds me, I need to find a good spot to display some of my husband's gun collection. He's very proud of it, you know. Taught my Emily to shoot when she was just a child, and you see how good she is."

"We won't keep you, then. You've been very helpful, and the best of luck with the new house."

"I'm going to need it. All the money we've spent hasn't helped so far. It's such a shame about you not speaking Spanish though…" Ben rose to escort her to the door before she could think of other ways he might be of service.

"She sounds like she'd fit right in with your client list, Ben. Sure you don't want to take a crack at it? Think of all those delightful trips to Cabo," said the Other Rufus in a way that made me think he meant exactly the opposite.

And the flood of Kovacs kept coming. The next person through the door was a very worried looking Kathy Kovac.

"I do hope you have good news about when the police are arriving. Brooke is inconsolable about all the disruption this has caused to her big day. I still can't believe someone decided to murder Rush before the ceremony. No one thinks about anyone except themselves these days."

"We've had no word yet about when the police will arrive, Mrs. Kovac," said Ben, at a loss as to how address the total lack of consideration shown by the killer, "but I'm sure they'll get here as soon as they can. In the meantime, if you can give us an idea of where you were yesterday afternoon it will help them whenever they do manage to make it out here."

"I wonder if police can marry people. You know, like judges. Everything is still ready in the chapel. We have the most wonderful flowers. They cost a fortune, but my husband does love to show people a good time." For his PA's sake, I hoped so. "Mike and I were married in a grotty little church and now we've got all this," she said gesturing as if she were the chatelaine of Crackshaw herself. "It just goes to show."

"Yesterday afternoon?" prompted Ben gently.

"Oh yes, let's see, yesterday afternoon….I went up to our suite to have a nap. Being the mother of the bride is even more exhausting than being the bride herself you know, but it was impossible to sleep with the horrible noise of those bagpipes. Tucker is a sweet boy, and he's been enormously helpful, but God help me, if I don't want to strangle him sometimes. I can't imagine that there's any amount of practicing that would make that instrument sound good to anyone. It's even worse than listening to opera and let me tell you opera is painful. And I should know. I'm on the board of the Kovac Concert Hall downtown—I had Mike buy the name with a large donation, so we'd be invited to all the galas, but I didn't realize I'd be expected to listen to fat people screech at each other for hours on end. It's so awful that they should be paying us. But my sister-in-law is livid with jealousy, so I guess it's worth it."

"I agree that bagpipes are an acquired taste," replied Ben, "but do you remember what you did after you couldn't sleep?"

"Yes, I grabbed a copy of *Me*—that's Brooke's magazine you know. *Me* hires only the most beautiful girls so she loves working there. She's always had a problem with girls being jealous of her because of the way she looks. And she gets to go to all the fashion shows and meets so many famous people. Of course I'd always hoped that she'd marry one of those famous, or at least rich, people she meets through work, but still…I guess you can't choose who you fall in love with. Percy may not be much in the money department, but he is good looking, I'll say that. And that real estate developer she dated before Percy ended up in jail, so it probably worked out for the best. They don't put bankers in jail so that's a plus.

"Oh you'd be surprised," said Ben. "So you took the magazine and went where?"

"I decided since I couldn't sleep I'd go to the Morning Room and have some coffee."

"Did you meet anyone or talk to anyone?" asked Ben.

"Yes, my son came in and we had a chat about the business. He's a big part of it, naturally. Mike always says that family are the only people you can really trust and besides, Greg is a brilliant businessman. After we were done talking Anne and her sister-in-law—I can't remember her name— came in and we discussed future plans for Brooke and Percy. They went to go look at some plant or other, and I sat a while longer and then decided to go try on my dress to make sure it still fit after all this food. Like I always tell Brooke, if you want to keep a man you have to keep your figure." Or not. "Then Mike came in and told me what happened and that he'd be speaking to everyone in that room with the Libor name."

"Thank you very much for speaking with us," said Ben and got up to forestall any further cultural critiques or information about the prodigious talents of the Kovac family. "Oh, did you happen to hear anything that sounded like a gunshot."

"Not that I remember," she replied. "But you know I had so much on my mind, and I wouldn't have paid any attention anyway. Mike shoots stuff all the time."

They thanked her again and she departed.

"I have a feeling she knows about as much about the

LIBOR as her daughter does about the SS," said Ben. "Also, I don't think there is much point asking about the gunshot. It would have been nice to narrow the time down, but I doubt anyone would have remembered a distant shot even if they had heard it. Especially as everyone seems to have had so much else on their minds."

Next up was the much maligned musician.

"If this is about my bagpipes, I haven't played them since you asked me not to," Tucker said.

Ben explained.

"That's easy. As I'm sure everyone in the castle can tell you, I went up to my room to practice. We have a concert coming up next month and there is nothing worse than a bad bagpipe player." Or any bagpipe player. But as an under-appreciated musician myself, I could sympathize with the general public's lack of taste in such matters. My instrument would be as much admired on the hunting field as his was in the highlands. In New York City and wedding castles not so much.

"Anyway, I hope the police clear this up quickly. It's been a terrible ordeal for Brooke and her family, although I can't say that any of them will mourn the loss of Rush. There was a lot of bad blood there."

"Yes, that incident at the sword fight," said Ben. "I was surprised by it, but Greg still maintains it was an accident."

"Don't you believe it. And if Greg didn't kill him, the old man did. They have horrible tempers those two and I don't see anyone crossing either of them without consequences. I shouldn't really say anything, but I was on my way to the kitchen on Tuesday to let them know that Sergio Emilio Augustus wanted a cheese sculpture of Brooke, when I overheard Rush suggesting to Mike that he might want to make a large donation to Rush's acting career. I gather he had just caught Mike, shall we say, being very personal with his personal assistant. I can't imagine that went over well. And then Brooke confided in me that she had gotten drunk one night and slept with Rush and now he was threatening to tell Percy before the wedding if she didn't grant him ongoing access to her favors. She was terrified and went to Greg about it because that family sticks together like a Lego kit. Personally, I think the sword might have been a warning and maybe Greg or his father decided that the message hadn't been received. The police are going to have their hands full there and I'm so close to it all that I'm frightened I'll end up run through like Rush."

"I wouldn't worry," said Ben. "With the police on their way it would be foolish of the murderer to try anything else."

"It's a big relief that I had planned a vacation in Cambodia for after the wedding. It should be far enough away, and I can always extend my stay until after they catch the killer. And maybe Brooke can get married there next. I expect she's gone off the idea of castles."

"I think we've all gone off the idea of castles. Anyway, thanks. And thanks for laying off the bagpipes," said Ben. "By the way, did you happen to hear anything that sounded like a gunshot?"

"I don't think any musician really hears anything except the sound of his glorious instrument when he's playing," replied Tucker sententiously.

Chapter 23

There was a gap after Tucker left, so I took the opportunity to climb into Ben's lap and give his face an invigorating wash. I find that nothing helps focus the human mind like a face full of viscous, slimy drool. I would have climbed into the Other Rufus's lap too, but he had his computer on it and was busy reviewing his notes.

"The more I read, the more I can't imagine how this case is ever going to be solved. If at least someone would have heard a shot, we could have given the police a specific time to zero in on, but from what we've heard—or more precisely not heard—it seems unlikely. But continue to ask anyway, you never know. And thumbs up on your diplomatic skills. I had no idea you were such a smooth character; no wonder you snagged a girl like Cressida."

"Smooth had nothing to do with it. The way to a girl's heart is through her hound. I honestly think the main reason Cressida likes me is because I like Rufus." I was happy to hear that Ben understood the seminal role I play in all my human's affairs, romantic and otherwise; but it was less a case of that he liked me than of that I liked him.

As agreeable as this discussion about me was, it was abruptly shattered when the much-feared Mike Kovac marched into with the room with same purposeful aggressive energy as his son. I think both sleuths hoped he had left his pistol behind. I know I did. In spite of our name, we bloodhounds are not big fans of blood, especially our own. I slithered off Ben's lap and lay down behind a well-padded club chair.

Sensing the restless impatience of the man, Ben quickly got to the point.

Our host's frown deepened as he listened. He obviously found it deeply offensive that he, The Knob King of the Midwest, confidante of Defense Secretary McMinky and meeter of presidents, was to be questioned by a couple of jumped-up Ivy League chowderheads. On the other hand, he was clearly conflicted as he processed the fact that whatever he said would be conveyed to the police.

"I have nothing to hide, but I can spare only a few minutes," he announced at length, oblivious to the fact that those who declared they had nothing to hide usually did.

"Understood. If you can just give us a quick rundown of where you were after lunch and who you might have seen or spoken to," said Ben, "it would be very helpful."

"That's easy. I was working with Caitie."

"The bridesmaid?" asked Ben quizzically.

"No, the bridesmaid is Katie—K-A-T-I-E, my PA is Caitie C-A-I-T-I-E. We were working in one of the galleries in the south wing. The plaque on the door said it was called The Belvoir Gallery—it's about the only one where you can't hear those blasted bagpipes. After that I went to get in line for the phone. You better believe that even though my wife and daughter had their hearts set on this place, if I'd known about the phone situation, I never would have agreed to it. I don't know why they just couldn't pick one of those castles in Europe they looked at. Anyway, the line wasn't moving so I went outside to look for bars on the property. There've been rumors that they exist, but as far as I can see, they are just that, rumors. I was on my way back to try and get some more work done, when Sergio Emilio Augustus—what kind of name is that and where my daughter finds these people, I'll never know—accosted me and told me what happened. I mean the fact that she's marrying someone called Percival is bad enough..." I raised my head ready to snap if he dared to diss the name Rufus. It's a ridiculous name but only we Rufuses get to say so. "Anyway he asked for my help getting everyone to the Great Hall. But first I went to tell Kathy. And then Caitie."

"Did you see Rush or anyone else when you went outside?" asked Ben.

"Alive or dead?" he snarked. I'm sure Ben was tempted to answer "either."

"Alive. Or hear anything that sounded like a gunshot."

"I didn't see Rush" he said, flushing slightly at the name, "but I did see my son, although I don't think he saw me. I assume he was looking for bars also. As far as a gun, if I had, I'd just assume it was hunters. Now if that's all, I'm a busy man." And with that he rose to signal that the interview was over. Ben also rose and accompanied him to the door. But it wasn't deference that made him do it, but a hunch and some quick thinking.

"Caitie, could you just step inside for a second," said Ben, giving her boss no time for a debrief. For once she looked anxious rather than sulky as Ben walked her to the couch and quickly got right to it. The less time she had to think, the better.

"Mike and I were working after lunch."

"Where?" asked Ben. This seemed to flummox her for a few seconds.

"There are so many rooms, and they all look alike, so I'm not exactly sure," she replied uneasily.

"I hear you," said Ben, "this place has a ton of rooms and so many of them do look alike that it's difficult to know exactly where you are or in which wing. I just hope you were able to get some work done with the sound of those bagpipes playing. There have been a lot of complaints.

"Ugh! Bagpipes. There's nowhere to get away from the horrible noise they make. But we were very absorbed in what we were doing so we just ignored them. It's wonderful to have the opportunity to work with someone as brilliant as Mike. Not everyone appreciates how clever and intelligent he is." She emphasized the everyone.

"Did you work together all afternoon then?"

Here she hesitated again.

"Yes, pretty much. But I did go to my room for a while. I was there when Mike knocked on the door and told me what happened and to go the Great Hall."

"Thank you, Caitie," said Ben rising. "That's all we wanted to know."

"You know I think with everything that's happened I might have gotten a bit confused," she said. "Mike always gets mad when I forget things."

"I wouldn't worry," said Ben reassuringly. "There wouldn't have been any particular reason for you to remember everything exactly. But you didn't happen to hear anything sounded like a gunshot though, did you?"

"Did Mike say we heard a gunshot?" she answered flustered. "I don't know. I think he'd be the one to ask."

Ben walked her to the door and again told her not to worry.

"Here's what we've got," said the Other Rufus when Ben returned to our den of inquiry. "Brooke says Greg was with her, Mike says Greg was outside, and Greg says he was in the armory, then talking to his mother, then wandering around, and then back in his room. The only thing we can corroborate is that at some point he was talking to his mother. I'm starting to feel like I too need a bar. Just not the phone kind."

"And then there's Mike's PA," said Ben. "I'm glad I got to her before Mike did. Her manner suggests that she was at pains not to tell us anything that might contradict him. I have a strong feeling that Mike is not a boss you want to contradict, no matter how much she sings his praises and or whatever else they get up to together. And although she doesn't know where she was—legit in a place like this—Mike told us they were in a gallery in the south wing to get away from the bagpipes. If he was lying about his whereabouts that would be a good choice. It's the wing furthest away from the wedding activities and doesn't seem to be in much use."

"So not much chance of seeing anyone who can say you weren't there."

"Yes, but that Cress and I were messing about in all the wings, including that one, and we didn't see either of them, coming, going or in situ. Although to be fair, given both the size of this place and the fact that like everyone else we weren't paying attention to when we were where, we could easily have missed them."

"I've noted all the contradictions in bold." Said Rufus the Scrivener. "The Kovac family is looking decidedly sketchy.

"Maybe all the Kovacs did it," said Ben only half joking.

"But if that were the case, they'd have gotten their stories straight, wouldn't they?"

"Not if they wanted to confuse us," replied Ben.

"Or confuse us more. Like with all the murder

weapons," said the Other Rufus.

Further discussion came to a halt when Katie with a K entered. Her eyes were as red as her clothes were black. Ben explained why they asked to see her and avoided all use of her name just in case.

"Rush was such a beautiful person; he was an angel, and so kind," she sobbed, providing further evidence of Rush's extensive acting ability. "New York guys can be such assholes—I should know, I've been engaged to several. Not at the same time of course, but Rush was so different. As soon as we laid eyes on each other he recognized instantly that we were soulmates. I have no idea who would want to do such a thing to him, except of course that creature Emily who was jealous of our relationship. I'm sure she did it. I'll tell you anything I can to help you catch her."

"Well actually, we won't be catching anybody. That's the job of the police," corrected Ben who had no wish to make a murderer believe they were hot on his or her tail. "But it would help if you could tell us where you were after lunch yesterday and if you saw or spoke to anyone, particularly Rush."

"After lunch, Riley and Kiley were making ridiculous claims that Rush was in love with them. I have no idea why they would say things like that. I mean Riley might have wanted to get back at me for hooking up with her fiancé, which was totally not my fault because he said they were on a break and anyway he's her ex now, but I always thought Kiley and I were solid. Things were getting ugly, so we decided to play a marathon game of cribbage to settle the matter. We were in the Games Room when Brooke came in and told us about the tragedy." A tear trickled down her face as she remembered the scene.

"I'm sure it must have been a terrible shock," said Ben sympathetically, "so I won't keep you any longer." He helped her up from the couch since she seemed to be unable to accomplish that feat on her own. Whether it was from grief or lack of calories was anyone's guess, but she clung to Ben's arm as he walked her to the door.

After he had detached his charge and sent her on her grief-stricken way, he flung himself back down on the couch.

"I told Dris to tell our bloodhounds—sorry Rufus—our retrievers, that we don't really need to speak to the other two bridesmaids. Apart from anything else I don't think any of them would have had the strength, even collectively to kill anything, let alone Rush."

While we all awaited our next interrogee, I took advantage of the lull in the proceedings to slobber on the Other Rufus' laptop and to poke Ben in the ribs and roll over to call attention to the fact that I had a belly that needed scratching. Neither of them seemed terribly upset when this idyllic scene was abruptly intruded upon.

"What the hell is this about," demanded Jason using his outdoor voice. "The market's open and I was in the kitchen watching the financial news. On an f------g television set if you can believe it. It's like the only one I found in this f----- up place."

Ben explained why they had torn him away from the fascinations of finance.

"If it will get us out of this f----- hell hole sooner, I'm all in. Brooke is such a bitch, I'd say she did it herself, except that now she's pissed off that she can't get married to investment banker boy. But let's see, yesterday after lunch I was reading prospectuses in the study, the one with the paintings, and then decided to take a break and go to the Train Room to see if any of them worked. Can't make any money in transpo these days, but the model train set up in that room is epic. After that, I think I went looking for Pops. I checked the kitchen because I was sure he'd be in there teaching those twats how to make edible pies, but no luck. Roamed around a bit. Didn't find him. And then the woman with all the scarves and the silly accent no one can understand told me to go to the Great Hall. Although the way she pronounced it, it's a wonder anyone went. Apart from her and the kitchen staff I can't remember if I saw anyone else."

"Thanks," said Ben. "We won't keep you. Can you tell us though if you heard anything that sounded like a gunshot."

"No," he replied and made for the exit with the self-important stride of a man who knows his time is more valuable than everyone else's.

"Great someone else without an alibi," said the Other Rufus. "And why does no one realize that in this place saying you were in a room with paintings is like saying you were in a room with walls. Still, at least his story was pretty straightforward."

"Except that he also might be lying. Cress and I were exploring the rooms around the Train Room and didn't see him. Could we have just missed him? Maybe. But when we went to look at the trains he wasn't there either."

"Mendacity does seem to run rather freely through the Kovac DNA," said the Medical Rufus. "But why is it that you and Cressida seem to have been here, there, and everywhere that afternoon."

"What can I say, I'm an architect; an obsessive interest in buildings is an occupational hazard. And it's only a matter of time before one of my firm's clients wants me to design something that looks like Crackshaw Castle, even if it's only a doghouse.

"I wouldn't give Rufus ideas if I were you," said my namesake, "I don't think Cressida would appreciate a castle in her living room." I of course already had the blueprint in my head.

Any further discussion of my new doghouse was cut short when the door opened and Sergio Emilio Augustus came in. Although he didn't so much come in as make an entrance.

"If this has anything to do with finding someone else to officiate, I told Brooke the wedding is already in tatters, and I wash my hands of it."

"That's only to be expected from someone with your reputation," said Ben in a flattering tone of voice, "but it's nothing to do with the wedding. At least not directly. We're making notes for the police about where everyone was on Wednesday afternoon."

"Oh, well, that's alright then. I was in the East Parlor holding an emergency meeting with my staff and the video people to find workarounds for the weather situation. We had to organize an entirely new shooting schedule. The planning for each and every moment of a Sergio Emilio Augustus wedding is meticulous and unacceptable weather like this caused the whole thing to collapse like a house of cards. We obviously had contingency plans, but they were for rain, not snow. And then on top of all that, our officiant goes and gets himself murdered." He said it like the florist had delivered the wrong shade of peony.

"I can imagine how annoying it must have been," said Ben sympathetically and with not a trace of irony. If architecture didn't work out, he had a great future in the diplomatic corps. "Were you and the staff in meetings all afternoon?"

"Most of it, yes" replied the matrimonial maestro. "But after the meeting ended, I went to the chapel to personally inspect the flowers and decorations. I find that if you leave these things to others some idiot will have placed the hydrangeas in completely the wrong place or something else equally as catastrophic. It was just after I left the chapel that I was informed about that moron getting himself murdered and that my staff was expected to get everyone to the Chamber of Libations; even under normal circumstances getting anyone to do anything at this wedding has been like herding cats. And now of course all my hard work is utterly ruined, and no one seems to know when we can get out of here and I'm due in Bali on Tuesday.

"Did you happen to meet or speak with anyone other than your staff?"

"If I did, I was much too preoccupied to pay attention. There was just so much to be done and Sergio Emilio Augustus never interacts with wedding guests. I have staff for that. You should check with MahRee. She's in charge of guest relations; the French are good at that sort of thing."

"Can you tell us if you remember hearing anything that sounded like a gunshot?" asked Ben.

"Are you mad? In the middle of Sergio Emilio Augustus wedding who has time to be listening for gunshots. Unless of course they are part of the ceremony."

He was as charming as one would expect of someone whose commercial success depended on convincing clients that he didn't want their business. I got the distinct impression that my companions were glad to see the back of him as he swanned off to wherever aggrieved wedding planners swanned off to when their weddings had been spoiled.

The revolving door continued.

"Cressida said Rufus wanted to speak with me," said Emily as she tentatively stuck her head into the room. At the sound of my name I bayed, flung some drool, and climbed up next to Ben and placed my head in his lap to offer my assistance. He explained the reason for her presence and gestured for her to sit on the couch opposite. Getting up to do so politely was not possible with a large hound head glued to your lap.

"Oh that's easy," she said, "after lunch I went to the Orangery to watch the new romcom *Sleepless in Slovakia*. I had started watching it on my iPad last week and thought it might cheer me up." Here she paused and looked uneasy. "The movie inspired me to try to talk to Rush. Maybe we just had had a misunderstanding, you know, like the characters in the film. So I went to his room, but he wasn't there and when I was coming down the stairs, I saw him in a coat leaving. I didn't follow him or anything."

"Did you see anyone else," asked Ben as he scratched me between my flews in response to a firm thwack on the arm.

She fidgeted and twisted her hair.

"Jason. He left just after Rush did. I know my brother is very protective and he was upset about what happened Monday, but I'm sure he wouldn't have hurt Rush." She didn't sound all that convinced.

"I'm sure not," said Ben, although he too did not sound all that convinced. "Did you happen to hear a gunshot during the afternoon?"

"No," she fidgeted some more.

"Then thanks for the information, Emily. We appreciate it." The Other Rufus did the escorting out this time as I moved more of me onto Ben's lap to make sure he and his hands remained where they were.

"Another bolded entry for your notes," said Ben when the Other Rufus returned. "If I had to choose which of them was lying, my money'd be on Jason."

"On the other hand, she did have a gun. Maybe we didn't find it by the body because she had to put it back in its presentation case."

"That's true but Jason could have taken it also."

The debate ceased when MahRee glided into the room. She made her way to where we were sitting with the self-assurance of a woman who is confident that her presence among men is an honor to be bestowed.

"Messieurs et Gros Chien," she began without preamble as she sat down. "You desire to speek wiz me, non?"

Ben explained.

"Ah mais oui," she replied in response to Ben's explanation, "après le lunch, we 'ad zee meeting. Zhen I go to meet zee good looking one who do zee cérémonie. He offer to me to 'elp wiz zee English. Malheursement, he eez not in zee petite parlor where he say we meet." Here she gave a Gallic shrug and adjusted her scarf. "Me, I do not wait. I go to le ballroom de soirée, and zee other rooms to shek le décor zhen Serge Emile Auguste come and zay find zee guests and zhey must go to Gran 'all. Voilà c'est tout."

"Did you happen to hear a gunshot during the afternoon?" asked Ben.

"Zhee what? Zhees word I no comprend."

"Un coupe de feu," replied Ben who had had the rudiments of the language drilled into him in a fairly merciless way at Exeter.

Her eyes widened.

"Mais, non! Certainement pas! C'est un marriage pas le wild west, n'est-ce pas? Et eef you speak le français, pour-quoi you speek zhee Anglais avec moi?" she exclaimed. A torrent of indignant French followed in which the words "une langue barbare" could be heard.

"Merci Marie," said Ben as the Other Rufus rose to walk her out.

"Nothing illuminating there," said Alternative Rufus when he returned, "except that you apparently have a good accent and Rush seems to have been spreading himself rather thin."

"It's a wonder he had any time for acting. Although I suppose it was all acting," said Ben.

Next on deck was Dr. Bruce.

He strode confidently in our direction like a veteran batter facing a pitcher just up from the minor leagues.

"I was told you wished to consult me on a matter of some urgency," he said addressing the Other Rufus.

"Not exactly. Charles Winthrop suggested that we gather information for the police about everyone's whereabouts on Wednesday afternoon," replied the Other Rufus.

Dr. Bruce's eyes narrowed, and he stiffened perceptibly. "Henley and I were in our room doing a regression. This wedding has been very stressful for her."

"The entire time?" asked the Other Rufus. "Only I knocked to see if you had any atropine."

"Henley was in a critical therapeutic phase of a very deep regression," declared Dr. Bruce authoritatively. "When a patient is in that stage they cannot be interrupted for any reason. I don't expect you to understand since you're not a clinician and don't see patients." To his credit, the Other Rufus did not take the bait and continued to tap away quietly at his laptop. "In any case, that's where we were until you found us in the music room and that is what I will tell the police. There is no need to disturb Henley. She is in a very fragile state, and she will tell you exactly the same thing." Given Henley's jubilant reaction to the news of her brother's corporeal cancellation, it would appear that Dr. Bruce had a very different definition of fragile than the rest of us.

"This is all voluntary," said Ben well aware that they had about as much authority to extract information from the guests as I had to extract food from the refrigerator. "Did you happened to hear a gunshot at any time?"

"I was concentrating on my patient, not on extraneous sounds," he answered curtly. Then he rose and I lifted myself to indicate that Ben had my permission to do likewise. Both men walked to the door and as Ben had expected Henley was waiting outside. Before he could say anything, however, Dr. Bruce beat him to it.

"Henley, Rufus and Ben are preparing notes on everyone's whereabouts yesterday after lunch. I explained to them that we were in our room all afternoon until we went to the music room and that you have nothing to add and that you are not in a state to be questioned. At least until the police arrive."

"Of course, whatever you think best Bruce," she replied, her face a shimmering moon of devotion.

"No joy there," said Ben when he had reclaimed his seat on the couch after wrangling me off his spot. It is an inviolate rule that whenever a human vacates a couch, a chair or a bed, a hound must occupy it immediately. Whether due to the strong, pleasing scent of the newly departed human or the desire to cause them the maximum amount of inconvenience, I'm not at liberty to say. "Henley will tell whatever tale Bruce tells her to. So either he was lying about being in the room or Greg was lying about seeing them come in from outside. I think the police have about as much chance of solving this case as Rufus has of earning an obedience title." I couldn't have said it better myself.

The rest of the sleuthing passed with much less drama. A parade of guests trickled in and out while I alternated between bone chewing, pseudo snoozing, and demanding that Ben massage various portions of my anatomy. No one had anything useful to add to what was already known and everyone had a different theory about who had done it.

"I suggest we leave the staff and the hired wedding entertainers for the police," said Ben after the last guest and the last theory had departed. "There are just too many of them and I don't see anyone in that group being the killer. After all, we're strangers to them."

"You forgot about that waitress. The one who didn't seem to be Rush's biggest fan. It's probable that the knife stuck in Rush's neck came from the kitchen and considering that she made every effort to bathe him in food and drink, I'd say she was acquainted with him. I'll ask Buck and Cressida to find her and see if she'll talk to us."

While we waited, I considered whether I had time to shred a copy of *Cesar's Way* that I had noticed on a lower shelf but abandoned the project when our quarry arrived. She looked questioningly at the Other Rufus.

"If this is about the guy who got sick, I don't know anything about it. I don't do any food prep, just serving."

"No, it's not about that," said Ben. "We're just trying to get a sense of where everyone was yesterday afternoon. We're hoping it will help the police let us go sooner."

"I'm all for that; the weather might have disrupted activities for the guests, but life goes on for the rest of us. Tables still need to be cleared, food prepared and served, guests asked if they'd like anything, tables set for the next meal, etc., etc., etc. This place sucks even worse than a cruise ship and if any of us had known what we were in for there wouldn't have been many takers. And that's even without getting snowed in with a murderer." Despite her discontent, she was a pretty girl, tall and graceful with abundant dark hair and a look not unlike that of Brooke. It would have been tempting to think that Rush had a type, but evidence suggested that Rush's type was anything with two X chromosomes.

"We couldn't help but notice that you seemed to be acquainted with Rush," said Ben.

"Yeah, I guess you could say that given that we were engaged," she said venomously. "Or at least I thought we were. I was beginning to plan our wedding—nothing like this monstrosity, even if I had the money—and then suddenly he was gone. It wasn't like we'd had an argument or anything, he just left my apartment one morning and blocked my cell and socials and changed the locks to his apartment. Look, I'm an actor, or trying to be, and trust me good looking guys like him litter the landscape like beer bottles at a frat party. The trouble is they don't really want a girlfriend; they want an audience. But Rush was totally different." Her voice momentarily took on a dreamy quality. "He was so...so...well genuine. Not at all self-absorbed in the way guys who look like him usually are. He was interested in you. How you were. How your friends were. Supportive after every failed audition and no hint of jealousy after a successful one. He once even traveled all the way to New Jersey to see me do a bit part in a local theater. I guess he had more acting talent than I thought."

"Did you know he was here when you took the job?" asked the Other Rufus momentarily looking up from his screen.

"Absolutely not. When we arrived some of the other girls started talking about the hot guy who was performing the ceremony. I went to have a look and anything I can say about how shocked and appalled I was just sounds like a horrible cliché. And all those bridesmaids fussing over him made me want to vomit. Preferably on him. And yes, I wanted to hurt him. I wanted revenge. I'm just not sure I wanted this much revenge. The jury's still out on that one. But I couldn't have killed him even if I'd wanted to. None of us could have, actually. Between Mrs. Morgan the caterer and the wedding planning people, and even the film maker guy, they made sure they got their money's worth out of us."

"We won't keep you then," said Ben.

"I wish you would though," she sighed as she reluctantly rose to return to her duties, giving me the obligatory scratch on her way out.

After she left my human appeared and I greeted her with my usual show of camaraderie.

"That should be all of them," she cried as she crouched over with her hands covering her face to avoid being French kissed. If it were yoga, it would be called The Pose of the Bloodhound Owner. "Let's take Rufus out for a toilet break and then the rest of us are dying to hear about what you've found out. Lunch was ages ago, so I sent Barclay and Driscoll off to the kitchen for sandwiches."

I thought this was an excellent plan, especially the sandwiches part so I smacked her in the leg with my tail to let her know I approved. Someone could make a fortune selling protective gear for people who live with bloodhounds. My human once showed up for a routine checkup with a black eye (my nose), a bruise on her face (my snout), bruised knees (my tail), bruise tracks on her legs (my nails), bruises on her chest (the point on my head), bruises on her abdomen (my elbows) and miscellaneous abrasions on her body (being pulled over and dragged during an especially frisky walk). The doctor wanted to call the police.

But I digress.

"I'll come with you," said the Supernumerary Rufus. "At least as far as the kitchen door. Just let me print out my notes."

When he was finished, I marched the four of us to the kitchen where I was pleased to see that sandwich preparations were actively underway. Equally welcome, at least to my humans, was the fact that some snow had been cleared from the area around the doorway and the sound of snowblowers could be heard in the distance. And while it wasn't exactly June, the chilly air was distinctly less so. Nevertheless, I cavorted in the usual way while my human pleaded, also in the usual way, for me to speed up the identification of acceptable real estate upon which to empty my capacious internal cavities. Her words fell on deaf ears. Bloodhound ears are good for many things but registering the wishes of their humans is not one of them.

By the time I consented to be brought indoors I was once again white as the sheets I habitually shed all over.

Chapter 24

With Driscoll and Barclay bearing large trays of tasty smelling sandwiches, we made our way to the quiet and cozy den that had been the scene of our previous conclave.

"We're all ears," prompted Driscoll when we had settled ourselves. This was of course manifestly untrue. If anyone was all ears, it would be me and even I am not all ears.

The Other Rufus consulted his notes and proceeded to relay the results of this afternoon's investigation to his rapt audience while Ben idly fed me a steak sandwich.

"We also came up empty with everyone on the sound of a gunshot," said the Extra Rufus when he had concluded his remarks.

"But that was a longshot in any case," said Ben, "no pun intended. Given the distance, the sound of bagpipes, the lack of attention paid to something that would be put down to hunters, it's not surprising. Also, someone would have had to be in completely the right place at the right time to hear anything.

I could see Driscoll calculating the odds.

"My money's on The Knob Prince," he said at length. "I think he decided to finish what he started at the sword fight. He was spotted outdoors by a witness who is more credible than his sister, although she might be in on it too."

"If she was, then you'd think she and Greg wouldn't have contradicted each other though," countered my human as she fed me a slice of ham.

"That's true, but maybe they thought they'd have plenty of time to come up with a story before the police arrived," replied Driscoll, "so they had to improvise. I've got Greg at even money 1-1 and at 3-1 if they were both involved."

"I agree that Greg is an appealing choice given all the contradictions," said Ben, "but I'm following the money. Henley and Bruce have a strong financial motive."

"Yes, but even with Rush dead it doesn't mean Henley would automatically get her hands on her trust fund money," said my human.

"That's true," said Ben, "but with Rush alive she definitely wasn't getting it, and now she's at least got a shot with your uncle. He and Bruce looked mighty chummy the other day. And now that she's gotten sober, Mr. Winthrop might feel she's entitled to the money; although given Bruce's treatments I'm not sure sober is exactly the right word to use."

"Then the question becomes, was it both of them or one of them and in that case, which one?" said Barclay between bites.

"And let's not forget about what happened to Mr. Winthrop," said the Other Rufus. "Was it a poisonous mushroom or some other substance that found its way into his food. And was it accidental or intentional?"

"Maybe the plan was to get rid of both Rush and Mr.

Winthrop," said Ben. "I can't see a group of bankers caring much about delving into the details of Henley's sobriety or the purpose to which she intends to put the money. I would imagine that Bruce attesting to the fact that she's gone through his rehab program and is no longer using would be sufficient. They also alibi each other and she'd say anything he told her to. Then there is the matter of them being seen coming in and not being around when Rufus knocked on their door."

"Yes, but maybe they were outside for a reason that had nothing to do with the murder," said my human, "and Rufus just happened to miss them when he knocked. It's still a mystery though about why she was in a state when she was seen coming in, but seemed fine, in fact more than fine, after she was told about her brother's death."

"Maybe she was upset by the actual, physical killing part but then recovered when she thought of the benefit?" said Ben.

"All good points," said Driscoll. "This is a tough one. I'll give them 2-1 as a paired entry and 3-1 as singles. Although Dr. Bruce is as slippery as an eel." I paused in mid-tuna sandwich. I am exceptionally fond of eel. Whether sushi'd or sashimi'd my human always makes sure to order extra from my favorite Japanese restaurant. I sniffed the sandwich trays in case I had missed it.

"Rufus, stop drooling on the table," said my human. The Other Rufus reflexively wiped his mouth with a napkin.

"You seem to be good at playing devil's advocate, Cressida," said Driscoll as she dealt with a puddle of drool. "Who do you like?"

"If I were to place a bet, it'd be on Mike Kovac," she replied. "He's a bit of a rough customer under his bespoke Italian suits and he's devoted to his daughter. Also, there's what Tucker told Ben and Rufus about Rush trying to blackmail him. And he's got a gun and doesn't seem afraid to use it.

Plus, from what my mother told me, I don't think the family would be all that heartbroken if Brooke didn't marry Percy. Granted I don't think that's the primary motive or anything, but it would give Brooke time to reconsider."

"I agree with you that Mike's a strong candidate," said Ben, "and probably the obvious one. But he's not stupid and I don't see him announcing he's got a gun if he's just used it to shoot someone."

"I still think the evidence for him outweighs his peacocking with the gun," said my human. "I'm also sure we passed the Belvoir Gallery several times yesterday afternoon and we didn't see him or his assistant."

"You mean the Beaver Gallery," corrected Barclay.

"I think they're all beaver galleries considering what's on the walls," said Driscoll.

"Yes, I agree that the 8th Earl of Crackshaw did seem to have a thing for the ladies, particularly those missing multiple items of clothing, but he was English, so Belvoir would be pronounced beaver," said Barclay. "Like the Duke of Rutland's place."

"How on earth do you know that?" asked Driscoll. I noticed he emphasized the "you." I don't think Driscoll had fully recovered from the shock of the Boadicea incident. However, I sympathized. Jocks, like bloodhounds, are not rated highly in the brains department. "Are your people chummy with the Duke's?"

"No. Or not as far as I know," said Barclay, "although they do get around quite a lot. But summer of sophomore year I traipsed about the UK with a girlfriend who was deep into Downton Abbey. We had to see every bloody stately home in Britain."

"It's appalling the things you had to do to get laid," said Driscoll.

"I know, but in my defense, I was young. Anyway, I can't remember a thing about the place but the name kind of stuck in my head."

"It would," said Ben.

"But to get back to Mike," said Barclay with another sandwich stuck in his hand—like me he was an excellent trencherman—"don't forget that there's a money aspect with him too. At least assuming it's true what Tucker told you about Rush's pay to play scheme."

"But you know it's also possible that Kathy Kovac knows all about her husband's extra curriculars," said the Other Rufus, "and as long as the cash keeps coming, she doesn't care."

"I like Mike," said Driscoll. "I make him 1-2."

"What do we think about some of the others?" asked Ben.

"They're more or less all longshots, I think" said Driscoll. "Chime in if anyone has anything to add, but I have Mr. Winthrop at 10-1—sorry Cressida, but he was a bit unaccounted for that afternoon. As far as the other the Kovacs, I have Brooke at 15-1…"

"Which reminds me, "interrupted the Other Rufus, "when Percy surfaces, I suggest we refrain from discussing the specifics of our investigation. Somehow it doesn't seem polite to suggest that he might be marrying into a family of murderers. Plus, there's the whole blabbing to Brooke thing and I'm sure none of us want to keep Rush company in the wine cellar."

Everyone agreed, especially with respect to the latter point.

"To round out the Kovac entry, "resumed Driscoll, "I have Pete at 12-1 but that's purely on the basis of lack of an alibi. He's a dark horse and I can't see him having done the deed unless Rush threatened to commit some pie related crime. Then as to the remaining members of the Kovac cadet branch, I have Jason going off at 8-1. The whole playing with trains stuff is suspect and he's a fiercely loyal brother."

"Also, he runs a hedge fund so he probably belongs in jail for something," said Barclay.

"Not everyone can play with boats for a living," replied Driscoll.

"I do not play with boats for a living. I sell racing yachts, which is completely different. And at least my job isn't playing with toys with a bunch of friends."

"Gaming apps are not toys," protested Driscoll. "And what would people do in meetings without them? But anyway, now we're working on a robot that does your laundry."

Everyone's ears perked up. Except mine, because I love doing laundry, although my definition of it might be somewhat different.

"We're getting off topic," said Driscoll. "To round out the Kovac stable, I have Emily at 8-1. A woman scorned and all that and we know she has a gun. And to finish with the fillies, there's the other woman scorned—or at least the one we know about—Rush's ex-fiancée. She'll go off at 15:1. I don't fancy her myself but you two spoke with her, what do you think?"

"I think we both believed her when she said that her idea of revenge didn't stretch to something quite this permanent," said Ben.

"Although you must admit, it was a pretty next level ghosting," said the Other Rufus, "and we have no way of knowing whether she was being truthful when she said she had no idea Rush was here."

"What's Rush's deal with women?" asked my human. "I

mean apart from the usual New York guy dickishness? Present company excepted of course."

"I'm not a psychiatrist," said the Other Rufus, giving Driscoll a quelling look to silence him, "but even in college, Rush displayed the traits of a narcissistic sociopath when it came to girls. And I don't think living in New York, and especially being an actor, helped any. It's not only that he enjoyed watching the obvious effect his looks had on women, but he also seemed to get a real kick out of figuring out who women wanted him to be and then creating the character to match. Knowing Rush, I'm sure he just thought of it as honing his craft."

"Well Shakespeare did say that all the world's a stage," said Driscoll. "He just took it very literally."

"I agree with Rufus's diagnosis," said Ben. "Rush always took pleasure in turning on the charm and then studying its effect on people without regard to their feelings. He liked the power it gave him. But blackmail is a dangerous game."

"Anyway, what odds do you have on everyone else?" asked my human, clearly now intrigued by Driscoll's bookmaking approach to homicide.

"The field is 20-1 which I think is pretty decent considering how big it is and how little we know for certain."

"And speaking of the field," said my human, "I wonder what they've all been up to while we've been hunting a murderer."

"Or murderers," corrected Driscoll. "I wonder if I should offer odds on the Kovac family as a whole" he mused. "Anyway, to Cressida's point, I move that Buck and I do some reconnaissance to make sure everyone's still alive and to gather intelligence on what's been going on in our absence."

"Don't do anything exciting while we're gone," added Barclay.

The only one who got up to anything exciting while they were gone was me. I uncovered a partially deconstructed bone I had hidden under a cushion and went to work. I think the scattering of bones makes a place feel homey. Even a castle.

I chewed while the others chatted, tossing around theories and counter theories like so many bits of unappetizing kibble. There was still a distinct lack of consensus when the door opened, and Percy slunk in.

"I ran into Dris and Buck and they said I'd find you in here. I need a drink."

"That bad?"

"Worse. I'm finding a little Kovac goes a long way. Brooke is in a foul mood, her father and brother are discussing knobs, and her mother is trying to find out how much money I make."

"Well hold that thought," said the Other Rufus. "I want to check on your father and you can come with." I decided that I, too, would come with. The sandwiches were gone, and I felt in need of a digestive biscuit.

"I see we have company," said Percy giving me a scratch as I walked politely by his side in a way I never do when I'm attached to a leash. "You can't have too many Rufuses; I just hope he doesn't find another body, although at the moment I have a couple of strong suggestions for him."

We got to Uncle Charles's room and the Other Rufus knocked and this Rufus bayed. I wanted to reassure the occupants that no weapons-brandishing villain awaited them outside. Aunt Anne opened the door.

"What perfect timing! I was just saying to Elizabeth that I hoped you'd look in. Charles says he thinks he is up to eating something and we didn't want to leave him alone to go to the kitchen." I belched tuna fumes to let everyone know that I highly recommend the tuna sandwiches. Then I helpfully prewashed the two plates sitting on the coffee table that contained the remnants of the ladies afternoon's lunch.

"I see they've sent food up for you," said Percy. "I suppose it's more or less safe."

"We all have to eat and I think your father didn't have anything more sinister than a case of food poisoning," replied Aunt Anne as she organized the now immaculate dishes on a tray. "We'll be back as soon as we can. Cereal, bananas, and toast?"

Uncle Charles nodded. He was sitting in a chair and although he was fully clothed, he still looked pale. While Dr. Rufus did his thing, I laid my head in Uncle Charles' lap near a pocket in which I could detect the strong odor of biscuit. Also the odor of Golden Retriever, but no one's perfect.

"What a way to spend your birthday tomorrow son," said Uncle Charles as I munched a biscuit and he massaged my dewlap. "Your mother and I will give you our gift when we're out of this mess."

"The only gift I want tomorrow is your recovery. And the police."

"Still, it's such a shame about your great uncle Percival's will. Losing an inheritance and a wedding in one go is hard luck. Not to mention having to carry the old boy's name as a reminder. I always considered the will's marriage provision exceedingly arbitrary; people frequently find a spouse and marry quite happily after the age of twenty-eight. I can have a look when we're home and see if there's a workaround."

"That's OK Father. I'm doing well and there's nothing I want except for all of us to get out of here unharmed." I knew there was a reason I liked Cousin Percy, apart from his questionable taste in women.

"Well, you're looking much better Sir," said Dr. Rufus,

"so I don't see that there's any reason for you not to make a full recovery. But I would recommend that you see your doctor when you get home." With the important business concluded, the conversation turned to neutral subjects, no one wishing to introduce any topic that might distress the invalid.

The ladies soon returned with a tray of easy to digest foods and we returned to HQ.

"Perce, why don't you keep Cress company," said Ben after Percy had his drink, although time spent with his father had lifted his spirits more than the whiskey. "Rufus and I—or more likely Rufus, Rufus and I—will go see what's become of our absent colleagues."

Ben had read my mind. I, too, was eager to see what the remaining groomsmen and a castle full of snowbound humans had been up to. Whatcha doin' is my middle name.

But our initial search proved surprisingly unrewarding—the place seemed eerily deserted. It wasn't until we reached the entry hall the reason for our lack of success was made manifest. There was a clothing rack standing next to the door and upon it hung an odd assortment of scavenged coats, sweaters, hats, boots, and other bits and bobs of winter attire. Sergio Emilio Augustus might have given up on the wedding and its guests, but the staff clearly had not.

Just then, the door flew open, and a red-cheeked and snow-covered Driscoll and Barclay blew in, hooting and hollering. Barclay took one look at me and closed the door quickly behind him.

"Aha! We've been looking for you two," exclaimed Ben. "I thought you were supposed to be gathering intelligence."

"We were," said Driscoll. "We discovered that some of those models throw a mean snowball. And they're vicious as well. I may have to offer them at 25-1 as a separate entry. Maybe one of them is another of Rush's rejects."

"Anyway, we're off to the Games Room," said Barclay as he rehung his garments for use by the next snowball combatant. "We have it on good authority that it's the place to be." I would have thought the place to be was pushing models into snowbanks, however, a visit to the Games Room sounded promising. There were ping pong balls to be stolen, board games to be upended, and who doesn't love chasing a bloodhound with Park Place in his mouth.

The Games Room was big and abuzz with the repressed energy of the chronically cooped up. There was ping pong, air hockey, video games, shooting games, pinball, foosball, and even a roulette wheel that immediately caught Driscoll's attention. There were also board games and card games galore. All pretty old school, but old is new when you've grown up with games on screens. Not that anyone ever gets to play a game on a screen when I'm around since in addition to our other talents, we bloodhounds are incorrigible screen blockers. Whether it's a television, a laptop, or a phone, if we can see it, you can't.

But I digress.

There were several animated tables who were engaged in loud and lively games of Clue. Or a version of it.

"I think Colonel Kovac murdered Officiant Rush in the Chamber of Revels with The Large Dog" declared the participant whose turn it was. Even more egregious, someone had the audacity to cross out the picture of a wrench, write LARGE DOG across it, and draw a caricature of me. I protested in the strongest possible terms. We Rufuses are a peace-loving lot and in spite of the fact that I hadn't taken an oath to do no harm like the Other Rufus, I never did. At least not intentionally. Nevertheless, I was sorely tempted.

My companions circled the Clue tables like inquisitive sharks investigating a new species of fish. Other weapons included a sword, an arrow, a pistol, a mushroom, and a hypodermic needle. The rooms had likewise been modified to include the Chambers of Revels, Libations, and Repast, to which had been added things like Gallery With Pictures of Naked Women, Small Sitting Room With Pictures of Naked Women, Den With Pictures of Naked Women, and Salon with Sculptures of Naked Women. I am embarrassed to say that these included the types of crude drawings that one would expect. The suspect cards had also undergone considerable alteration. In addition to Colonel Kovac, there was Bridezilla Brooke, Pretentious French Chick, the Knobster, and Pie in Your Eye Pete, among others. And in an aspiration move, Mr. Boddy had been replaced by Mr. Wedding Planner.

I had a feeling that Colonel Kovac was going to find a charge for replacement Clue games on his bill.

We returned to the table with the offensive picture of me.

"Are there any sporting ladies and gents at the table?" asked Driscoll pulling out his phone while I stared again at the odious card. I was incensed. My ears were too short and my occipital point had been exaggerated so it looked like I was wearing a dunce cap. "I'll give you 1-2 on Colonel Kovac and a very attractive 15-1 on Bridezilla Brooke, although she's 3-1 as a paired entry with her brother the Knobster." He began to rattle off the odds like a carnival barker on the midway and soon had a crowd of eager punters gathered round.

"But what about Percy?" piped up a voice. "Maybe he whacked the officiant to get out of marrying Bridezilla Brooke."

"Or you," said another aspiring sleuth pointing at Driscoll. "You could be offering odds on everyone else to divert suspicion."

"Point taken," replied the always fair-minded Driscoll. "If you like me, you can always take the field at 20-1.

"Does the field include the dog?" asked some rude jokester.

"And what are the odds for a paired entry of Rufuses?"

interjected an even ruder jokester.

"Sorry Rufuses," said Driscoll apologetically unapologetic, "both Rufuses are naturally included in the field, but I'll give you 50:1 on a longshot paired entry."

"I'm pretty sure the plural of Rufus is Rufi," said a studious looking young man in spectacles, "but what's the minimum bet?"

"A mere tenner. Well worth the price," answered the oddsmaker. Everyone reached for their phones.

"Nooooooo!" howled one of the Cluesters. "There's no WiFi!"

"Yes, we know," said a Colonel Kovac's accuser.

"No WiFi, no Venmo!"

A shocked silence gripped the group.

"What do we do now? We have no way to place bets," moaned a gangly young man. While there was no actual gnashing of teeth, expressions of extreme disappointment swept through the crowd.

"IOUs?" suggested someone.

"Jewelry maybe?" said someone else.

"Or my shoes! They're Louboutins!" cried a young woman jubilantly.

"How about cash?" suggested Ben.

"Cash! OMG! That's f-ing brilliant."

"Yeah, but does anyone have any?"

A new wave of consternation seized Driscoll's punters.

Pockets, wallets, and purses were ripped open and plumbed to their furthest depths.

"Look! I found a ten!" shouted someone triumphantly waving an ancient and tatty bill like it was the flag of a conquering army.

Driscoll collected a small pile of the precious paper—much of it very much the worse for wear—from those Luddites who possessed them and IOU'd those without, until all who craved a wager had been accommodated.

In the meantime, I decided to make myself scarce before someone noticed that a card had gone missing.

Chapter 25

I have nothing much to report about the rest of our snow day. I frolicked in the drifts and ate a lot of food. My humans drank a lot of alcohol. Mostly it was a game of waiting, speculating, and trying not to get killed.

It was on Friday that things really kicked off.

The day dawned—and given my penchant for early morning risings, I mean that literally—much warmer as spring once again asserted its dominion over the season. I consumed my usual hearty breakfast, which as we know, is the most important meal of the day—or one of them—and our customary breakfast numbers were augmented by the less than cheery bridegroom who elected to eat with us rather than with la famille Kovac.

"Happy Birthday Perce," said Driscoll, nearly pouring champagne on the birthday boy's head in his eagerness to fill his glass and everyone else's. For once I did not attempt to insert my tongue into the beverage. The bubbles made me sneeze and I had a feeling I would need to keep a clear head.

The morning and lunch passed peacefully enough, but when I was conducting a post-prandial nap in the library to keep the recently ambulatory Uncle Charles company, I heard a great hullabaloo. It began with the distant sound of wheels spinning to gain traction in the snow and ended with members of the local constabulary pounding on the front door. Strictly speaking, they rang the loudly chiming doorbell, but pounding sounds much more dramatic.

Our visitors were quickly enveloped by an excited crowd and Uncle Charles had to push his way through before he was able to reach the man who appeared to be in charge.

"Charles Winthrop," he said, exuding his usual confident authority as he extended his hand. "I'm the father of the young man who was supposed to be getting married this week and also the senior law partner at Winthrop, Brewster, and Ames."

"Detective Ingo de Vries," replied the man, shaking Uncle Charles's hand firmly. "I'm the senior detective of the East Snodsburgh PD." He was a roundish, middle-aged, dark-haired man almost as tall as Uncle Charles.

"I suggest we adjourn to the library," said Uncle Charles. "I can fill you in on the preliminaries and my son and his friends have compiled some information that we hope will make your job easier." I hung back a bit and twitched my nose to catch a whiff of the guy in order to determine whether he was someone whose acquaintance I wished to make. A strong and powerfully agreeable odor made its way through my olfactory channels and up into my brain. I bayed and sliced through the crowd.

"Who's this fine fellow?" asked the detective, a look of delight illuminating his otherwise serious face.

"This is Rufus," replied Uncle Charles. "He belongs to my niece Cressida Pennington." In the circumstances, I let the whole "belonging to my niece" thing slide. She and I both knew who belonged to whom. As did anyone who had spent much time in our company. But I gave Uncle Charles a pass since as someone with a Golden Retriever, he wouldn't know any better.

"I handled one of these bad boys when I was in the K-9 unit," said my new best friend as I leaned against his leg and he massaged the inner workings of my dewlap. "Amazing animals."

"Well that's one way of putting it," commented my human who rocked up trailing Cousin Percy and the rest of my fellow sleuths in her wake.

"The library is this way," said Uncle Charles. "There are hot drinks for you and your men. In spite of the storm the staff has kept us well supplied, so let them know if you need anything."

We settled ourselves around a large, round table of polished mahogany and I paid the detective the extreme compliment of parking my posterior next to his chair. I would have sat on his feet but I was too big to sit upright under the table.

"This is my son, Percival, his groomsmen Ben, Barclay, Rufus, and Driscoll, and my niece Cressida," said Uncle Charles.

"The bloodhound is a groomsman too?"

"No, sorry. We have another Rufus." He gestured towards the Extra One. "He's a doctor, by the way." I heard Driscoll mutter "radiologist" under his breath.

"Excellent," said the detective. "I have one on the way, but with the roads the way they are, I'm not sure when he'll get here."

"Let's begin with the lists," said Uncle Charles as he took a sheaf of papers from his son. "This is the wedding planner's list of all the guests and their contact information as well as his permanent staff and the staff he hired for the occasion—musicians, waitstaff, miscellaneous actors, etc. This one is the videographer's list of his people, and this one is the castle's chief of operations's list of everyone who worked this week."

"I also thought you might like to see this," said Cousin Percy, as he handed over a piece of paper. "It's the schedule of wedding events and I've marked down the names of who won which of the various competitions that were held. When you see the body and what was in it, you'll understand why we thought it might be relevant. Everything was going according to plan except that we had something of a mishap during the sword fighting competition. The swords we were using were supposed to be the ones with blunted edges that the castle keeps on hand for movie shoots. But Greg Kovac—that's my bride's brother—seems to have gotten hold of one with real edges and rather had a go at Rush with it."

"Rush?" said the detective.

"Sorry. Rush Deveraux, the victim. He was supposed to officiate. Not my choice, by the way. Anyway, Rush wasn't hurt badly, and Greg said it was an accident, so we took his word for it. But in light of subsequent events...well now we're not so sure."

"As my son said, apart from the incident at the sword fight, things were going as planned until Wednesday afternoon. Weather conditions had begun to deteriorate, and the events scheduled for that time period had to be cancelled. I'll let the rest of you take it from there."

"I guess it all started with me," said Barclay. "Not the murder, I mean, but I was passing the front door and Rufus—the dog one—seemed to want to go out, so I opened the door for him."

"You seriously didn't know any better than to let an unleashed bloodhound out into open country? That was an incredibly foolish and dangerous thing to have done young man," snapped the detective giving him the look that had cowed the criminal classes of East Snodsburgh into submission. He was almost as irate as my human.

"So I've been told. Multiple times." He looked guiltily in my human's direction as she picked up the story.

"Ben and I—he's my boyfriend as well as being my cousin Percy's Best Man—had been looking for Rufus to take him for a walk, but then we ran into Barclay and he told us what he'd done." Her eyes darted in his direction with an unpleasant look in them. It's one of my human's more laudable traits that as much as she might complain about me, she is slow to forgive others where I am concerned. "So the six of us formed a search party to go look for him."

"Any idea what time it was?" asked the detective.

"We've thought about that," said Ben. "We all had our phones, but none of us can remember checking the time. I think we'd been out for maybe half an hour..." here he turned to his fellow bloodhound hunters who nodded their heads tentatively..."so working backwards we probably left the castle somewhere around 2:30 ish. But it might have been earlier. Anyway, we'd been looking for about half an hour give or take when we heard Rufus baying. It probably took us another half hour or so to follow the sound and locate him."

"And when we got there, Rufus wasn't the only thing we found," said Driscoll with a ghoulish glint in his eye. "He was standing next to Rush's dead body."

"So Rufus—the bloodhound—found the body?"

Everyone nodded in the affirmative.

"Who's a good boy," said the detective and scratched me behind the ear. "The killer obviously didn't reckon with a bloodhound being on the job. Without your hound, Miss, who knows when the body would have been found."

"I'm sure he is happy to have been of service," said my

human. "It happens so rarely." Or ever. Although that's not strictly speaking true. I make sure my human doesn't have to waste money on a gym membership because getting dragged around Central Park for an untold number of hours keeps her in peak condition. And she never has to worry about her weight because she only gets to eat half her food. On a good day. Still, it's nice to be appreciated. Maybe I should find dead bodies more often.

"You're absolutely right about not finding Rush," said Percy. "He probably wouldn't have been missed until dinner and we'd only have called the police after we spent time searching the castle for him. I'm sure nothing could have been done until morning, even if we hadn't been snowed in.

"Anyway," continued Ben, "it was late afternoon when we found Rufus and Rush. We stayed with the body and sent Barclay back to the castle to call the police; when he returned, we did as you instructed and took pictures and videos of the body and crime scene and bagged the items we found."

"I'll examine the photos in more detail later," said the detective, "but if anyone has their phone handy I'd like to take a quick look."

Six pairs of hands held up phones.

He selected one and began to scroll.

"He's very photogenic."

"Yes, Rush was actually an actor. He only got licensed to officiate for my wedding," said Percy.

"No, I mean Rufus." There was no question about which Rufus he meant. I thumped my tail and put my head in his lap. I did briefly consider climbing into it but deferred that pleasure until a later date as I felt it might hinder the investigation.

"Rufus, no," said my human which I generally interpret

as meaning "Rufus yes." "I'm sorry Detective, he's going to drool all over your pants, and I forgot his spit rag."

"Don't worry about it. I miss the slobber. And the smell." This was good to know since I intended to coat him liberally with both.

"I think you'll find this next document interesting," said Uncle Charles. "I thought it might speed your investigation if we could provide you with preliminary statements as to everyone's whereabouts on Wednesday afternoon. Since I'm an attorney I intended to do the questioning myself, but I came down with food poisoning..."

"Or just poisoning," interjected Driscoll.

"As I was saying," continued Uncle Charles giving Driscoll a disapproving look, "I became ill late Wednesday afternoon, which I assumed at the time was most probably due to the wild mushroom ragout we had for lunch and Dr. Rufus did not feel it was medically advisable for me to participate."

"Also," said Cousin Percy, "given what had happened to Rush, we couldn't be sure that the poisoning wasn't intentional and that whoever did it wouldn't try again. My father and Rush's father had been friends since college, so there is connection between them."

"In the end," said Ben, "it was decided that Dr. Rufus, and myself, would be the ones to ask everyone about Wednesday afternoon. In the interests of time we concentrated on the wedding party, the guests, and anyone else we thought would be of the most interest to you. Obviously, we know you'll be taking official statements but Mr. Winthrop felt that these informal notes could help you to focus some of the questioning. Any statements that are contradictory are in bold."

The detective ran a practiced eye over the papers.

"The people with the surname Kovac seem to have a lot of bold."

"Yes," said the Other Rufus. "Brooke Kovac is the bride, Greg is her brother, Mike is her father, Pete is her uncle, and Emily and Jason are Pete's children. Sorry Perce, but all of them gave us conflicting statements as to their own whereabouts or the whereabouts of others. Even Brooke."

Percy didn't look all that shocked. "They didn't get to where they are by being generous with the truth," he shrugged.

"Also, you should know, Detective, that Mike Kovac has a gun," said Ben. "He showed it to everyone to reassure them that he could protect us. And Emily Kovac won a Rohrbaugh in the pistol shooting competition."

"Nice," commented the detective.

"And as you saw in the photos, there was an arrow, a sword, a knife, and a syringe, but no gun," said the Other Rufus. "However, I observed what is probably gunshot wound to the chest. We don't know if the missing gun is significant, but it might suggest that whoever was known to have one couldn't leave it lying around. But I'm not a pathologist so I don't want to speculate as to cause of death."

"He's a picture doctor," said Driscoll unable to contain himself. The detective looked perplexed.

"I'm a radiologist," explained the other Rufus. "Or more accurately, before my smart mouthed friend points it out, I'm a radiology resident."

"So barely even a doctor," said Driscoll. "But my money's on the gun. If I were to kill someone that's how I'd do it."

"Not me," said Barclay. "I think it's a much better idea to put a poisoned pill into someone's prescription bottle. That way you wouldn't need to be around."

"Yeah, but what if someone you wanted to kill isn't taking any medication," said Driscoll. "And even if they were. then you'd still have to steal a pill and poison it. I'll bet Rufus will back me up that it's not all that easy to do. It only works in books."

"Well..." began the Other Rufus but was cut off.

"Gentlemen, I think we're getting off the topic," said Uncle Charles. "We don't want to waste the detective's time."

"Sorry," said Driscoll. "But getting back to the subject of our suspects, it seems that only a few of them were either seen leaving the castle or admitted to leaving. So that should narrow things down."

"Not necessarily," said Percy. "This place is massive, it's possible that people were elsewhere when our murderer went in or out."

"Agreed," said Barclay, "but I think that would be risky. He or she couldn't know that they wouldn't be seen. For once I agree with Dris."

My human had remained silent during this exchange. One of the occupational hazards of being a writer is an inclination to listen and observe rather than to speak. People who hadn't heard her chattering away with friends as I had, were inclined to think she was either quiet or shy. She was neither. But a writer's mind, like a bloodhound's nose, never takes a holiday.

But now she spoke up.

"Ben this might be a good time to tell the detective what we found." She knew how much her boyfriend liked springing surprises.

Ben looked around the table gathering eyes like a

magician about to pull a mouthwatering bunny out of a hat.

"As many of you know, Crackshaw Castle is rumored to have numerous hidden secret passages, many of which were constructed by the late Earl to facilitate his dalliances with ladies who had the misfortune to be other gentleman's wives."

Barclay interrupted him. "I think the whole secret passage thing is bogus; it's just a myth dreamed up by the Lemming Event Group's marketing department to add mystery to the castle. Dris and I have been all over this place and haven't found a single one."

"That's because you didn't have Rufus," said Ben. Everyone's attention swiveled in the direction of the good doctor.

"Don't look at me. I have no idea what he's talking about," said the non-secret passage finding Rufus.

"Not him, him," said Ben pausing and pointing a dramatic finger in my direction. It wasn't quite as captivating as the secret passage reveal he had originally planned, but it definitely got everyone's attention. "I was in Cress's room and she asked me to help clean Rufus's slobber off this one particular section of wall panel. Then he came up beside us and gave it a thwack with his paw and a shove with his snout and boom, the thing swung open."

"You always have all the luck," grumbled Barclay.

"Luck had nothing to do with it," said the detective. "If there was even the tiniest bit of air coming through that panel, any bloodhound worth its salt would be able to smell it easily." It was nice to have my nose appreciated instead of being apologized for, like when I stick it places no one thinks it belongs.

"But where did the passage lead?" asked Cousin Percy.

"At first it was more a case of what it led into. Our

passage led into a larger one and as we followed it, we saw other small passages joining it along the way. Given the Earl of Crackshaw's, shall we say, entertaining style, you don't have to be Sherlock Holmes to work out that that he required bedrooms with unconventional exits."

"We didn't say anything, because Ben wanted time to explore the smaller tunnels," said my human. "He was hoping to surprise you guys by popping up in one of your rooms. But then after the murder it was safer if we were the only two who knew about them."

"Although maybe you weren't the only two," said Barclay stating the obvious.

"Exactly," said Ben. "Especially when you hear where it came out."

Driscoll groaned.

"Don't tell me it's where we found the body. That'll blow the field wide open and wreak havoc with the odds."

Percy looked at him questioningly.

"Don't ask," said Ben.

"But that's not the only secret passage," said my human.

"You found another one?" exclaimed the Other Rufus.

"Again, not us, him," said my human reaching over to give me an affectionate pat on the neck. "The passage in my room came out under the fake ruined chapel—that's near the Overlook where we found the body," she explained to Detective de Vries—"and while we were there, Rufus seemed to be taking an unhealthy interest in some daffodils which didn't bode well for their health. I pulled him away before he could do any real damage and neither of Ben nor I thought much about it until the next day."

"You'll see from the schedule Detective, that there was a forest scavenger hunt," said Ben.

"Yes, and Ben and I were paired with Henley and Bruce, Rush's sister, and her fiancé," continued my human. "Rufus dragged us back to the Overlook and while we were busy showing Henley and Bruce the view, he dug up the daffodils.

"Then we heard his nails hit something hard," said Ben, "and when we cleared the dirt, we found a wooden door." Nails, I might add, that no one has ever been able to cut—many have tried, none have succeeded—and they are as useful for shredding important papers or inaccessible etchings as they are for uncovering secret passages. "The door led down to another tunnel. But this one appeared to be newer than the first one and didn't lead to any bedrooms but to a pantry off the kitchen. We think it probably belonged to the bootlegger who owned the castle during Prohibition."

"The bedrooms AND the kitchen! Do you have any idea what this does to my book," moaned Driscoll.

"Again, don't ask," said Ben to Percy. "The bottom line is that any number of people could have gone back and forth to the crime scene without using any of castle's doors. It complicates things but I hope the information helps, Detective."

"Thank you, lady, gentlemen, and hound," said the detective. "Yes, this has all been extremely useful." He turned to the Other Rufus. "I'd like to see the body now."

"We stored it in the wine cellar," said Ben taking the key out of his pocket.

"That seems as good a place as any given the lack of facilities" said Detective de Vries as he hoisted himself out of his chair. "And I'm happy to see it's got a lock. Lead on gentlemen." Or hound. I had epoxied myself to his left thigh.

"Not you Rufus," said my human.

"No, Miss. Let him come. There might be another way into the wine cellar that we don't know about, but he would. It's important to establish that the body has been securely stored." I liked this guy more every time he opened his mouth.

When we got to the wine cellar, Ben opened the door and handed the key to the detective.

"The stairs are a bit steep, I'm afraid," he said, "although, it's a lot easier going down them without a body. It took all five of us to get Rush down there and it wasn't easy even then." I of course had no difficulty navigating the stairs and flew down them like I was being chased with a nail clipper. Humans are ridiculously slow on level ground but on stairs they are positively snail-like.

The large room was chilly and musty-smelling and filled with rack upon rack of wine. I ignored these and trotted to the rear of the chamber where Rush's body lay in state. I bayed to let everyone know I had found him. Again.

"Is this just how you left it?" asked de Vries, when everyone had at last arrived.

"As far as I can tell, yes," said the Other Rufus. "Everything that we found in the body is in those plastic bags. We used rubber gloves and bags from the kitchen."

"Were the bags sealed immediately or did you do that later?" asked the detective as he pulled out a pair of gloves from his pocket.

"We did it immediately," said the Other Rufus. De Vries seemed to like this answer very much. "I removed the sword and the arrow from the torso, the knife from the neck and the note and the syringe from the arm."

The detective pulled back the sheet and closely examined the remains of Crackshaw Castle's least popular resident.

"This wound is from the sword, the one here is the arrow, and this appears to be a gunshot wound," said the Other Rufus pointing to the killer's handiwork. "I didn't bother examining the body for anything else since it would have been too difficult given the conditions and didn't seem necessary since I knew you'd have a pathologist. I'm only a radiologist, as my friends never cease to remind me, so I'm no expert, but I'd be surprised if the gunshot wound wasn't the cause of death."

"I'd agree with you there, Doctor. Everything else strikes me as being a little too theatrical and a gun is certainly the least risky and most efficient way to kill someone."

"The castle is rather over-supplied with theatrical people I'm afraid," said Ben. "Perhaps the theatricality is a clue."

"Possibly. And neither you nor anyone else heard anything?"

"No," replied Ben and he explained the potential reasons for this. "Plus, The Overlook is probably over a mile away."

"But we were able to hear Rufus baying," said my namesake," although I'm not sure how far away we were at the time."

"A gunshot is no match for a bloodhound in full cry," said the detective. "You'd be surprised how far their can voices carry." I wasn't surprised at all. And neither was my human. Or our neighborhood. "And you're sure none of you touched these items?"

"Absolutely. We were all extremely careful not to touch anything," Ben assured him. The detective's face might have relaxed into a small and satisfied smile. He certainly smelled pleased as he replaced the sheet and carefully picked up the bagged items.

Then he turned towards me.

"Let's take a stroll around, K9 Rufus." Music to my ears. Generally, people want to stop me from taking a stroll around.

And stroll around we did. Up and down the wine racks we went paying particular attention to those along the walls. As delightful as this was—I'm very partial to sniffing bottles at our local liquor store—I smelled nothing but wine.

"Looks like there aren't any hidden tunnels down here," said Ben. He sounded disappointed. "Still, I supposed that's a good thing since it means no one could have tampered with the evidence." He turned to de Vries, "We were also careful not to tell anyone where we had stashed...I mean deposited Rush."

Everyone made for the stairs which forced me to abandon an investigation of an especially fine Chateau d'Yquem '01. It had an excellent nose.

As we all assembled above ground, I noticed that I was a bit untidy, so I shook the dust, drool and cobwebs from my snout. A large juicy wad hit Detective de Vries square in the face.

He smiled like it was Christmas morning.

Chapter 26

We returned to the library and Detective de Vries, still holding the bags from the body, caucused briefly at the door with his men. They departed and he headed back to the table where we were all now waiting.

"I assume you'd like to take official statements, Detective" said Uncle Charles. "Ben knows the castle best, so if you let him know how many rooms you will need, I am sure he can show you those that are most appropriate." It was a prudent suggestion given that Crackshaw Castle had more naked women on its walls than a bordello.

"Thank you, Sir, but I've I asked my officers to round everyone up and send them in here first. K9 Rufus, you're with me."

He gathered up the documents we had prepared for him, and I followed him to a spot by the library door.

The inhabitants of the castle began to slowly file in. Some were apprehensive, some were relieved, and many were exuberant with an anticipatory energy, eager to see what the next act of the drama would bring.

As they entered, I welcomed each of them to my murder investigation. The character of The Royal Hound Rufus the Red was no more. In his place stood K9 Rufus, The Relentless and Indefatigable Sleuth Hound, finder of bodies and hunter of clues. I meticulously nose wanded my guests as Detective de Vries checked off their names against Uncle Charles's lists and studied their faces. When he was satisfied that everyone was present and correct, he placed the evidence bags on a table beside him and called for silence.

"Ladies and gentlemen, I am Detective Ingo de Vries of the East Snodsburgh Police Department. I am here because as all of you are aware, a homicide occurred on Wednesday afternoon. First, I want to let you know that all your rooms have been unlocked and we have a warrant to search them. Pursuant to this, you may notice some disturbance in your belongings for which we apologize in advance." I of course had nothing to hide; for those like my human who had a tendency to leave their embarrassing lacey bits about, perhaps not so much. Some of the things she claims count as underwear aren't even worth the trouble it takes to shred them.

"Second," continued the detective, "we will be taking statements from all of you in due course. But now, to get to the reason I asked you here: it struck me immediately that whoever killed Mr. Devereaux did not know that a bloodhound would be on the scene, nor did he or she appreciate the power of the bloodhound nose. I had a brief look at the notes regarding most of your whereabouts on the afternoon in question, and even from a cursory glance it is apparent that not everyone has been entirely truthful. There may be completely innocent or even not so innocent explanations for this which it will take time and patience to investigate, and I understand that many of you are eager to depart."

"Does that mean we can go," Jason Kovac called out.

"No, I'm afraid it doesn't, although we may be able to considerably accelerate your release by the simple expedient of asking Rufus for his assistance." The Other Rufus rose from his seat.

"Not you, you donut," said Driscoll. I bayed to call everyone's attention to the error but also hoped that the mention of donuts meant that some would be forthcoming, however much it would irritate our resident pie maker. In the meantime, I turned my attention to Detective de Vries who had donned a new pair of gloves and selected the plastic bag containing the arrow from his stash of murderous goodies.

"This arrow was found embedded in the victim's torso," he said. All eyes and not a few phones turned themselves upon us. The detective leaned over me, opened the seal on the bag and quickly slipped it over my pulsating nostrils. When I had had a good snort, he withdrew the bag.

"Rufus, find!" he commanded. As you probably know by now, I'm not much of one for obeying commands of any kind, but this time I was happy to make an exception. I raised my snout and sniffed the air more for dramatic effect than for any useful purpose. Then to increase the tension even further, I meandered about, conscientiously snuffling this one and that one along the way. A silence thick enough to be cut with one of the caterer's cleavers hung in the air. Finally, I stopped in front of my quarry and let fly with a lusty finding bay much like the one I use to let everyone know that I found a fresh pile of horse manure in the park or Ben cooking dinner in the kitchen.

The crowd gasped and all heads and phones swiveled in my direction.

"This is nonsense. Of course my scent is on that arrow. I helped with the archery competition," said Tucker.

"Fair enough," responded the detective. "Let's see what K9 Rufus has to say about the next item." He reached for the bag containing the sword and I obligingly returned and stuck my snout into it.

Everyone was staring at Greg expectantly. He looked both belligerent and uncomfortable. Far be it for me to disappoint an audience; I sniffed the air, snuffled the people, and came to rest in front of him. Once again, I bayed.

"That must have been the sword I accidently used during the sword fighting competition," he snapped peevishly. "Yes, I cut Rush's arm, but I didn't kill him. And even if I had, I certainly wouldn't use a sword to do it."

I listened attentively to his explanation. Now although I might not have wanted to disappoint my audience, I also did not want to compromise the evidence. There was a second scent on that sword. I pivoted but rather than return to the detective and his evidence bags, I came to rest in front of the scent's owner. I bayed once more. Tucker seemed to be rather displeased with me.

"As I said before," he scoffed "it's all nonsense. I helped with all the competitions so my scent will be everywhere."

"Point taken," said the detective calmly. He picked up the bag with the knife and made his way around the library.

"Does anyone recognize this?" he asked. There was a murmur of assent as he made his way over to the kitchen staff.

"Yes, It's from the kitchen. But I had nothing to do with this. I don't know any of these people," the caterer said, averting her eyes from those of the detective. I had a feeling that this might not be strictly speaking true, but I let it slide. "One of the waitstaff knew the victim, I believe. Perhaps you should talk to her," she said indicating the jilted fiancée.

"Yes, I knew Rush," the girl admitted, causing a bit of a stir. "But I'm sure that knife could have been handled by any number of us."

I agree, so we won't trouble K9 Rufus with this particular item at the moment."

He moved back to the other bags.

"But now let's see what K9 Rufus thinks about the syringe that was found stuck in the victim's arm." I returned to the detective's side and stuck my snout into the bag. As far as everyone was concerned this was going to be a no-brainer. And they were correct. But Dr. Bruce appeared unmoved.

"Yes, It's probably my syringe. I have no argument with that. I just have no idea how it came to be stuck in Rush's arm. I certainly didn't put it there. And even so, how do you know it's what killed him?"

"That is certainly a fair question," answered the detective. "But there is someone who might be in a position answer it." He opened the door and spoke to one of his men, and presently a small, grizzle-haired man entered the room.

"Obviously, there's an autopsy and forensics to be completed," said the police surgeon, "however, upon a preliminary examination of the body, I would say cause of death is most likely a gunshot wound to the chest. Which is not to say that these other items could not have hastened or contributed to the victim's demise."

"K9 Rufus, over here please," called the detective, interrupting my slobbering on My Attendant who I discovered sitting in the back of the room. I missed having a servant. Or at least another one.

"I can see you were distracted, K9 Rufus," said Detective de Vries when I returned to his side. "Have another sniff." He was correct, the pleasing scent of my former attendant had distracted me, but I didn't really need a second sniff. For form's sake, however, I complied.

This time, I didn't dilly dally but made straight for the mad musician and bayed in his increasingly agitated face.

"You made him do that!" cried Tucker. "He'd already ID'd Bruce!"

It was at this point in the proceedings that the disturbance broke out.

No sooner were the words out of Tucker's mouth than Riley, Kiley, and Katie were on him like a trio of angry hornets, hitting, slapping, and scratching. But it was when Katie began to beat him with a stiletto that the momentum shifted and Tucker swung from defense to offense. Although it was three against one, at least in theory since the three barely added up to one, Tucker began to gain the upper hand when Brooke decided to enter the fray to protect her girls. Tucker kicked her in the shins to discourage her after which he discovered that he had a lot more than a gaggle of excessively slender women to deal with. No one was going to lay a hand—or a foot— on Brooke without there being serious consequences. Greg punched him in the nose. Riley meanwhile, thinking that perhaps she would hedge her bets, landed a blow on Dr. Bruce's head with her Manolo, prompting Henley to hurl herself out of her seat and rush to his defense. There was a good deal of yelling and screaming, most of it not printable— words beginning with the letter F proving especially popular— and none of it was helped by the fact that by now everyone was on their feet yelling encouragement to their favorite combatant. And if you weren't fighting or trying to break it up, you were filming, and if you weren't filming you were placing bets with Driscoll.

The melee spun out of control with surprising speed.

"In here, now!" yelled Detective de Vries to his men.

Since restoring order was obviously going to take some time and riot control was not part of my job description, I took the opportunity to slip unobtrusively out the open library door. I am a patient hound, but enough is enough. I intended to put an end to this nonsense once and for all.

But nothing, or at least nothing concerning me, was going to get by the eagle eye of my new partner.

"Murphy! Follow that hound!" cried de Vries as soon as

I had stepped over the threshold.

Now I am acutely aware that we bloodhounds are not generally thought highly of in the intelligence department; I have it on good authority that humans believe that the point on the top of our heads contains our only working neuron. Nevertheless, contrary to both prevailing wisdom and much evidence, I do actually possess an abundance of working neurons, it's just that they all happen to be connected to my nose rather than my ears (although naturally I do hear important words like snack, walk, car, and pizza, etc.). But there is a world of difference between learning pointless commands like "sit" and "stay," not to mention the truly horrific "heel," and doing something useful— like uncovering things that are hidden from view. Now very often humans wish these things to remain hidden from view which is why they hid them in the first place but that makes uncovering them even more fun.

But I digress.

Followed by Officer Murphy, who did not appear to be one of those humans built for speed, I arrived at my destination and did what I had come to do, much to the officer's astonishment. My activities also meant that I was now in possession of something he wanted, but if getting something away from a bloodhound were that easy, my human would have a lot more panties. I pushed passed him and took off down the hall, and while the arm of the law might be long, its legs were not. I'm not a greyhound by any means, but two legs are never a match for four, especially when the four legs has something the two legs wants.

I scratched at the library door—the universal open sesame of the canine world—and bounded into the room.

My arrival caused almost as much of an uproar as the recent riot.

"Look there's Rufus! He's got something in his mouth!" cried out a woman who appeared to be one of the models.

"What is it? I can't see," said the Wall Street modelizer sitting next to her.

Now to be fair, things pretty much do disappear when I carry them in my mouth, so I moved swiftly over to Detective de Vries and dropped my prize at his feet.

It was a gun.

Chapter 27

Pandemonium descended upon the room.

"The dog did it! I knew it!" cried someone triumphantly.

'It's always the one you least suspect," said another. "And he looked like such a gentle dog too. You just never know."

"What's his motive, do you think," asked a guest off to the left.

"Maybe Rush patted him on the top of the head," speculated a young lady in red.

"But why is he confessing?" asked a quizzical lad. "He would have gotten get away with it."

"Guilty conscience maybe?" said the young lady in red. I hated to break it to her that if I had one of those my human would have had a lot more shoes in her closet and food on her plate. Also couch cushions; but who's counting.

The detective held up his hand for silence and another officer donned gloves to bag my find.

He handed it to De Vries.

"Over here K9 Rufus," he said, "it's all yours." Everything always is. But for once no one had to bribe me with a snack to come. I came. He opened the bag, which was really quite unnecessary since I obviously knew whose scent was on the gun. But I like drama as much as the next hound, especially since everyone's phone was now in zoom mode, ready to capture my every snort for social media posterity. I had a sniff and again took my time to prolong the suspense. But eventually I parked myself in front of the gun's owner. This time I increased the decibel level and lowered the register of my voice to signify that I meant business. It wasn't quite in Wilbur the Gordon Setter territory, but it was close.

"This is ridiculous!" cried Tucker, his voice rising. "This creature has it in for me. And anyway, a killer would have worn gloves so he's wrong!"

"The nose of a bloodhound is not wrong," responded the detective, defending the honor of my kind for which I trotted over and favored his kneecaps with a smack of my tail. If any unpleasantness were to arise, it was his legs I would be hiding behind. "Wearing gloves may prevent leaving fingerprints or DNA but it does not prevent a bloodhound from detecting scent."

"It doesn't matter anyway. Everyone can tell you I was playing the bagpipes all afternoon," he said looking around the room for support.

"That's true," said one of Percy's friends. "I had to take some aspirin."

"But no one actually saw him playing them," contributed an aspiring sleuth. "It could have been an audio file." I'm sure the police appreciated trying to solve a murder with the help of a crowd who treated their efforts like interactive dinner theater.

"Well then tell me how I left my room, went down all these corridors and out the front door and then back again with no one seeing me," said Tucker.

"I think we can solve that little mystery pronto," said the detective. "Perhaps if Mr. Prescott and Miss Pennington would care to accompany K9 Rufus and myself to Mr. Twistleton's room, we might shed some light on the matter."

Who knew weddings could be so much fun.

"That's a very special animal you have there, Miss," observed the detective, as we headed to Tucker's room. I basked in the praise since I so seldom get it.

"He's definitely special," replied my human, although I had a feeling she really meant "special." If no man is a hero to his valet, no hound is a hero to his human.

We found the door to Tucker's room wide open. Just like I had left it. Equally wide open was a section of the far wall that led to the pitch-black tunnel where I had found the gun. We bloodhounds have no need of superfluous things like flashlights when we explore secret passages. We have noses.

"It's just as I thought," said de Vries. "The murder weapon would have been impossible to find without the assistance of both of you two and especially of K9 Rufus." I'm sure the "both of you" was just meant to be polite. "Mr. Twistleton was really quite clever. If not for the brilliant efforts of K9 Rufus, we'd have been facing a potentially ambiguous cause of death and no murder weapon; and then we would have lost valuable time sorting through a collection of incriminating weapons and contradictory statements."

"And Tucker would have been all the way to Cambodia by the time you even started," said Ben.

"Mr. Twistleton was planning a trip to Cambodia?"

"Yes, he happened to mention that he planned to take a vacation for after the wedding."

"Cambodia and the US have no extradition treaty," said the detective. "Even, assuming we knew or could prove he had killed Mr. Devereaux, which is doubtful, we'd have a problem arresting him. It's a good thing he didn't know that wearing gloves doesn't matter to a bloodhound."

"Nothing matters to Rufus in general," said my human, who was as an astute observer of me as she was of her own species, "but I wouldn't trade him for anything." This was good to know. I hope she remembers it the next time I add some extra ventilation to her sneakers or drag her into a snowbank to make her squeal.

By the time we returned to the library order had been restored and Driscoll was explaining to the crowd around him that the betting window was closed. For the sake of his bank account, I hope there weren't many takers of the field at 20:1.

"K9 Rufus was kind enough to show us how you were able to exit and enter your room without being seen, Mr. Twistleton, so I'm afraid you will be coming with us," said the detective.

"But I have no motive!" cried the bitter bagpiper, jumping to his feet. "Although there are plenty of people in this room who do," he added malevolently. This got everyone's attention and his audience rustled in anticipation. "We all saw how Rush publicly humiliated Emily." There was a murmur of assent. "A woman who is hurt and scorned is dangerous, especially when she knows how to handle a gun. And then there is her protective father whose proficiency with a bow and arrow we all saw, as well as her belligerent brother." Then he twirled like a dervish and pointed a finger. "And how about Rush's sister and her charlatan of a lover..."

"I am not a charlatan! I'll have you for libel, young man," exclaimed Dr. Bruce, ignoring the fact that at the moment, libel was the least of Tucker's worries.

"…her charlatan lover who needed money for his ridiculous business scheme."

"That's rich coming from someone whose previous ventures included a rabbit café and a line of inflatable swimsuits," observed Percy "not to mention someone who has been trying to raise money for an urban pogo stick sharing business."

"What!" cried an alarmed animal lover. "He had a café where they ate rabbits!"

"No, sorry," said Percy. "It was a café where you could drink coffee and pet rabbits. Like a cat café only with rabbits."

Tucker's face grew red.

"We weren't talking about me, and besides pogo sticks are going to be the next big thing in personal urban transportation. As I was saying, Henley and Bruce needed money and I overheard her telling her pill pushing boyfriend that she had a big fight with Rush about releasing the money from her trust fund. And I know for a fact that they were planning to murder Charles Winthrop who would have taken over management of the trust if Rush wasn't around. Just look at her. Not only is she not grieving for her brother, she seems positively delighted that he's dead." The phones now swung towards Henley and Bruce, visions of virality playing out in everyone's head.

It was now Henley's turn to go red.

"Am I happy my brother is dead? Yes. He was a prick. But that doesn't mean I had anything to do with his death. It would have been impossible for me to kill someone since I have no past life regressions of murderers. And besides, I was in a deep regression when my brother was killed. I was a Hawaiian princess and saw visions of large, voraciously hungry animals stealing pineapples." I have no idea why everyone suddenly pointed their phones at me. "So I don't need that money anymore. I'm off to Maui to help feed feral goats." This was clearly news to Dr. Bruce; his usual suave and self-satisfied manner vanished, and a look of astonishment crossed his face. "I'm sorry Bruce, I was going to tell you after the wedding. I know you told me that I suffered an overdose on Wednesday, but it was a good thing really. It gave me clarity."

"I guess nearly killing someone explains why he lied to us," whispered Ben to my human.

"She's obviously unhinged," declared Tucker, "and unhinged people are capable of anything. With all the drugs she takes, who knows, maybe she doesn't even remember killing her brother. But if that's not enough people with motives, there's the bride and her family. They could all have been in on it." He turned to Percy. "I didn't want to tell you this cousin, but your beautiful bride-to-be slept with the man who was going to marry you."

There was a collective gasp of shock at this new revelation. The crowd was certainly getting its money's worth.

"Sex, drugs and money; it's classic, I love it" exclaimed a girl at the far end of the room.

"It's like Netflix, only live," said the amped up individual sitting next to her. "It's terrific!"

Percy didn't think it was so terrific. He turned an angry face to his almost wife who suddenly had as urgent a need to bend down and adjust her shoe as my human recently had to bend down and adjust my collar.

"Yes, but that's not all; I overheard Rush threaten to tell Percy about it before the wedding. And we all saw her brother try to kill Rush with a sword. He probably decided to finish the job with his father's gun. Any one of these people could have done it and framed me."

Those accused protested vehemently. Mike Kovac rose from his chair and had to be restrained by his wife.

"And what about the waitress who publicly tried to murder Rush with a knife? I'm sorry Detective, this place is crawling with people who had a motive to kill Rush but I'm not one of them."

Now it was Uncle Charles' turn to rise.

"It won't do, Tucker. You do in fact have a motive and a rather substantial one, at that."

He turned towards the detective.

"It didn't seem particularly relevant until now, but my wife's uncle, Percival Ogden Wigglesworth, was an eccentric gentleman who happened to be unlucky in love. He courted a woman for years but delayed proposing to her until it was too late, and she ran off and married someone else. He was 28 at the time, and losing the woman he loved at that age caused him to develop a fixed belief that a man ought to be married before that age. Mr. Wigglesworth was a man of considerable means and as he remained unmarried and childless and as my wife was his favorite niece, he made a will in favor of her son. It had two stipulations: first, that the child be called Percival and second that he be married before the age at which he had lost his own chance at love. If you will refer to the schedule of events that we prepared for you, Detective, you will see that Thursday was to have been my son's wedding day and today is my son's 28th birthday. As a result of recent tragic events, however, my son has reached the age stipulated in the will and remains a bachelor."

"That is unfortunate," agreed Detective de Vries, "but how does Mr. Twistleton figure into this?"

"I was just coming to that," said Uncle Charles. "Under the terms of the will, should my son still be unmarried at the age of 28, the next legatee would have been Percy's younger brother if he had had one, which he does not. That being the case, next in line is the son of my wife's younger sister, Eleanor Twistleton, who is Percy's first cousin Tucker. Tucker stands to come into a large amount of money if he marries before the age of 28, which given that he is currently only 25 would not be difficult to achieve." Although I appreciated Uncle Charles's optimism with respect to Tucker's matrimonial prospects, I can't think there is much demand for bagpipe playing bridegrooms who are crass enough to pat hounds on the top of their heads.

"I won't stand here and listen to this!" yelled Tucker, his voice heavy with indignation. "You don't have a case. Not only is there no proof that I knew anything about the will, but there is no legal evidence of anything."

"That's where you're wrong, young man," replied the detective evenly, "the evidence of a bloodhound's nose is admissible in a court of law; so yes, we do have a case." This was thrilling news! I wondered if I would get to sit in the witness box when I testify. I think I'd quite enjoy that although the judge might need a good pair of earplugs.

"That's the dumbest thing I've ever heard. There is no solid evidence that I had anything to do with this, and there's not a jury in the world who would convict me on the say so of a dog." This guy was really getting up my nose in more ways than one. The nerve of him calling me, a Royal Bloodhound, a dog!

There was a discrete cough at the back of the room.

"Actually," said Ethan, "there kind of is. Proof I mean." All eyes, digital and biological turned towards the director. "After lunch on Wednesday I went up to one of the turrets to set up a camera for my B roll."

"B roll?" said the detective.

"Sorry, it's supplemental footage that I'd be able to insert into the main action of my film to add additional visual interest and variety. Anyway, the wedding scenes were to be shot in the castle's chapel and my breakdown called for additional scenes to be shot at the ruined chapel at the Overlook. I had no idea we were in for a blizzard, so on

Wednesday after lunch, before our production meeting, I decided to go up to one of the turrets and set up a high-powered telescopic lens I've been wanting to try. It cost a fortune, but what's money when it's in the service of art and especially when it's crucial to the realization of one's artistic vision. I'm sure when Francis Ford Coppola was just starting out..."

"That's all very interesting, Sir, but if we could just stick to the facts," said the detective.

'Sorry. It's just that with this awesome new plot twist, the lens is cheap at the price," explained the director, visions of the Palme d'Or fandangoing in his head. "Anyway, I thought that having long range static B roll footage of the ruined chapel and Overlook as the light and weather conditions changed over time would be cool. I mean drones are so overused, that they've become a cliché and I'm going for something much more classic you understand."

"The facts, please, Sir."

"Yes, about that, after I set up my camera, I went to our production meeting and afterwards there was the commotion about the murder. Then the blizzard happened. I was finally able to dig out my camera this morning and when I took a look to see if there was anything usable for my revised film, I realized that I'd hit the jackpot—I've got the white wedding murder in the can so my B roll is now my A roll!"

"I think what you have, young man, is neither an A roll nor a B roll but a prosecutor's roll," observed the detective.

Tucker jumped back up from his chair. "I don't have to sit here and listen to this!"

He ran towards the door but before he could reach it, his foot connected with a foreign object. He swan dived into the carpet. Personally, I would like to think that my rawhide saved the day, but where he thought he was going with so many police officers around is anyone's guess. Then again, he probably wasn't thinking, like me when I see a fast-moving rodent and forget that I have a human attached to my leash.

I'm not a vindictive hound, but just to rub it in, I sat on him and drooled on his head while the officers cuffed him. No one calls me a creature or dismisses me as a mere dog and gets away with it.

Chapter 28

"Ladies and gentlemen…" began Detective de Vries.

"Or Lords and Ladies," called out some lively spirit.

"As I was saying," continued the detective favoring the lively spirit with a stern look, "I would ask that you please all remain here for the time being. We want to take some photographs and review the, ah, B reel, and we will be taking statements from all of you for the record. We will, however, make every effort to bring the investigation to a swift conclusion, at which time you will be free to go."

This was exhilarating news, although being free to go in theory and free to go in practice were two entirely different things. As much as I admired Detective De Vries, even he could not miraculously clear roads or restore transportation links. But since the practicalities of the leaving part seemed to have not yet occurred to anyone, a celebratory mood swept through the room like the gaseous products of my digestive system after a surfeit of liver. People rose and gathered in clumps, chatting eagerly about how they always knew it was Tucker because anyone who could play *Get Off of My Cloud* on the bagpipes was obviously capable of other criminal behavior. But the majority of those present made a beeline for me, offering congratulations, taking selfies, and gathering tidbits for their soon to be engorged social media accounts. I was probably going to be Instagrammed more times than last week's lasagna.

Kudos, accolades, and acclaim, rained down upon my head, while my fellow sleuths and assorted relatives hovered nearby discussing recent events.

"I have a question Mr. Winthrop," said Driscoll. "Now that Percy is a geriatric bachelor and thanks to sleuth hound Rufus it appears unlikely that Tucker will enter into the matrimonial state any time soon as he will be otherwise engaged, who cops the loot?"

Mr. Winthrop sighed. "Under the terms of the will, the money will be used to endow the Percival Ogden Wigglesworth Chair of Newt Studies at Princeton."

"Newts? You did say newts?"

"Yes, I'm afraid so," said Aunt Anne. "After the crushing blow of losing the woman he loved, Uncle Percival threw himself into newts. It was newts this and newts that; morning, noon, and night, it was all newts. The common newt, the great water newt, the smooth newt, he could talk of little else. It made dinner parties quite a challenge. By the time he died in a freak newt collecting accident on the Orinoco, Uncle Percival had amassed one of the largest newt collections in the world. I've been told his books *Pond Scum*, and *Behind Every Great Man is a Newt*, are seminal works in the field."

"He always did say to never underestimate the power of the newt," said Uncle Charles. "I guess he was right; the newts won in the end."

"That means that the students at our alma mater will be taught by an Old Newtonian!" said Driscoll, provoking groans from his friends. But all this talk of newts made me wonder if there were any in Central Park, and if they were slower than squirrels. Also, what they smelled like and if they tasted like chicken. But any further newt-related reveries were interrupted by the arrival of Brooke.

She took Percy's arm.

"I have wonderful news! Sergio Emilio Augustus says he might be able to squeeze us in in January for a wedding on Mustique."

"Tell him not to bother," replied Percy.

"Why? It's not hurricane season if that's what you're worried about. And I have no intention of eloping."

"Neither do I. At least not with you."

"What's that supposed to mean?"

"It means we are not getting married on Mustique or Mars or anywhere."

Spots of anger appeared on her beautiful face.

"If it's because of Rush, it was only one night, and I was drunk, and he was very persuasive. So it's not really my fault."

"No."

"Then what? Is it because I lied to your friends about Greg being in my room? I was sure he had done it—he and daddy have terrible tempers—and I was only trying to protect him. Anyway, he said he was nowhere near the scene of the murder, he had snuck out to smoke some weed. Daddy disapproves and he wanted to avoid a fight."

"No, it's not about you lying."

"But why then? We look so good together. And it'll be perfect; Daddy is going to bring you into the business, so we'll have plenty of money. Greg doesn't like it of course but he'll come around, so don't worry about that. Anyway, he has no choice." It was Cousin Percy's turn to go red. I guess knobs weren't his thing.

"You seem to have it all planned. Except for the fact that I no longer want to marry you."

She stomped her foot—metaphorically speaking of course, since actually stomping would have risked breaking the heel of her pricy Spreco di Denaro stilettos.

"You ARE going to marry me! I've worked way too hard to get Sergio Emilio Augustus to agree to accept me as a client." As someone who generally gets their way and is not fond of being thwarted, I sympathized. Many a time I've said, "We ARE going racoon hunting in The Ramble." But fortunately for me, insistence and persistence are better suited to steamrolling dog-loving humans than reluctant matrimonial partners.

"No, I am not, Brooke."

"But why? And don't give me that, 'it's not you, it's me thing.'"

"I wouldn't dream of it. It's definitely you. And the reason you have no idea why, is why."

Percy returned to his family and friends with the look of a man who thinks he might have dodged a bullet only to find it was a cannonball.

"I broke up with Brooke," he said. "I don't know what I saw in her but I after this wedding I have no desire to see more of it."

"Champagne all around!" crowed Driscoll, who was never known for his tact. "As soon as they let us out of here we'll drain the cellars dry. Or at least the ones without the dead bodies in them, although I expect Rush will be on his way to the morgue by now." My human was about to point out that Ben no longer had the key when Jason approached her. He glanced furtively at me.

"Can I have a word?" I could see by the look on her face that my human would have liked to say no, but under the watchful eye of her mother, manners prevailed. Manners are hugely inconvenient which makes me grateful I don't have any.

"Rufus has a powerful sense of smell, right?" This was a bit of an understatement considering that I had just unmasked a murderer, but I let it go.

"Yes, bloodhounds have the strongest sense of smell of any dog breed," said my human unsure of where this was going and a bit unnerved to see the hedge hog stripped of his usual bluster and confidence.

"Umm… can he pick up the scent of other things? I mean other than the smell of people?"

"Rufus can pick up the scent of most things," she replied, neglecting to mention especially if they are edible. Or things that might be edible.

"Well can he, say, pick up the scent of things like drugs. Is he like, a drug sniffing dog?"

"I don't think Rufus is a drug sniffing dog, but then again, I didn't think he was a murderer sniffing dog either. So with him, who knows. He's full of surprises."

"So here's the thing. My job is stressful and requires intense concentration and long hours, and I find that doing a line here and there—nothing major you understand—keeps me going. You don't achieve returns like mine"—here he resumed a bit of the swaggerish Jason my human had come to know and not love—"without some occasional extra help. On Wednesday afternoon I was looking at prospectuses, like I told your boyfriend, but I went to my room for a quick pick me up, and when I came down, I saw Rush leave. I was furious about what he'd done to my sister, so I ran back upstairs, grabbed my coat and was going to follow him and teach him a lesson. I don't usually tell people this," (meaning he told people this all this time) "but I know kung fu. I picked it up one summer when Dad sent to me China with a pie-making delegation. Anyway, by the time I got outside, I didn't see where Rush went, so I went back in. But my question is, if the police have Rufus sniff my room will he know that I had coke in there Wednesday just like he knew what Tucker had touched on Wednesday. And will he know that I went outside."

My human is seldom at a loss for words—and since many of them generally yelling at me, it was kind of nice to see her fall silent.

"First, I think you should probably tell the police what you told me about following Rush. Second, as far as drugs, the police haven't asked Rufus to sniff the rest of the rooms and as I said, I think drug sniffing dogs have to be specially trained and Rufus isn't." She omitted to mention that I'm not non-specially trained either.

"OK, good to know. This has been such a shit show from start to finish that I don't want it getting any worse." I myself of course was having a splendid time; nevertheless, speaking as one who puts on a shit show several times a day, I deeply resented the disparagement. I was just about to wipe my wet face on his pants when Detective de Vries appeared.

"I want to thank everyone for their patience. We won't be too much longer and then we can start taking statements, after which, as I said, you will be free to go." There was a collective groan that he wasn't there to announce our liberation.

As he turned to go Mike Kovac buttonholed him.

"Can I have a quiet word outside, Detective?" My curiosity piqued, I followed them both out, leaned heavily on Detective de Vries leg and shoved my snout under his right hand.

"I'll come straight to the point," said our ex-host. "I had nothing to do with the murder, although I can't say I'm sorry the bastard is dead. I know it's part of the drill to take statements from everyone, but man to man, I'd appreciate it if you'd take it as a given that Ms. Plovis, my PA, was with me all afternoon like we told Percy's interfering friends. It can have no bearing on the case where we were or what we were doing if you get my drift. And a man in my position can't afford for something like this to become public knowledge. Now I know you trust your men, but we both know that everyone has a price and information of this kind can have serious repercussions for my business. Not to mention that the young lady in question thinks I'm going to marry her. Women, huh." He took out a card. "And of course, if you or your family ever need anything, I'd be more than happy to help." I was more than happy to see that de Vries ignored the card.

"Statements will be taken from everyone who was in the castle at the time of Mr. Devereaux's death. Anything that does not have a bearing on the case will be ignored and I would remind you that lying during a police investigation is an offence. Now if you'll excuse me." He spun around to resume his duties while I spun around to resume mine. There were still people in the library who hadn't petted me.

But all good things must come to an end and finally Detective de Vries poked his head in to announce that we were all free to leave our book-lined prison. Cheers erupted. Then a general stampede towards the liquor. The castle soon rang out with a degree of merriment not seen since the night the 8th Earl entertained a group of friends with exceptionally attractive wives.

"That's a fine hound you have there, Miss" said Detective de Vries, as he fed me a farewell piece of steak. "We'll be in touch if we need anything further as the case progresses."

"Thank you. And if you're ever in New York I'm sure

Rufus would be delighted to see you."

We then joined the others in our happy hideaway. Although Cousin Percy's friends were far too well brought up to tell him exactly what they thought of his choice of bride, the vigor with which they celebrated her exit said it all.

Chapter 29

It was a late night. The partying went on into the wee hours and in an unprecedented burst of consideration, I allowed my humans the luxury of sleeping past dawn.

Later that morning, when we were all sitting, or in my case standing, around the breakfast table the caterer appeared and tapped Uncle Charles on the shoulder.

"I'd like to talk to you," she said tersely. Puzzled, Uncle Charles rose and seeing as I was fond of Uncle Charles, I followed them. You never know, maybe she was going to try to force feed him a mushroom.

Once outside the room she grabbed his arm.

"You really don't remember me, do you Charlie," she snapped. "People like you never do." She clearly had something on her chest that was about to come off it. Uncle Charles turned and for the first time, really looked at her.

"Lisa?" he said, surprise mingling with shock. "It can't be."

"I'm afraid it is Charlie. I never expected to see you again either, not that you and Payne ever tried."

"Did you know…" here his voice trailed off.

"No. I work with Sergio Emilio Augustus quite often and as far as I was concerned this was the Kovac wedding. One of the waitstaff mentioned the name of the groom, but Winthrop is a common enough name, so I didn't think anything of it. Then you came looking for ice. You paid no attention, did you? Spoke to me like I was some faceless flunky."

'I'm so sorry Lisa, and I know Payne was too."

"Easy to say now, isn't it? I never went back to college you know. I was gutted, and my parents, well they were devastated. But it's funny how these things turn out. I started working in restaurants to get by and ended up going to culinary school. Now I run a successful catering business. But that's not what I wanted to talk to you about. Just in case you were thinking of trying to find someone else innocent to blame this time too, I was responsible for your illness. The mushroom I used wasn't intended to make you as sick as you were. I just wanted to ruin the ceremony for you. Petty of me I know, but there it is."

And with that she was gone. Uncle Charles stroked me gently on the neck. They say dogs provide comfort and although I generally expect the process to be reversed, I gave his hand a lick. We walked slowly back to the dining room.

"What did she want?" asked Aunt Anne.

"She just wanted to let me know that she identified the source of my food poisoning. It was as we all thought, a bad mushroom," replied Uncle Charles.

"So Tucker didn't try to kill you?" said Driscoll. He sounded disappointed. "But then maybe there's another murderer in our midst," he said hopefully. "Another mystery for us to solve."

"The only mystery for us to solve is how we are getting home," said Ben. "Has anyone given thought to the fact that our return trips were to be organized and paid for by the father of the bride who is now father of the ex-bride."

"I heard some of the models say that there would be buses to Pittsburgh and vouchers for onward travel, "said my human, "but there is Rufus to consider." This time everyone knew to which Rufus she was referring.

"Maybe Detective de Vries can help get us to a rental car agency," said Ben. "After all Rufus did solve his case."

"I don't think that will be necessary," said Cousin Percy. "Have your luggage sent down at around noon and meet me in the entry hall."

"What about lunch?" asked Barclay. "Just asking for Rufus, you understand. The murder- solving one."

"Don't worry about it," replied Cousin Percy.

"All right then," said my human. "I'd better go pack."

I returned to The Rufus Suite slightly saddened to be going back to once again being merely Rufus rather than The Royal Hound Rufus the Red or K9 Rufus. I drowned my sorrows by helping my human pack and drooling all over her clothes. Then catastrophe struck.

She walked over to the chest of horrors and turned to Ben.

"I'm obviously going to leave all the dresses. Who knows, maybe Sergio Emilio Augustus will be able to re-purpose them for another one of his wedding extravaganzas, but do you think they would mind if I took all these cute jackets for Rufus?" I bayed to point out that Rufus would mind taking all these cute jackets for Rufus. "

"I can't imagine they would be able to use them again,"

said Ben. "And Rufus would cut quite a dashing figure strolling around Central Park in them." Oh, the perfidy of the human race! Leaving aside the fact that strolling is the very opposite of what I do in Central Park, I can only hope that my human intends keeping them under lock and key lest they inadvertently go the way of her underwear.

I sulked while my human continued packing and precisely at noon we joined the others in the entry hall to await the arrival of Cousin Percy.

"I've had this idea," said Driscoll. "I want to gamify Rufus. He could hunt down murderers and toss them off turrets. We'd pay him a royalty of course."

"I'm sure Rufus would appreciate being able to help with the rent," said my human with a smile as she gave me an affectionate pat. I liked the idea in principle, but if I had my way—which I usually do—I'd be helping with the purchase loins of venison and filets of salmon instead.

The discussion of me as an app ceased with the arrival of Cousin Percy.

"We all seem to be here, so everyone follow me please," he said.

Outside stood three large black SUVs, the kind celebrities use when they want to be inconspicuous.

"I hope you're not thinking of driving us to New York," said my human. 'I'm not sure anyone wants to be in a car with Rufus that long. He had a liver omelet for breakfast."

"No, we're not driving to New York," said Percy cryptically.

"Well then where are we going?" asked the Other Rufus.

"You'll see. Mother and Father, we'll go in the lead car. Aunt Elizabeth, if you, Rufus, Cressida, and Ben can please take the second car. And you guys," he said addressing the rump end of his now defunct wedding party, "can bring up the rear. Which considering what asses two of you are, seems fitting."

We climbed into our respective cars and the caravan made its way cautiously down the winding and slippery drive before turning onto the open road. But where was it the open road to? I wouldn't have minded another stay at a posh hotel, but truth be told, I missed my bed, although my human might quibble with this since she labors under the misapprehension that it's hers. In any case, I decided to await developments in the way I usually awaited developments, by taking a nap. And although our vehicle was not short of space, it might as well have been a Mini Cooper since I took that nap stretched out on top of my humans. Everyone always assumes since I am a large dog, I require a large space, but the reality is that the only space I require is the one my humans occupy.

I was only vaguely aware of the groans of discomfort, lamentations about the lack of Febreze, and complaints about my sharp elbow joints being in places sharp elbow joints should not be, when the car came to a halt.

We had arrived.

A large private jet sat on the airfield's tarmac, and this time we had a welcoming committee that consisted of more than just an aircraft crew.

Our convoy immediately came under attack by a swarm of men shouldering cameras and trailing the kind of ladies and gentlemen of the press who looked even more meticulously groomed than Brooke's bridesmaids. There was not a hair out of place nor a crease in their clothing. At least for now.

Our driver opened the door and they all started shoving and jockeying for position.

"We want to interview Rufus!" they shouted.

"Which one?" asked Driscoll, as he and his companions emerged from their car. "We have two."

"What! There are two bloodhounds!" This seemed to fire them up even more.

"Ladies and Gentlemen," he said, "allow me to present The Rufi. To my left," he said gesturing to my namesake, "we have the Medical Rufus, a physician whose insanely expensive medical education and keen clinical eye enabled him to rapidly diagnose that a person who is not breathing and has no pulse is dead." The Other Rufus shot him an evil look. "To my right," continued our master of media ceremonies, "and needing no introduction, is K9 Detective Rufus, slayer of small mammals" (OK, here he was stretching things a bit, although I may have once killed a cockroach by accidentally stepping on it), "whose extraordinary powers of deduction and astonishing olfactory abilities enabled him to unmask a murderer with a single sniff."

Never one to shirk my duties, except when I want to, I graciously gave a large number of interviews, posed for innumerable pictures, and stood majestically beside each reporter as they did their on camera "stand ups." Driscoll ushered me around to each group and adjusted my ears to their most attractive position. And when he shared the lurid crime pics from his phone our guests would have whooped for joy had their Botox permitted it.

Needless to say, by the time we finally ascended the stairs to our jet, I was in such a frisky mood that my human almost completed the journey face first.

After a suitable interval of fawning and photographing by the crew, we all settled in, buckled up, and perused the drinks and luncheon menus.

"Son, I appreciate your desire to make sure we had comfortable transportation home, but you really shouldn't have," said Uncle Charles. "It's terribly extravagant and your mother and I would have been perfectly happy flying commercial."

"Oh, I'm not paying for this," replied Cousin Percy as he took an envelope out of his pocket. He extracted a sheet of Crackshaw Castle monogrammed wedding stationary and read the following:

"Percy, accept this parting gift as my way of saying thanks for not marrying my sister and trying to get your hands on our family business. Now stay the hell away from her or you'll end up like Rush. Greg."

"What an amiable fellow," said Uncle Charles. "Forget what I said. Your mother and I will be very happy to fly Air Kovac."

"Here's to Rufus," said Cousin Percy raising a glass of champagne after we had taken off.

"To Rufus!" chorused everyone.

Just then a smiling flight attendant appeared and looked at my human.

"He'll have the salmon. Light on the hollandaise."

The Royal Hound Rufus the Red always gets his man. And his salmon.

THE END

9 798218 486013